What the Critics are saying:

About *Another Love*
by Ann Jacobs

"ANOTHER LOVE is a heartwarming, yet heart-wrenching, tale of second love… Ms. Jacobs has written another winner." - *Denise Powers, Sensual Romance*

About *Make Her Dreams Come True*
by Joey W. Hill

"It's a tender, moving romance that is arousing and hits the senses at every turn. This is a very hot, hot erotic romance, with a little kinkiness thrown in. I think every woman would like to have a "take control" man at least for a while. This is a definite keeper for me." - *Patricia McGrew, Timeless Tales*

About the *Death Row* serial
by Jaid Black

"Black's books combine bold sexuality with terrific worldbuilding. When I'm in the mood for ultra hot romance, this is what I go for." - *Susan Sizemore, author of I Burn For You*

Discover for yourself why readers can't get enough of the multiple award-winning publisher Ellora's Cave. Whether you prefer e-books or paperbacks, be sure to visit EC on the web at www.ellorascave.com for an erotic reading experience that will leave you breathless.

WWW.ELLORASCAVE.COM

Ellora's Cave Publishing, Inc.

PO Box 787

Hudson, OH 44236-0787

ISBN # 1-84360-522-8

Enchained

ALL RIGHTS RESERVED

Ellora's Cave Publishing, Inc., 2003.

© Mastered, Ann Jacobs, 2002, 2003.

© A Choice Of Masters, Joey W. Hill, 2003.

© Death Row: The Mastering, Jaid Black, 2003.

This book may not be reproduced in whole or in part without author and publisher permission.

"Mastered" edited by Allie McKnight.

"A Choice Of Masters" edited by Sheri Ross Carucci.

"Death Row: The Mastering" edited by Martha Punches.

Cover art by Bryan Keller.

Warning: The following material contains strong sexual content meant for mature readers. *Enchained* has been rated NC-17, erotic, by a minimum of six independent reviewers. We strongly suggest storing this book in a place where young readers not meant to view it are unlikely to happen upon it. That said, enjoy…

ENCHAINED

MASTERED

WRITTEN BY

ANN JACOBS

Prologue

Control. He had to have it, in bed and out, and she was the last woman on earth he'd expect to shed her armor and bend to his loving dominance. Worse, she was his good friend and confidant, and as often as not his colleague because his detectives chased down the criminals she ultimately prosecuted.

So why was it that Sandra kept his cock twitching every time he got within smelling distance of that musky perfume she wore? And why did he wake up nights hard as stone from dreaming of her bound and helpless and moaning with pleasure with every stroke of his tongue on her sopping cunt?

Rocky tamped down the futile fantasies that flooded his mind as he walked his good friend to the door of her apartment after drinks and talk at Bennie's, his cooling off aided by the soft spring rain that kissed his skin and left shimmering crystals beading in her glossy black hair.

But when he bent his head to give her a friendly goodnight kiss at her door like he'd done a hundred times before, Sandra responded like anything but the cool, collected lawyer he knew. The way she traced his lips with her tongue and tangled it with his had his cock primed and ready for action.

As though shocked by the sudden wave of sexual electricity that had overcome her, she pulled away and opened her door. "Goodnight, Rocky," she said as though nothing had gone down between them. Her nervous laugh belied her casual words as she beat a hasty retreat.

For a long time Rocky stood staring at the closed door, reliving that kiss and mentally kicking himself in the ass for having read his good buddy wrong.

Cool? Collected? Control freak? Hell, no. She walked the walk and talked the talk, but what the fuck? Nobody who didn't have a damn strong interest in sex kissed the way she'd kissed him tonight. And ice queens sure as hell didn't have tongue piercings.

Chapter One

Nothing at the courthouse had changed much in the year since he'd left the testifying to his underlings. Keys still clanged as guys emptied pockets and dumped the contents into baskets before walking through the metal detection machines. Anxious-looking people milled around in the halls taking surreptitious glances at uniformed city cops and sheriff's deputies. Small-time crooks and perfumed hookers huddled in corners with lawyers in ill-fitting suits, ties askew.

The smell of stale tobacco, unwashed bodies and cheap cologne lingered in chief of detectives Rocco Delgado's nostrils long after he'd stepped inside Courtroom B and found a vacant section of a side wall to lean against.

The eyes of the women jurors seemed glued on the defense lawyer as he delivered his closing statement. Their tongues were practically hanging out their mouths, and Rocky even thought he saw one drooling. Disgusting, what a guy like Tony Landry could do with movie-star good looks and a deep, mesmerizing voice that Rocky bet could coax a nun right out of her panties.

Rocky stood there, half listening to Landry while he visually zoomed in on chief prosecutor Sandra Giancone. His tie suddenly felt too tight when he considered how some guys on his team had screwed up taking a key witness's statement. They'd screwed her case in the process, but no one would guess it. It always amazed him how nothing seemed to blow Sandra's cool.

Nothing, that is, except the idea of taking their friendship out of restaurants and movie theaters into her bed or his. He'd been about to give up on seducing her until that kiss last week when he'd discovered the flat acrylic retainer in her tongue.

Only a slight tremor in her voice when she stood and made her summation to the jury gave away the desperation she must have been feeling, facing the likelihood that another guilty man would walk.

She'd made a damn good argument. He'd buy it any day over Landry's silky-smooth allegation that the State hadn't proven its case and the jury must therefore set a big-time drug trafficker free. But then Rocky didn't get a hard-on looking at a hunk in a tailor-made suit.

He imagined most of the women on the jury had soaked their underwear, imagining Landry crawling into their beds. And that they'd gotten the lawyer's point when he emphasized that he'd neatly impeached a big chunk of the evidence Sandra had needed to prove the defendant's guilt beyond reasonable doubt.

On the other hand, Sandra had a way of bringing his cock to instant attention. Rocky's balls tightened when he thought about the lady replacing that retainer in her tongue with a vibrating barbell. The idea of her rubbing it sensuously over his naked body was a massive turn-on, and he damn well intended to make that happen soon.

His unflappable friend would need to let go some of her scary self-control when this case was over. She'd need to be mastered, and his cock was just the tool to do the job. Now if he could only convince her…

Fuck, he was dreaming. The lady might be keeping that tongue piercing as a souvenir of some long-ago fling.

Nothing else about her gave the slightest hint that she might get into the BDSM scene he'd inhabited off and on for years. No, Rocky told his eager cock it wasn't likely ever to feel the inside of Sandra's cunt, let alone the delicious sensation of her pierced tongue sliding over it, wet and eager for a meal of his come.

He'd better cool it or he'd embarrass himself with a hard-on nobody in the courtroom would be able to ignore. Putting the lid onto his fantasies, Rocky forced himself to concentrate on what Sandra was saying.

By God, she might get lucky and pull this case out. Her argument sure as hell would have convinced Rocky that the creep on trial belonged behind bars for the rest of his natural life and then some, if he hadn't already known that for a fact. But then Rocky knew his detective whose testimony Landry had just impeached, and he had confidence that the man would never perjure himself, even if his family situation suggested otherwise.

The jurors didn't.

It was obvious from the tight set of her lips when she walked out of the courtroom that Sandra knew Landry had cemented doubt in those jurors' minds. She hid it well, though. He doubted the reporters who were now ganging up on her outside the courtroom could tell.

"Do you think you've got a conviction?" one shouted at her from the back of the horde.

"Did Landry's discrediting the detective hurt your case?" yelled an especially stupid young woman who shoved a microphone in Sandra's face.

It was all Rocky could do to restrain himself from knocking aside everybody who stood in his path, plowing into the melee, and knocking the pesky reporters out of Sandra's way. Damn, it was as if they wanted to make her break—wanted her to snap and say something that would spice up the evening news.

"No comment," she snapped again and again, her smile tight-lipped as she and the rest of the prosecution team shoved their way through the crowd with the help of some uniforms.

Rocky stood and watched, hurting for her and for his detective who had inadvertently fucked up the case. Tonight he'd coax her once more to shed her cloak of determined self-control. If she'd let him, he'd be there for her and give her the love that had been growing inside him, love that was yelling to be revealed—and he'd provide however much or little sex as it took to shake that scary, brittle control of hers into oblivion.

Maybe he'd even hide the toys he kept below deck on the forty-foot motor cruiser he'd bought with his inheritance from Uncle Marco and treat Sandy to a relaxing cruise on the Gulf. He could always hope she wouldn't notice *Neptune's Dungeon* discreetly stenciled on the stern–or if she did, she wouldn't catch the name's significance.

* * * * *

"No comment." Sandra could have saved valuable breath by tape recording those two terse words and playing them nonstop while she walked from the courthouse to the state attorney's offices for the second time in two hours.

A cool breeze caught wisps of her simply styled pageboy and whipped the strands against her cheeks. Another annoyance, she thought, brushing back her hair as she tried to ignore the horde of TV commentators and photographers dogging her trail and spoiling this otherwise gorgeous February day.

Sandra hated reporters. Vultures. That was all they were. This time they hadn't even waited for the jury to come in. She hadn't needed to hear the verdict rendered moments earlier to know Landry had ripped her case to shreds.

This was one of those days when she wished she'd listened to Mama and forgotten about saving the world from bastards like the one who'd just gotten off scot-free. She should have settled down with a good old Italian-American *paisano* to raise her own brood of macho boys and sweet, subservient girls. At the very least she ought to have tossed away her ambitions and gone with her old Master when he'd moved his construction business to Arizona last year.

Maybe she should have taken Rocky up on one of his frequent hints that they nudge their long-time friendship into an affair. Too bad he seemed like such a nice guy. Too bad nice didn't get her off.

Her second-guessing wasn't happening because some hotshot defense lawyer five years her junior had just ripped apart her case. That humiliation was nothing compared with what she knew was coming from the state attorney, whose political ambitions went far beyond his present elective office. Sandra had no doubt he'd see her loss to the flamboyant attorney as a diminishing blow to his chances for moving up to Congress next year. She'd gotten a hint of just how angry her boss was when his secretary had buzzed her on her cell phone as soon as the trial was over and summoned her to an urgent meeting.

Sometimes Sandra wanted to strangle that pompous ass, but as always she vowed to keep a tight rein on her feelings. She wouldn't let anybody get to her. Taking a deep breath once she got past the receptionist who she hoped would hold the reporters at bay, she opened the conference room door.

"Good. You're finally here. We can get started." The scowl on Harper Wells' patrician-looking face gave Sandra another hint as to the level of verbal abuse she and the other members of the prosecution team should expect.

She schooled her features into what she hoped would be seen as a neutral expression. No way would she ever give Wells or anybody else the satisfaction of getting past her defenses. "Fire away," she said as she took a seat at the conference table between Andi Young, her second chair, and Kristine Granger, the law clerk who'd assisted with preparations for the trial.

A quick check of the other faces around the table confirmed that everyone who'd been even peripherally involved with preparing the case had received their boss's summons. Even the detectives who'd screwed up collecting evidence—and Rocky, their boss, who wore an ominous scowl.

Damn! This was apparently going to be even worse than Sandra had imagined.

It was. She clenched her fists under the table to keep from using them on Wells when he threatened her with firing or demotion for having let Landry get the best of her. She gathered from his comments that he'd run up against a brick wall with the flamboyant defense attorney before, and this loss added insult to the earlier injury.

Then Wells turned on the police investigative team, his mouth curled in a mask of disgust. "I'm filing a complaint with the Tampa Police Department, Delgado. I'll have all your heads on pikes before I'm through with you," he concluded following a lengthy and loud recitation of every real and imagined error that might have contributed to the not-guilty verdict.

Sandra glanced across the table, noted the hard set of Rocky's square jaw and the white-knuckled fists he didn't bother hiding from plain view. From the fierce expression in his deep-brown eyes, she imagined he was one step away from exploding. And she didn't blame him. Wells was out of line, blaming Rocky because Landry had dug up the detective's family problems to impeach his testimony. If anybody was to blame for that, she was.

"I should have thought to ask Detective Sergeant Kelly if anything in his private life might be subject to scrutiny. I didn't. If you need to blame someone, blame me," she said when Wells paused in his loud diatribe. Not that she imagined the big, rough-edged chief of detectives needed defending. She'd put her money on Rocky over Wells any day—at least in a back-alley brawl. No, she spoke up to keep from witnessing an explosion of testosterone that could easily have resulted in bloodshed.

As the state attorney turned back to Sandra, he slammed a fist onto the table, sending reverberations through her fingers, up her arm and into her throbbing head. "Yes, you should have. Why in hell can't I get attorneys as good as Landry?"

Because you're a self-serving bastard, maybe?

Careful to keep her expression neutral, Sandra looked Wells in the eye. "I doubt the state attorney's office pays nearly as much as Landry makes in private practice."

"That may be. Still... Don't let this happen again or you're out, Giancone. I don't need lawyers who can't get convictions. All of you get the hell out of here now."

"Wells was in fine fighting form today," Rocky observed a few minutes later when he and Sandra waited in the hallway for the balky elevator. "It's past quitting time. How about we head over to Bennie's Place and commiserate over a drink or two?"

"All right." Sandra had no desire to rehash the trial or its replay, but she could seriously use a drink—and a few hours with the big chief of detectives who was the closest thing she had to a best friend. Truth be told, she could use a man...the right sort of man. Maybe tonight if Rocky suggested again that they share a friendly fuck, she'd say yes.

Maybe she'd even enjoy it.

* * * * *

Bennie's. For over ten years now she'd been stopping in for a bread bowl of Selena's famous stew at lunchtime, drinks after long days in court. Located across from the courthouse in downtown Tampa, the pub attracted a horde of lawyers and judges and the occasional detective or cop. A cool blast of air greeted Sandra as she and Rocky stepped through faux-western swinging doors into a bar paneled with dark wood. Candles flickered at the centers of the round tables in the center of the room.

"Over there." Rocky led the way around the tables and through the maze of mostly empty barrel chairs to the dimly lit corner booth he always chose when it wasn't already occupied. "Need the peace and quiet after the day from hell we went through from Wells, right?" he asked after Sandra had slid around to the back of the horseshoe-shaped red leather seat close enough to him that she could smell the woodsy scent of his aftershave.

"Yes. Right." The crackling silver light from a sphere on a neon beer ad behind him bounced off his gleaming scalp. Suddenly she wondered...

Except for the coat and tie that looked as though it didn't really belong over his massive shoulders or surrounding his thick, tanned neck, Rocky might have been a dockworker...a pro wrestler...anything but the highly respected cop he was. In some ways he reminded Sandra of her old Master. Of the hot, committed relationship she'd ended a year ago after refusing to quit her job and follow Him to his new home in Arizona.

She recalled the orgasms she hadn't had with her last lover, a local corporate attorney. Ice maiden. That was what he'd called her. Little had he known how hard she'd tried to find release when they fucked in the plain-vanilla way that left her cold—or how frustrated her failure to come had made her.

The jerk never would have believed her if she'd told him how she'd gone wild with men who'd hardly been fit consorts for the respectable, unflappable Sandra Giancone. Hard, macho types she'd never dare show up with at bar association parties or Harper Wells' mandatory social-business gatherings. Men who took control of her body the way she'd never let them intrude on her professional life—until Master had come along.

Men with dark, dangerous edges honed to razor-sharpness in Tampa's underground community. Could Rocky be...?

For the next half-hour Sandra and Rocky rehashed the case while she polished off two syrupy strawberry daiquiris.

"Want some dinner?" Rocky asked when it seemed they'd said all that could be said about their shared business dealings.

The last thing Sandra wanted was food. Her stomach already was queasy from having drunk those daiquiris on

19

her empty stomach. "No. But I could use some..." She dared not tell him what she needed right now. "Coffee."

"I think you need more than that. You need to loosen up. Relax." Rocky's voice compelled, commanded, despite its deep, melodic tone.

What I need is for him to clamp his cuffs on me, force me to let go.

Sandra's nipples tightened and her pussy got wet when she imagined him taking control, taking her the way she hadn't been taken for far too long. Because he'd hinted more than once that he wanted to fuck her, she imagined he'd pick up on even the subtlest of invitations. "Relax how?" she asked, her tone deliberately challenging.

"In bed." His declaration, as bald as his cleanly shaven head, came out as a low rumble, and he drew her hand to his lap and settled it over the bulge of his rigid throbbing cock.

When he shot her a predatory grin, his straight teeth flashed a brilliant white against swarthy skin dotted along his square jaw line with a heavy five o'clock shadow. And his dark eyes glittered, promising...

Danger?

More like mastery. Oh! How Sandra needed to be mastered. In bed, not in court the way Landry the wonder lawyer had bested her this afternoon.

Testosterone practically oozed from the big detective whose conventionally cut dark brown sports jacket did little to disguise his hulking shoulders and massive chest. The winking silver stud in his left earlobe did nothing to offset his blatant maleness. She imagined Rocky without his clothes, certain now he had everything it took to turn her into a mass of quivering jelly. Not just the cuffs she imagined he carried in his pants pocket and the big, hard tool now pulsating beneath her palm.

He'd have the confidence to know what she wanted, the balls to take her and make her like it. If she was really lucky, he might even be a true dominant male — a Master.

Sandra's pussy wept more, drenching her pantyhose. She barely managed to resist the impulse to squirm against the leather-covered booth when she imagined Rocky restraining her with his iron-muscled arms, dragging her head down to his crotch and making her swallow his hot male flesh.

His cock would be long and thick and maybe uncut as so many Latino men were. Her mouth went dry at the thought, and her whole body began to tingle with greedy anticipation. His thick, slick cream would slide down her throat, trickle down her chin.

After she sucked him off, he'd pin her to the mattress and fuck her long and hard. He'd make her come the way no gentle lover had ever managed.

Yeah. The big dangerous-looking cop could make her come. No doubt about it. Problem was, he'd likely strip away the control she'd worked so hard to come by. And conquer not just her body but her mind.

Her nipples beaded up, their sensitive tips pressing against the lace of her push-up bra.

The hell with the aura of control she'd managed with such determined effort to create around herself. She could get it back tomorrow. Maybe. "Why don't you take me home?" she asked, giving his cock a playful squeeze.

Maybe if she held on to her control. Maybe if she let it down only enough to gain momentary release...

Chapter Two

Having put the same proposition to Sandra numerous times before and gotten coolly rejected, Rocky had trouble believing she'd given in so easily tonight. But he hadn't questioned his luck when she'd tweaked his cock at Bennie's. He wasn't about to hesitate now that she'd handed him the key to her apartment and invited him inside.

Shit, but her place left him cold. He looked around a living room that reminded him of the kind of hotel suite salesmen rented to hawk their wares.

Everything was beige, except for a few startling black accents. A few wood-framed black-and-white photos marched neatly along the foyer wall. A geometric pattern stood out startlingly against stacks of big pillows massed on either side of the fireplace.

He'd be afraid of sitting down for fear of knocking one of the loose pillows out of place on the backs of a sofa and two love seats that sat at precise ninety-degree angles to each other and the fireplace. Or of even suggesting that they light a fire in the pristine, beige marble grate and sprawl out together on the utilitarian woven carpet that looked anything but cozy for a fuckfest.

The place was brittle. Cool, calm and collected. Like Sandra.

He wanted to toss those sofa pillows onto the floor, muss the room the way he intended to destroy that cool facade she'd shown him every time they'd worked together—hell, every time she'd turned him down whenever he'd suggested more than a drink at Bennie's or a friendly meal and a movie.

He wanted to break down that control, discover the hot-blooded woman he sensed lay just below the brittle veneer he sensed was close to cracking.

"How the fuck do you stand living like this?" he asked, spreading his arms wide to encompass all the blandness that offended his need for color and disarray in his surroundings.

She followed his gaze around the room, her expression confused, as though she was unclear as to his complaint. "It was this way when I bought the place last year. I saw no reason to replace perfectly good things. Come on. The bedroom's more inviting."

It was, but only because she was in it, shedding the jacket of her courtroom armor. Her deliberate movement called his attention to hard little nipples outlined against the pale silk of her blouse, and to a dark shadow at the apex of her thighs that showed when her skirt slid down her legs and onto the floor.

First, she hung her jacket neatly in the closet. Then the gray skirt that had skimmed her stocking-clad knees joined it among a bunch of equally somber colored suits. He noticed the subtle differences between black, navy-blue and brown garments that divided reds from blues and from one lone bright-green dress. Holy shit! She even hung her goddamned clothes by color.

Then he looked back at her in time to see that silky blouse slither off her narrow shoulders, followed by a cream-colored, unbelievably soft-looking slip. The gaze she shot him as she toed off high-heeled black pumps and wriggled her toes against the deep beige pile of the carpet seemed more challenging than aroused.

He'd never seen a woman strip down for sex so methodically. Or stand before him so dispassionately, as though determined to control each action she took. As though wanting sexual release but not willing to invest the least bit of emotion into the act.

His cock wilted. And it stayed that way until she reached behind her back and unfastened her lacy bra, leaving herself naked except for the sheer, dark pantyhose that cloaked her cunt in mystery. Seeing her full breasts with their dark puckered nipples topping rosy areolas made his mouth water. Watching her hook her thumbs into the waistband of those pantyhose and slide them down, almost like a striptease without background music, engaged his libido once again.

Even so, she stood there. Calm, collected, neat. Rocky couldn't imagine digging his fingers through Sandra's smooth sable hair, knocking even one strand out of place. Surely a hand would come down from above and grab him if he dared muss up that perfect picture. Surely he'd be struck dead if he snatched the silken strands up into his fist and used them to drag her full red mouth down on his swollen cock.

Perfect, that's how she struck him, standing there naked as though for his detailed examination. He couldn't resist assessing her the way he might assess a perp in order to fix every detail of description firmly in his head.

He noted gently arched eyebrows above her big, dark-brown eyes. A modest Romanesque nose and a slender neck he longed to nip with his teeth. She had surprisingly full breasts for one so slim, with small, rosy nipples jutting proudly from lighter areolas. A trim waist and flat belly, olive-skinned like the rest of her, made him assume she did her tanning naked.

Her pussy was neatly trimmed, bare but for the narrow strip of curly black hair in the center of her mons that he figured would tickle his nose while he ate her out. Her firm thighs would clamp around his cheeks, lock his face to her pussy, warm his ears while he heated her clit. The thought had his balls tightening with anticipation.

Yeah. He'd break that iron control of hers, bend her to his will. She needed to let go, and so did he. He'd make her come and come and come, until he shattered the defenses she seemed so intent on keeping in place even here and now.

"Well?" she asked once she stood naked before him.

Oh, shit. He'd been there staring at her cunt like a love-starved teenager, and he was pretty sure she knew. He shot her a grin. "My turn?" he asked, raking her naked body once more before methodically stripping off his own clothes.

Sandra gasped when he dropped his pants and boxers.

"Well, hell. If I'd known all I needed to do was strip naked to get your attention, I'd have done it a long time ago," he said, laughing.

As recently as yesterday Rocky's knowing grin would have annoyed the hell out of her. Tonight, though...damn. He had muscles on his muscles and... Sandra swallowed convulsively when she saw it: a shiny, hefty looking silver ring through the head of the biggest, thickest cock she'd ever seen. It stood, a rigid, rampantly aroused symbol of male power, its bulging purple head a stark contrast with his taut bronzed belly.

She'd guessed wrong. He was circumcised after all.

Her mouth watered at the thought of tasting that delectable plum-like treat that crowned his long, thick shaft.

She didn't see a hair on his body except for broad slashes of black brows and lashes that set off his obsidian eyes. Just looking at him got her pussy sopping wet. When she imagined him wearing black leather and dangling a pair of glittering handcuffs ominously from his huge, callused hand, her breathing grew irregular and her knees started to buckle.

"Sit." His terse command left no room for argument, no doubt that he expected her to obey.

Sandra had picked herself another dom. She'd wondered several times if Rocky might be, but reminded herself he always seemed the quintessential nice guy and chided herself for wishful thinking. He was, though. No question about it, now that he'd shed the trappings of civilization.

Speechless, all she could do for a moment was stare at his beautiful cock, his big balls bulging in their velvety looking sac. Her pussy clenched with anticipation, and her juices rained down the insides of her thighs. Her nipples tightened and her mouth watered.

His eyes glittering, he took one step toward her. "I said 'sit'," he ground out, as though it tested his patience not to force her to obey.

Oh god. He was going to take her, make her give up the control she fought so hard for...and she wanted him. Desperately. Couldn't give in, though. But she had no choice. She sank onto the edge of the queen-size bed, not bothering to turn back the woven coverlet.

"Lie back," he ordered as he went to his knees and spread her legs wide apart.

Part of her perversely wanted him to realize he'd unearthed a closet sub. "Yes, Master," she whispered before she could call back the words.

Resistance wasn't an option. Not now when every cell in her body screamed for mastery. Sandra did as he said, felt the heat of his work-roughened fingers when he spread her legs and knelt between them. His hot, moist breath bathed her in sensation when he spread her outer lips and lowered his full, sensual lips to her clit.

Her pussy gushed out more of her honey, as though begging him to taste it. Instead, he clamped his mouth over her sensitized clit and sucked it in, forcing her to open further to him and lock her ankles behind his massive neck. The musky smell of man and woman—of sex—permeated her brain, robbed her of reason.

Half afraid of a rebuke, she clutched the top of his perfectly shaped head, so smooth compared with the sandpapery texture of his cheeks against her swollen labia. But he only flayed her harder with his tongue and sucked her deeper into his mouth until he'd apparently drunk his fill.

Then he blew on her clit once more—and laughed.

"How's that for a first real kiss?" His deep-voiced words reverberated off her sensitized flesh, building the tension in her belly, her aching nipples.

"F-fine. I like the way you kiss. Thank you."

He looked up at her, at the same time pinching the sensitive tissue of her clit sharply between his thumb and forefinger. "Thank you, what?"

"Thank you, Master." Vaguely she recalled her year-old vow to be no man's sub again, but at the moment she wanted nothing more than to become Rocky's sex toy.

His gaze locked with hers, glittering with unmistakable lust as he used his long pink tongue to lick her creamy juices off his lips and chin. With surprisingly gentle fingers he probed her slit, slipping one briefly into her cunt before circling her anus.

"I'm going to fuck you here, too," he told her.

She couldn't help trembling at the thought of his huge ringed cock splitting her ass. "You're too big."

He slipped one finger into her rear passage, just far enough to rest against her tight anal sphincter. "Relax. You'll love it," he said as he stretched his muscular body over hers and took her mouth.

He tasted of her love juices, salty and slick. The distinctive smell of him reminded her he'd just had his clean-shaven head between her legs until she'd wound up in this state of ferocious wanting. God, but she needed to come and come and come, the way she hadn't since the last time with her old Master.

The way she could only come when her lover made her helpless in fact as well as powerless to resist his command.

Their tongues tangled, probing the caverns of each other's mouths. His deep kiss stole her breath, and her nipples throbbed from the contact with the satiny skin stretched across his hard-muscled, hairless chest.

Now. She needed him. Needed him to make her take him. Wanted him to swallow up her will, make her helpless against his demands.

"The–the drawer," she blurted when he came up for air. "Over there." Not moving, because he hadn't said she could, she glanced toward the bedside table. Toward the toys she'd never been able to make herself throw out along with her old Master.

Abruptly he rolled over and got up. He dragged her to her feet at the side of the bed, then forced her to her knees and caught her hair in one meaty fist. "Play with my toy while I take a look at yours." With that, he fed her the round, swollen head of his huge cock. "Slide the ring around with your tongue. Yeah, baby. I like it like that. Go on. Dig your pretty fingers into my ass. Careful. Go easy or you'll make me come."

Sandra heard the drawer open, felt the rock-hard muscles of his buttocks tighten beneath her fingers. His cock swelled against her lips when she followed his order and worked her tongue under the silver ring that disappeared inside the dimpled indentation of his slit and re-emerged behind the underside of the corona. Each time her tongue nudged the smoothly polished metal, its captive bead moved upward until it nestled in his slit, its progress stopped by distended flesh with its oozing lubrication.

What would he choose? The cuffs? The tie-downs that could stake her out to the four posts of her bed for his ravishment? One of the dildos her old Master had teased her with?

More slick fluid oozed around the bead onto her tongue, and she lapped it eagerly while she gently squeezed his balls. She wanted to make him come, swallow his essence. To serve his pleasure and enhance her own.

She sensed he was about to come when he pulled her off his cock and to her feet. "Lie face-down on the bed and spread your legs," he ordered, his voice a gravelly whisper.

His touch was almost gentle when he stuffed a round bolster pillow under her hips. When he wrapped velcro cuffs around each ankle, securing their nylon leads to opposite bed posts, he took his time, kissing and nipping and licking his way back to her pussy. If he didn't stop, he'd drive her wild.

But he obviously wanted her wild, because he hooked rubber padded clamps to her labia and secured them to long velcro bands around her thighs. She lay helpless, wide open to serve his pleasure.

"Now give me your hands." He knelt between her splayed legs and rubbed his big cock against her sopping slit.

Confused, she did as he ordered, and he grasped both of her wrists.

"Say you want me to be your Master. Tell me you want me to fuck you like this."

"Yesss. Please fuck me, Master." Her pussy clenched with anticipation when he cuffed first one hand and then the other, secured them to the bedposts and stretched out on top of her. She lay beneath him, spread-eagled, helpless...his willing submissive. At each point of contact with his powerful body, her hot skin tingled.

She thrilled at every hot, moist breath as he made his way down her cheek, her neck. The sensitive skin of her back prickled as he licked and nibbled his way to her butt cheeks, those huge, callused hands following the path he'd just taken with his teeth and tongue.

Exquisitely gentle yet unmistakably in control, he made her burn with each touch of his hands, his mouth, his powerfully muscled satin-smooth body. Her breasts ached for his attention, but they were out of his reach as he sat on his haunches between her outstretched legs, his pulsating cock resting against the crack of her butt while his velvety sac nestled within her stretched, wet outer lips.

"Please me and I'll take you to my dungeon," he said, his voice a throaty growl. "Relax."

When he sat back, the sudden burst of cool air brought up goose bumps on her wet, swollen pussy. Then she felt it. Something cold and wet and rigid made its way along her slit. His warm, rough fingers that had been massaging the flesh around her asshole slid away, making room for the invading object.

"Pretend I've got two cocks, baby. This one's about to fuck you in the ass. Loosen up and let me in."

Her anal sphincter clenched, then gave way to the unrelenting pressure of a large, sculpted metal plug that had been a farewell present from her former Master. It stretched her almost unbearably, this cold invader she'd never wanted to use to find her own release.

"Easy. You know you want it. Your cunt's hot and wet and swollen. After I fuck you I'm gonna lick up every drop of that sweet honey."

Slowly, inexorably, Rocky worked the butt plug deeper. The throbbing of his big ringed cock against her thigh set off another gush of moisture. The hot, slick juices that dripped onto her clit and drove her so wild she nearly forgot the icy pain from the foreign object invading her ass.

Then the plug began to warm within her body. Gradually pain gave way to pleasure as he worked it further into her rear passage until finally she felt its flared edge flush against her body while Rocky's own rock-hard cock throbbed at the entrance to her drenched pussy.

"Oh, yesss. Fuck me now. Please, Master."

"Say you want my cock in your cunt." He slid its head along her dripping slit, pausing to massage her clit with the warm, slickly wet silver ring embedded in its tip. "Say it."

"Yes, Master. I want your cock in my cunt. Please." She tried to lift her hips, suck him inside her pussy, but the restraints had rendered her helpless, deliciously without the power to control him or even her own emotions.

"I'll give it to you, baby. First I've got to protect us," he said, pausing a few seconds to don a condom before positioning himself and entering her in one smooth, sure motion.

His movement was maddeningly slow, stretching her inch by delicious inch, moving in and out and hitting her G-spot with each inward stroke. With each silky thrust he pressed deeper, until finally his cock pressed against the opening of her womb and his heavy satin-smooth balls rocked against the sensitized flesh of her clit with his every thrust.

His heated skin scorched her back when he lay over her, his hands sliding beneath her to capture her aching breasts. Finally. He rolled both nipples between his thumbs and middle fingers, gently at first, then harder. Sensations began to converge and mingle, an incredible mix of pleasure and pain—an almost unbearable assault. The fullness that had begun in her ass and pussy migrated to her breasts and belly and every cell in her needy body. Without her conscious direction, her cunt began to convulse around his cock.

Whether she wanted to push out the monster invader or hold it inside her forever, she couldn't say.

"That's it, baby. Let go. Squeeze my cock. Make me give you my cream." His whispered words reverberated against the sensitive skin below one ear before he sank his teeth into her neck just below her jaw, hard enough to trigger the best orgasm she'd had since...

Since ever.

Her stretched inner walls were still contracting around his cock when she felt it start jerking wildly inside the passage made painfully tight by the presence of the now-hot anal plug.

Rocky's scream of satisfaction made Sandra come again. After all, she'd succeeded this first time in pleasing her new Master.

But apparently he wanted more. Having loosened her bonds long enough to flip her onto her back, he discarded the condom, straddled her face, and fed her his cock, still wet and hot and slick with his come. Then he reached between her legs and inserted a nine-inch dildo into her wrung-out pussy.

Full almost beyond bearing, she tried to concentrate on swallowing his big, thick cock with its heavy PA ring and breathing around the velvety-smooth ball sac that lay heavily on her nose. His beard-roughened cheeks abraded the insides of her clamped-off labia while the satin-smooth surface of his ears and head brushed against her inner thighs while he sucked and nibbled at her swollen clit.

He had every orifice of her body stuffed. Possessed. Incredibly aroused again, amazingly since she'd just come moments earlier, Sandra redoubled her efforts, licking and sucking and swallowing until her open mouth cradled his smooth groin...the velvety skin where his cock began to rise from his scrotum.

She was still coming and swallowing the last of his thick, salty cream when she felt him fasten a soft leather harness around her waist and between her legs, tightening it enough to secure the plugs in her butt and pussy.

Fully relaxed for the first time in recent memory, she barely noticed when he loosened her bonds and laid his bald head on her belly to sleep.

Chapter Three

When the early morning sun awakened him, Rocky sat and watched Sandra sleep, satisfied that for the moment he'd managed to allay that brittle air of desperation he'd sensed in her at Bennie's — and before. Hell, until she'd called him Master in that husky, half-scared whisper he'd never considered they might share the sexual appetite he'd honed while working undercover vice twenty years earlier in Tampa's underground of upscale sex clubs and fetish parlors.

Yeah, he'd found he fit right in as a male dom. So much so that the plain vanilla sex in his one short marriage to a high school sweetheart had left him frustrated and wanting. Hell, Gina had hated sucking him off and scoffed at the trouble he took to stay shed of all his body hair. She'd even sworn she didn't like the feel of his tongue on her pussy, which he knew had been a lie since he'd certainly swallowed enough of her honey on the few occasions when she'd let him eat her out.

His ex-wife would have had his ass in jail if he'd ever tried to tie her down or put a dildo up her butt. He imagined most good Italian girls would have done the same — at least those whose mothers had taught them well that sex was for making babies, not having fun.

Funny. He'd figured Sandra for one of those good Italian girls, only focused on her career instead of traditional girly things. In his wilder moments he'd even pictured himself taking her home to Mom and Pop, making them happy that he'd finally taken up with a good Italian woman. One who didn't sport a shaved head with a huge rose tattoo and some very visible facial piercings, like his most recent submissive had flaunted.

Boy, had Sandra given him a fuckin' delicious surprise when she turned out to be a sub. A sub who gave every outward sign of being a cool, collected lady who'd never entertained the first delicious, dirty thought. A sub who'd make his mom nod her head and smile.

Rocky ran his fingers through her silky black hair and grinned. Maybe he'd get an urge to rid her of it, explore all the erogenous zones he'd discovered on Desert Rose's smooth scalp–ones she'd so enthusiastically demonstrated on his own bald pate. If he did, he could always buy her a wig to wear in public. He'd indulge his penchant for piercings to her body parts that only he and she would ever see.

What he wanted to do with Sandra was control her mind. Win her complete trust that whatever he did to her would bring her pleasure. And he wanted her to acknowledge publicly that they were lovers, to flaunt him in front of the pretty-boy lawyers she worked with every day.

Hell, he wanted to discover firsthand with her what he'd realized by observing other Masters and slaves over the years: that if the match was right, they'd soon get past the need for physical manifestations of his control over her. And that the big O could get bigger and better when it came from the heart as well as the gonads.

First, though, he had to establish his dominance. He reached into her toy drawer and selected an ornate pair of round clamps with wicked-looking teeth coated with soft, pink rubber. Then he stroked her satiny breasts, pinching the nipples to hard little points before pulling them through the center circles of the clamps. When both clamps rested flush against her rosy areolas, he tripped the tiny switches that caused the teeth to close, then bathed each jutting nub with his tongue.

"Ooh. Bite me, Master. Please." Her sleepy plea came from lips still reddened from last night's finale.

He worried the closer nipple between his teeth, then clamped down on it until she let out a little scream that jump-started his arousal, making his balls draw up and his cock rear up against his belly. At the same time he tugged on the belt that ensured that her ass and cunt wouldn't dispel the high-end stainless-steel toys. He dipped a hand between her legs to jostle them and remind her the dildos still were there.

God, but she was already dripping wet. Her slick, hot cunt beckoned with its musky smell of sex. And his cock throbbed. But he could wait. First…

Abruptly he pulled away, standing naked in the morning sunlight. "Take off the harness," he ordered. "Then you may get up and shower. When you're finished, take the dildos out, but leave the clips on. It arouses me to see your nipples hot and reddened like this." Unable to resist, he tweaked one of the swollen buds.

"Yes, Master."

If he stayed, he'd fuck her again as soon as the dildos came out of her cunt and ass. And that wasn't in his immediate plans. Reluctantly he picked up the clothes he'd discarded the night before and began to dress.

Today he'd test her, see how far she'd go in pursuit of pleasure. Taking the pad he'd found neatly laid out by the telephone on her bedside table, he composed his orders for the day. Then while she was still in the shower, he rifled through her drawers and closet and laid out what he wanted her to wear. He left the sheet of perfumed paper folded neatly on top of the stack of clothes on her bed. As he strode out of the bland apartment she called home, Rocky glanced at his watch.

Nine hours and two minutes before he'd see Sandra again unless Fate brought him to the state attorney's office on less pleasant business before the work week was over. Unless she decided she didn't want him for her Master after all and blew him off.

*   *   *   *   *

Friday. A quiet day, with only a few defense attorneys wanting to talk plea bargains when they could otherwise be out playing golf or doing whatever it was that got them off. Sandra wished something urgent would come along, take her mind off Rocky's message that she'd tucked into the pocket of her suit jacket.

She didn't want to consider that if she took Rocky as her Master, she could lose the focus, the hard-won self-control that had made her successful in her career. Unlike her old Master, He wouldn't fit neatly into the compartment in her life she'd carved for the sexual part of her life. He'd invade her work space...the solitary time she'd always valued.

Damn it. Recalling the last outing she'd attended with her boisterous family, she realized Rocky would fit right in there, too. And she had a feeling He wouldn't take well to her shoving Him into her sex compartment and excluding Him from the other parts of her life—parts where she'd already let Him in before becoming His sub—when they were no more than good friends.

Sub, hell. Rocky obviously intended that she be His

slave. She'd almost ignored the instructions He'd left on her bed, instructions she was certain He'd meant to test her, to see how far she was willing to go for satisfaction.

She hadn't been able to say no, not when she'd just come out of the shower, pleasantly sore and still tingling from the long-denied orgasms He'd given her. Blindly, she'd complied with every scribbled order despite her doubts about her own sanity.

"By the way, Ms. Giancone, you look good in that red suit," the office's resident young stud Craig McDermott told her after she'd helped him find a precedent for objecting to change of venue for a rape case he was to try the following week. The kid winked—she could hardly believe it—as he backed out of her office and shut the door behind him. Junior staff attorneys didn't wink at cool, collected Ms. Giancone.

Maybe, Sandra figured, she looked sexy because she had sex firmly on her mind. How could she not?

The suit Rocky had chosen for her hid the scanty underwear He'd ordered her to wear—a lacy garter belt and matching bra with cutouts for the nipples that only a man would choose. The sheer thigh-high stockings He'd chosen scratched deliciously against her inner thighs whenever she moved around on spike-heeled black pumps better suited for an evening out than a day in the office.

Good thing the nubby fabric of her jacket disguised her rock-hard nipples that jutted from the cutouts in her bra. Not so good that they rubbed deliciously against the rough texture of the material. But fortunate indeed that Rocky—Master—had instructed her to remove the nipple clamps He'd put on her this morning, presumably in the interest of discretion.

She found herself wondering if He'd stop by the office. He sometimes did. Would He want to see whether she'd followed His instructions to the letter, even to the severe skinned-back French twist He'd ordered her to wear to bare her throat and the silver hoop earrings that seemed much larger now than when she wore her usual pageboy?

Her cunt clenched when she imagined Him slipping a hand under her conservative straight skirt and checking out her bare pussy, now as smoothly shaved as His head, per His orders. As soft now as the rest of His big, muscular body. Especially His incredibly satin-smooth cock and balls. She fantasized that He'd insert his rough, callused fingers in her cunt, and that He'd grin with satisfaction when He felt the diaphragm He'd ordered her to obtain and insert for His convenience–and His pleasure.

Sandra's tongue tingled at the thought of taking Him in her mouth again. And she could hardly wait to rub His big, satiny ball sac with the smooth round barbell He'd told her to insert in her tongue today.

The mandarin collar of her jacket hid a love-bite she'd noticed was turning an interesting shade of lavender. She'd seen it this morning when she'd lifted the thick curtain of hair off her neck and shoulders. The memory of Him topping her, licking and nibbling and rubbing His hot flesh over hers made her mouth go dry while her own steaming juices ran along her slit, bathing the entrance to her stretched, sensitive rear passage.

Good thing she hadn't had a court appearance today. Sandra slid her tongue along the roof of her mouth. The tongue ring, heavier than the one she'd worn for her old Master's pleasure, made her slur her speech, particularly now when she'd worn nothing but the acrylic retainer through her piercing for almost a year. It made her diction less distinct but, she thought, gave her voice a softer, sexier edge. Maybe, she thought, that edge came from her need for the day to pass by quickly so she could serve Rocky.

Sandra pulled out the paper that listed His orders, staring at the last two instructions—ones she had yet to follow. Opening her purse, she stared down at the egg-shaped pink acrylic vibrator, another parting gift from her former Master...the one to which Rocky now held a powerful remote control.

At precisely two-fifteen, put the egg in your pretty little cunt and think of how much better My cock will feel there. But do not come. Your orgasms belong to Me.

Dared she disobey? No. Not while every cell in her body ached to please Him. Sandra held the vibrator, warming it between her trembling palms. Glancing at her watch, she saw she had less than two minutes to do His bidding. She slid her desk chair as close as it would go toward the desk, hiding the lower half of her body from the view of anyone who might pass by.

Could she do this and still function outwardly for nearly three hours like the cool, collected prosecutor who let nothing interfere with business?

She'd have to. Until she talked with Him, established ground rules for her servitude. Now the yearning ache deep within her cunt compelled her to follow His last orders.

Since there was no time to take the fifty-yard trek to the nearest ladies' room, Sandra reached under her skirt and slipped the egg between her sopping pussy lips. Shoved it as deep inside her cunt as she could push it with her fingers. Then she clenched her inner muscles, mindful that the thing might pop out and that He'd allowed her no panties that might help keep the vibrator from bouncing onto her office floor.

Just as she'd thought she could control the needy sensations that snaked through her body, the vibrator began a gentle motion, back and forth, around and around. Her breathing became ragged before she regained control and managed with difficulty to concentrate on studying the police report of a recent drug bust for which she was to prosecute the accused ringleader.

Over the next hour or so, the gentle hum in her cunt strengthened, made her squirm. She checked her watch. Damn, she had to endure this for at least another hour before she could leave.

Giving up on reading, Sandra considered Rocky's last command. Subservience to Him. Her acknowledgment of His mastery.

She opened her center desk drawer and lifted the thick gold collar she'd worn for her former master. Smiling, she opened the innocuous-looking cameo that had nestled in the hollow of her throat—and slipped her finger through the sturdy O-ring it concealed. The ring where he'd delighted in hooking a matching gold leash.

His leaving had hurt her far more than the worst stings of his whip against her tender flesh, but He'd been right to go because she'd failed him. She'd refused to give up her professional persona and admit her enslavement to the world. Now his once godlike image had faded in her mind, replaced by a picture of the big, rugged cop whose discipline she sensed from His gentle touch would always involve more mind games than whips and chains.

Sandra glanced down at Rocky's last command. My collar awaits you. If you want to wear it, give me your hand when I come for you.

Would He agree their relationship must be kept private? For a long time her former master had, until he'd realized that for her the ultimate humiliation would be acknowledging to those in the plain vanilla world that she was his BDSM slave, lower in his estimation than the pit bull bitch he kept for hunting hogs. He'd relished taking her to public dungeons cloaked, masked and hooded, with her entire head and body except her well-used mouth, her rouged nipples and her clean-shaven crotch concealed under skin-tight, shiny black latex. But he'd wanted more. He'd wanted to strip her bare before her colleagues.

She imagined Rocky would expect her to go public with their relationship, although she doubted He would go so far as to flaunt His connection with the BDSM world, considering His job. With luck, she'd persuade Him to accept that His mastery of her must remain private...secure...and limited to times when they were alone. With more luck He wouldn't insist that she publicly acknowledge her enslavement at one of the well-known local sex clubs while she knelt before less vulnerable members of the local BDSM community to accept His collar.

She couldn't—wouldn't—do it. Wouldn't risk the respect she'd struggled to gain in the vanilla community, even if it meant a lifetime without the delicious sensation of being controlled...mastered by a true Master. While she might once again endure the humiliation of being lent to strangers, ordered to do their sexual bidding as well as His, she'd never let Him bare her face.

When she reached across the desk for the phone to call Him and tell Him this wouldn't work, though, the motion set off more tingling in her nipples. And the vibrations of the egg inside her cunt intensified, as though He'd sensed her doubts...her misgivings. Before she finished dialing the cell phone number He'd given her this morning, He strode through her office door, a benevolent smile on His rugged face. And closed the door behind Him.

A moment earlier she'd been sure she wouldn't do it, but when she met His smoldering gaze she held out her hand. He sandwiched it between His callused palms.

* * * * *

"Have you prepared yourself?" Rocky's gaze slid from Sandra's breasts to her lap as he fingered the remote control in his pocket and set the vibrator speed to its highest level. From the way she squirmed in her chair, he surmised she'd followed his orders at least to that point.

"Yes, Master," she said, but he sensed doubt in the way her voice broke on the respectful reply.

God, was she hot. His nostrils flared at the heady smell of her arousal and her perfume, obvious to him but mistakable as a musky, sexy bottled scent by anyone who hadn't eaten her cunt and licked her clit to a hard little point. Her pink tongue darted out, wetting lips as red as he'd made her nipples this morning with the clamps and his teeth.

His cock swelled against the codpiece of the leather jock he'd put on a few minutes ago beneath his dress slacks, and his balls drew up painfully in their sac. "You have doubts, Sandy?" he asked, encouraging her to speak up now before taking the step that would set her on the path to becoming his submissive—perhaps even his lifetime slave.

"I–I don't want anyone else to know. Master." As though she feared him, she hunkered down behind her desk.

Damn it, he wanted to flaunt her to one and all. But her sanctimonious boss probably would choke and sputter if he ever found out one of his lawyers was into the BDSM scene. Before he could stay his hand, he turned off the vibrator, a clear sign of silent rebuke.

When she met his gaze, he sensed her fear. "No one can know I'm Your slave. To the world we must look like friends–or lovers."

He felt he had to balk at least a little, lest she realize he'd have done his damnedest to curb his own dominant tendencies if she hadn't revealed she was a sub. "And if this doesn't please me?" he asked sharply.

"You could disguise me if You want to take me to the dungeons, Master," she said, casting her dark eyes toward the floor. "My old master did."

Suddenly Rocky recalled a slender sub who'd come onto the scene a few years back. She'd belonged to a real sadist he'd often wanted to punch out because of the way he'd treated the woman known only as S. Hell, once he'd been invited to sit on her masked face and let her suck him off while her Master had fucked her in the ass and another dom had fucked her cunt. The asshole had beaten her unmercifully when she'd failed to get everybody off at once.

"We don't have to do the dungeon scene, little one," Rocky said, almost certain she'd been the nameless, faceless slave he'd once helped humiliate at her former master's invitation. "Come with me. I'll take care of you. We'll skip drinks at Bennie's and go straight to my boat. I've never collared a slave before. I can do it as well in private as in public." He set the vibrator to humming again inside her, getting hard when he imagined her cunt dripping, weeping for the satisfaction he wanted her to trust he'd provide.

"Yesss," she hissed, spreading her legs as though inviting him to take her here, where one of her coworkers might walk in at any moment.

"I know you're hot, baby, but here's not the time or place." He drew her to her feet, ground his painfully restrained cock against her pussy while he slid one hand inside her jacket and tweaked one of the jutting nubs that he'd been able to see even through the concealing red material. "Let's go."

"Yes, Master." She leaned back against his other hand that caressed her exposed nape, reminding him that since she wanted privacy, he'd be the one to prepare her to wear the ornate collar he'd designed and bought years ago when, as a naive kid, he'd expected his wife would take to his adopted lifestyle as enthusiastically as he had. The collar he'd never bestowed on any woman during the twenty years it had been in his possession.

The collar Sandra would wear for his eyes only. For his pleasure. She'd wear his ring where no one but him would ever see it. If he got real lucky she'd agree to acknowledge the depth of their relationship–just not their lifestyle. Then he could put a ring on her finger. Meanwhile he'd take all she offered.

* * * * *

In moments they were driving south on I-75 in Rocky's sturdy SUV toward an unknown destination, and Rocky was stroking Sandra's newly shaved pussy with his right hand while grasping the steering wheel expertly with the other.

"Did you have any trouble getting the diaphragm?" he asked, dipping two fingers into her cunt and getting a testosterone rush when her inner walls convulsed around his fingers and a fresh wave of slick, hot lubrication flooded his hand.

She squirmed a little, as though to intensify the "No, Master. I already had one."

"No Pill, right?"

"Not for years. And not now. I'm too old for them to be safe."

"Okay. We'll be careful. And if we have an unexpected dividend, we'll take care of it together. Understood?" Rocky wasn't keen on having a kid horn in on his fun with Sandra, at least right away, but he wanted her to know if they got pregnant, he wanted in on the decision as to what they'd do.

"Yes, Master. Oh, yesss," she hissed, arching her hips so her pussy came in even closer contact with his hand.

"Feel good?" he asked as he circled her swollen clit, already slick with the juices that perfumed the inside of the car and made his cock rear up against the constricting jock.

"Feels incredible. Makes me so hot, I can barely wait for your big, hard cock. Why do you shave off all your hair?" she asked, changing the subject. Her soft fingers drifted over the back of his head , driving him wild. "Not that I don't like it…"

He chuckled. "My hair was already thinning twenty years ago when I decided the skinhead look fit my undercover persona. Now all I have to shave to keep it smooth is an ever-shrinking horseshoe above and behind my ears. Sort of like a monk's tonsure. Besides, I love the feel of a woman's hands and mouth and wet, sweet cunt on my bare scalp. It's an incredible turn-on.

"As for my body, I like it smooth. It's a lot more sensitive than when it's covered with hair. How about you? Do my fingers get you hornier now, when they don't get tangled in your pubic curls?" He cupped her silky mound, desperate to bury his aching cock inside her cunt one last time before the placement of his ring would put that sweet hole off-limits for a time.

* * * * *

Suddenly He pulled off the Interstate, found a side road, and stopped under the shade of tall pine trees and scrub palmettos. In one hurried motion He slid out from under the wheel, fumbling with His zipper as He lifted her over his lap and removed the vibrator from her tingling, eager cunt.

"Unsnap my codpiece," He rasped against the sensitive skin just below her earlobe while He unbuttoned her jacket and bared her jutting nipples.

It took both of her hands to loosen the snaps that fastened the heavy leather over His bulging sex, and when His cock sprang free it sought her pussy the way a divining rod might seek water. Eager for Him to fuck her, she spread her outer lips in welcome. Already sopping wet, her cunt gushed more lubricating fluid at the first contact with His rigid, ringed cockhead.

He sank into her wet heat as though He couldn't wait, tugging her off Him by her exposed nipples then slamming her down on His swollen shaft again and again. Delicious sensations coursed through her from her nipples and her cunt, where He nudged her G-spot with His metal

PA ring each time He stuffed her with His monster cock. Her ass rested against His satiny balls, the contact setting off waves of sensation there as well.

"May–may I please come?" she asked as waves of pleasure coursed through her and threatened to explode.

"Am I your Master?" He asked, His breath hot against the sensitive flesh of her exposed neck.

"God yes. Master. Oh, please. Fuck me harder. Bite me. Make me come." With both hands she cradled the back of His head, willing Him to devour her, claim her as His own.

As though at her bidding, He sank His teeth into her tender flesh, sucking it in. Sharp pain there, and in nipples He now pinched cruelly between His thumbs and forefingers. Incredible sensations deep inside her cunt where His hot spurting semen bathed flesh made tender by the unrelenting battering of His huge cock head with its silver PA ring.

Delicious pain. Incredible pleasure. Sandra cherished His gift—His hot seed spewing into her, intensifying the waves of sexual fulfillment that radiated from Him to her spasming pussy and throughout her entire being.

She collapsed against Him, her head bowed, and breathed in the delicious smell of His cologne and sex and the supple leather of the car seat before remembering her place.

"Thank you, Master," she murmured a moment later when, on her knees on the plush carpeted floor of the SUV, she licked away the evidence of His climax and hers. Starting with His satiny sac, she sucked first one big ball and then the other into her mouth, licking and loving them. Then she lapped every inch of His thick shaft, around His prominent corona and over His satiny cock head to the slit with its heavy ring. A delicious dribble of the cream that had flooded her cunt now dribbled down her thighs.

The heavy pressure of His fingers as they burrowed into her tightly-restrained hair sent new waves of desire to tissue still tingling from the massive orgasm He'd just granted her.

Chapter Four

Moonlight filtered through the tinted windows of the SUV, the golden sphere muted to a bronze glow that reflected off the hard ridges of Rocky's naked belly. Then all went dark when He lifted her face away from His cock and lowered a velvety-textured hood over her eyes and face. With slow, sure motions He laced it snugly about her head, enveloping her in soft, black darkness.

Sandra hated the dark, yet with Him she felt safe...protected. The even cadence of His breathing, the powerful purr of the engine, the stimulating sensation of the gently vibrating leather seat against her bare, swollen clit—even the pervasive, arousing smells of the sex they'd just shared seemed more intense for her now, deprived as she was of the distraction of sight.

"There are two things I require of my slave," He said softly as he pulled the car to a stop a few minutes later. "The first is that you wear my ring. Since you wish to keep our relationship private, I will place it where only you and I will ever see it. The friend who will help me place it will never see your face, which is why you wear the hood. I'll explain my second requirement later."

His fingers laced through hers, He led her through the darkness. A cool breeze blew, its smell slightly salty and fishy. Moist, too. They must be near the Gulf. Sandra's swollen pussy lips and exposed nipples popped up goose bumps, she was certain, with the sudden exposure to sea air. Boards creaked below her feet and when a spike heel caught between them she'd have fallen but for Master's quick move to steady her against His hard body before setting her down on a surface that rocked gently in the breeze.

"Easy, there. And welcome to *Neptune's Dungeon*," He said, His tone one of pride and amusement. "She's a forty-foot cabin cruiser. I'm sure you'll appreciate the modifications I've made to accommodate my lifestyle...ours now, my beloved slave."

As though she were a bride, He scooped her into His arms, carried her down some stairs, and set her onto a flat, padded surface. "My friend is already here. Be still while I get you ready."

His touch exquisitely gentle, He rid her of her suit jacket and skirt, then bent and tongued the nipples and areolas left bare by the cutouts of her bra. The nubs hardened, aching already at the prospect of having one of them pierced to display His ring. "Which one will you have pierced, Master?" she asked idly, reaching up blindly and stroking His satiny scalp.

His bald head reminded her He was silky smooth all over...an incredibly sexy cloak of satiny hairless skin stretched over massive muscle and sinew. Soft and hard. Cruel yet kind. A Dom she could trust, must trust if she were to grant Him complete control over her sexual being.

And He'd already breached her defenses, broken down her self-will. Her cunt, still wet and tingling from His fucking, gushed more love juices when He laid His big hand on her newly-shorn mound. "You will wear my ring in your clit," He said, His deep voice quiet, almost worshipful as His hot breath traced a tingling path from her nipples to that swollen flesh before He caught it between His teeth and flailed it with His tongue.

Incredibly stimulated at the thought of Him putting the proof of His ownership there, in her tingling, swollen clit, she spread her legs wider. Her eyes closed against the blackness within the hood, she pictured His shaven head between her legs, tanned and glowing against her pale, hairless mound. His tongue tugging on the jewel — His jewel that He'd soon have inserted there to stake His claim — much like she longed to rotate the heavy ring through the head of His big, hard cock.

Gloved hands tightened what felt like a wide restraining belt across her middle, then fastened her arms into cuffs and hooked them to the sides of the belt. "She is ready now, if you'll just take your face out of her cunt and fasten her legs into the stirrups," said the owner of those hands. The piercer, Sandra guessed when her Master quickly stepped away and strapped her legs into what felt like the cold metal stirrups in her gynecologist's office.

The icy feel of antiseptic, the bite of a clamp, and one sharp pain when a needle pierced through her swollen flesh gave way to an intense sexual pleasure-pain that rocked her entire body with wave after exquisite climactic wave. A sharp tug on what she imagined was her new clit ring triggered another intense little orgasm.

"It's beautiful. You won't believe how hard my cock is, just from looking at your plump pink clit with my ring dangling from it. I can hardly wait to taste it. Taste you." She loved the feel of His hands cupping her breasts, His breath bathing the insides of her thighs in moist heat.

"Thank you, Master," she whispered into the velvet hood. "Now I am Yours."

Rocky skimmed his hands over Sandra's helpless body, his gaze on her swollen clit and its little gold ring with a jeweled captive bead. Reluctantly, for his tongue and fingers itched to play with her new toy, he positioned the sterile vinyl shield the piercer handed him and smoothed its adhesive edges down to protect her newly pierced flesh from bacteria that might lurk on his hands and mouth. Momentarily he regretted that for the next few weeks he'd have to protect her this way whenever they made love—and that for a few days he'd have to deny his cock the pleasure of her cunt while the piercing began to heal.

Turning to the piercer, an old friend who'd done his PA years ago, he thanked him for his expertise and sent him on his way. Strange, he thought, that he didn't want to share his Sandy. He'd participated in countless threesomes in the years since discovering his taste for the BDSM lifestyle, without once begrudging a fellow dom the courtesy of sharing his sub.

Rocky shrugged off the unfamiliar need to keep his woman to himself. Love…it brought on new emotions, he guessed. There'd be time to analyze it later if analysis was called for.

For now he had Sandra alone. A perfect sub, pinned to a table, her legs raised and spread for his pleasure. A slave who obviously loved every act he'd yet performed on her willing body. A sub. No, not a sub or a slave but a partner he'd pleasure in every way at his disposal. A partner he'd take care of, protect. One he'd cut his own throat before he'd hurt.

Rocky visualized the love-swing hung in the center of the rear salon, the mirrored floor, walls, and ceiling of the room that would reflect the acts taking place there from every angle. He pictured Sandy's pretty ass, positioned at just the right level for his cock to penetrate. Her breasts hanging free, the sensitive nipples blossoming, swelling between his fingers while he cradled the generous globes in his hands. Moving from the table, he quickly freed her bonds, loosened and removed the velvet hood — and dug his fingers into her tightly bound hair, dislodging pins and sending the jet-black mass tumbling in wild disarray around her gorgeous, wanton face.

Rocky couldn't resist taking her mouth, fucking it with his tongue the way he intended to fuck her tight little ass with his cock. Then he scooped her up, strode into the rear salon, and positioned her willing body face down, fastening the straps to secure her hips and thighs in the slings on either side of the center swing, her hands in cuffs attached to the thigh slings, and...

The collar. He'd forgotten in his haste to put her in the silk-lined leather symbol of her servitude. A symbol Sandy obviously expected. If she hadn't, she wouldn't have mentioned earlier that she'd only wear it when they were alone.

After removing her hood, he hurried back to the table where she'd just been pierced, retrieved the collar from its hiding place and squatted beside her head that now rested on the soft leather of the swing's downward slope. "Kiss it," he ordered, holding up the wide, thick collar with delicate silver embossing and a heavy, filigree patterned silver D-ring where occasionally he'd attach the matching leash.

She did as he commanded and kissed it, though her eyes widened as if she feared taking this final step into submission.

Soon enough he'd dispel her misgivings, he thought as he positioned the collar and started to close the three snaps. "Your hair's in the way," he told her, grasping a handful and lifting it free. "There. I promise to give you pleasure, never pain. To fulfill your every sexual fantasy. Now relax."

Using loops on the swing, Rocky hooked them through the collar's D-ring, completing her bondage.

* * * * *

Helpless to her Master's desire, Sandra experienced the extent of her subservient state, the pictures reflected back at her from various angles when she gazed at the mirrors beneath and behind her. Her pussy spasmed as she savored the sense of being possessed, anticipated what He would do next to enhance her pain and her pleasure.

Bound body, neck, and limbs to butter-soft black leather, with her bare breasts hanging free between her legs, all her most sensitive flesh would lie within His easy reach when He stood behind her upthrust ass. She imagined the cool silver of His PA ring nestling between the dimples on either side of her ass cheeks, a stark contrast to the heat of His cock. It would lie heavily, pulsating with life within her spread-out butt crack. His balls would bounce against her slit, sending new waves of sensation throughout her body from her swollen clit.

When the inner walls of her cunt contracted involuntarily, the movement made nerves vibrate against the part of the ring inside her clit. Sensation spread to her cunt, her ass, even to nipples whose needy tingling made her want to beg Him to touch them, suck them, flog them — subject them to the delicious torture of clamps and whips and floggers she had no doubt He possessed in this exquisitely furnished floating dungeon.

He'd adjusted the height of the swing so her raised, exposed pussy with its brand-new clit ring would hang more or less at the level of His cock when He stood behind her. Now He'd retreated across the mirrored room, still close by but too far away for her to touch even if her hands had been free. His dark eyes glowed with sexual promise when He met her needy gaze.

A calm sea lapped noisily against the sides of the boat while she fantasized about lapping Him up. His features were regular, classically handsome yet somehow made rugged by the total lack of hair on His well-shaped head and the hard set of those full, sensual lips. God, how she wanted to feel His lips on her breasts, her sopping cunt. She yearned to feel Him use His mouth to stimulate the throbbing bundle of nerves He'd just had pierced as evidence of His possession.

In slow motion, He unbuttoned the white dress shirt that stood in stark contrast with His satiny, swarthy skin. Powerful muscles rippled in His chest and across His flat, hard belly when He shrugged the garment off and reached for His belt.

Would He use that belt on her upthrust ass?

No, it seemed that wasn't in His plan, because He tossed it away and stepped out of His shoes. Deck shoes, she noticed, worn without socks. Not black but buttery tan, like the khaki pants now slithering down His hard-muscled thighs to reveal the heavy leather jock she'd freed His cock from an hour earlier so He could fuck her along that deserted road near I-75.

Her mouth watered at the sight of that bulging black codpiece, the narrow straps that ringed His muscular thighs and held the leather snugly to His satin-smooth groin. Eagerly, she waited, but He made no move to take off the jock or loosen the codpiece and free His huge, delicious cock and balls.

Instead He moved behind her and adjusted the height

of the swing once more before bending over her and running His agile tongue beneath the lower edge of her collar.

Reminded of His possession, her helplessness, Sandra soaked in each sexually charged touch of His tongue, each moist warm breath He exhaled along the sensitive flesh in the center of her spine. The light, arousing sensation of His callused fingertips exploring the hills and valleys of her widely spread thighs and calves. Slowly, as if savoring this exploration of His new possession, He ran His hands up her thighs, over the swing that cradled her belly, until they cupped her hanging breasts.

"Beautiful," he murmured, sliding the pads of His thumbs over her aching nipples with exquisite gentleness. "I love the taste of you," He added, taking a long, arousing swipe down her back with His satiny tongue. When He sank His teeth into her buttocks then soothed each love bite with a languorous lick, her cunt gushed fresh juices over the barrier that shielded her pierced clit.

He bent further and traced sensuous circles around her anus with His velvet-soft tongue. When He stopped and stepped away, she barely held back a yelp of frustration.

* * * * *

So beautiful. So helpless. So *his*.

His black collar stood out starkly against the pale olive tone of her satiny skin. Her breasts hung down, lush rose-tipped mounds begging for more attention from his hands and mouth. Between her stretched-open labia the tiny ruby in her new clit ring winked at him through the plastic barrier shield.

He could hardly wait for the piercing to heal so he could suck and lick and nibble that sensitive little bundle of sexual pleasure to his heart's content. But the brief denial would be worth it—and not only to proclaim his ownership. Sandy's clit was made to be adorned, so sensitive and responsive even to the piercer's cruel needle. His mouth had watered, he'd wanted so much to lick away the honey he'd seen gushing from her cunt at the moment she'd been pierced.

Rocky ripped open his codpiece, leaving his cock and balls free but for the snug leather cock ring that held the jock firmly to his groin. The lubricated condom he slid over his heated flesh did nothing to restrain the urgency in his tortured balls—the compulsion to mark Sandy his in every way.

"Fuck me, Master. Please fuck me now," she whimpered, her pink tongue darting out between lips swollen from his kisses as her gaze focused on the reflection of his rampant erection.

He picked a tube of lubricant from his bag of toys and smeared some of its contents over his sheathed cock, never diverting his eyes from hers. "I'm going to fuck your pretty ass. But first…"

Fuck if he didn't want to own not only her body but her soul. Stake his claim and spill his cream in her cunt, her mouth, her ass. "I'm going to make you come like you've never come before. And I'm going to do it without inflicting the slightest damage on your delectable flesh. After all, why would a master want to hurt his most precious possession?"

After setting the tube of lubricant on the floor behind her, he sank to his knees, dipped his head to her glistening slit while he reached under her and cupped both breasts.

Pulling lightly on the nipples, he lapped droplets of the love juices that seeped from her cunt. Her sheathed clit throbbed against his lower lip, and she squirmed, as if to make her newly pierced flesh more accessible to his seeking mouth.

"Oh, God yes!" She dipped her head and caught two of his fingers in her mouth when he offered them. As though they were his cock, she licked and sucked and swirled her tongue around, all the time rubbing her sopping cunt against his face, bathing him in her juices, driving him wild to fuck her until she'd wrung out every drop of semen from his swollen, aching balls. For a minute he felt guilty that he'd sent the piercer away instead of inviting him to join in the fun — but only for a minute.

He really did want her all to himself.

Tenderly he licked her slit, angling his head so his tongue could slide inside her sopping cunt. So he could ring the puckered opening to her ass, readying it for his cock.

"Please fuck me, Master. Put your big hard cock inside my cunt again and let me come." Vibrations from her throat tickled his fingers when she made her anguished plea.

"Relax, baby. Your cunt's off limits for a few days. But this tight hole's fair game. You're gonna love it," he murmured against her puckered rear end. Then he tongued her again, circling until suddenly he plunged the tip of his tongue inside the tiny opening. Standing, he reached for the tube of lubricant and smeared more of it over his sheathed erection.

His eyes glowed with hot desire when He met her reflected gaze. The deliberate stroking of the slick stuff over His jutting cock filled Sandra with fear — and delicious anticipation of the pleasure-pain she sensed was coming.

Her pussy clenched and gushed more honey when she felt Him ring her anus with a gentle finger dripping the same slick, wet lubricant he'd smeared over the massive length of his cock. Involuntarily her flesh tightened when he began to insert that finger slowly, reminding her that soon he'd stuff that tight, ungiving hole with the huge glistening shaft that jutted proudly from his buff, hairless body. Reflected at her from the mirrors on three sides of the room, that long, thick weapon seemed more formidable accentuated by the tight cock ring built into his black leather jock.

Her mouth went dry. The smell of sex filled her nostrils. Reflections of her, hanging helpless to His desire, and of Him preparing to fuck her, had her cunt dripping its juices over her throbbing clit and onto the mirrored floor. Her breasts tingled and the nipples jutted forward like tiny cocks seeking…

"Oh, yesss." He'd opened her, lubricated her, preparing her ass for His cock with His big, callused fingers. His ringed cockhead now pressed bluntly at her anus, its pressure slow, steady, insistent. With one hand He milked His cock. With the other, He stroked along her hot, wet slit, around her cunt and lower, to brush ever so softly against her swollen clit. "Please, Master. Make me come now, before I die."

"Easy," He murmured when she tried to rear back and give what He apparently was not yet ready to take. "Feel my ring in your clit. Imagine me sucking it when the piercing heals. It's going to feel good. So fucking good you'll wonder why you didn't pierce that jewel years ago." He paused, pressing a little harder against her anal sphincter when she started to whimper and moan. "Relax, baby. Take a couple of deep breaths. When you do, I'm going to slide my cock up your pretty ass."

"Oh, yesss. That feels good. So-oo good. Please, Master, fuck me now. Fuck my ass."

He was so big, so hot. She gasped when He pressed beyond her anal sphincter, certain He'd split her apart. The white-hot pain shot through her, followed by another wave of intense pleasure when He grasped her breasts and squeezed them in His big, strong hands.

"Open up, baby. You can take me. Damn, but your ass is tight." With each slow stroke He sank His rock-hard cock deeper. Her cunt constricted as though protesting its emptiness, and her clit swelled more against the incredibly arousing little ring.

With each slow, rhythmic stroke pain gave way to a delicious sense of fullness that began a chain reaction of erotic sensation. Sensations that careened from cell to cell, one after the other bursting into shards of pleasure that went on and on and on.

When she shattered, He buried His cock to the balls and let go, the jerking spasms of His climax feeding hers. Only much later when they lay in the big bed along one wall of the mirrored salon and she ran her pierced tongue lazily along the length of His satiny cock did she think about the lingering soreness–and marvel that she'd managed to take all twelve glorious inches of Him up her ass.

Chapter Five

Rocky woke the next morning, his hard-on nestled in the crack of Sandy's butt. A brisk breeze outside rocked the boat, reminded him where they were and that he'd planned more for this weekend than a fuckfest. He needed to get his ass up and get underway, because he had no intention of letting his new slave escape on the grounds of needing to get work done.

Neptune's Dungeon moved along lazily in the chilly water of the Gulf, operating on autopilot while Rocky brewed coffee and set out doughnuts and some fruit for them to nibble on while they talked.

And talk they would. Now that he'd found his soulmate, he had no intention of letting her go. Or letting work interfere — his or hers.

He reached inside his sweat pants and rubbed at the base of his cock and balls, making a mental note to toss that jock or have a leather craftsman he knew adjust the fit. Later on when they went back to his place in Tampa, he'd join Sandy in a steaming hot shower. Meanwhile maybe he'd have her soothe the raw spots with the pierced tongue that had first clued him in on her secret sexual appetites.

She was sleeping like a baby, curled up on her side with her knees pulled up against her beautiful breasts and her wet, rosy pussy exposed to his gaze. His collar stood out starkly against the creamy paleness of her neck, the attached leash loosely looped around a bolt in the mirrored wall.

"Time to get up," he said, bending down and unfastening the leash. Unable to resist tasting her again, he swiped his tongue along the small of her back and into the valley between her luscious ass cheeks. "We need to talk."

"All right, Master." Her sleepy voice reminded him of sex. Hell, everything about her reminded him of sex now that their preferences were up-front and they'd escaped the blunting cloak of civilized society.

She rolled over and came up on her knees, clasping her hands behind her back. Images of her downcast eyes and the vulnerable curve of her neck and back were reflected at him from all around the mirrored room while he looked directly on her upthrust breasts and the curtain of silky black hair that hung down and obscured most of her face.

Apparently her old master had trained her well. Jealousy bubbled up in Rocky—along with the unprecedented desire that this slave should belong to him and only him not only now and in the future, but in her past as well.

"Let's put this on you so you can come above," he growled as he draped an old silk robe over her shoulders.

It took all his patience, all his resolve, to resist tasting her swollen clit after he'd peeled off the plastic protective shield and eased an egg-shaped dildo into her very tempting cunt. Feeling deprived but determined they'd have the talk that should have happened before he'd ringed and collared her, he belted the concealing robe around her lush, submissive body and ordered her to come on deck.

* * * * *

From topside, *Neptune's Dungeon* looked like any other rich man's toy, Sandra thought once she'd gotten a good look at the gleaming white deck and mahogany fittings on what she guessed must have been an old but well-kept motor yacht. Its engine's purr and the slapping sound of gentle waves punctuated the silence of a glassy-smooth sea.

She liked the isolation…the feeling of oneness with her Master in a vast, watery playpen. The delicious invasion of His ring that pierced her clit, the gentle rolling of the deck accentuating every sensation within that little nub of nerves. Even the slide of His silk robe against her breasts and belly made her cunt throb and drip hot slick juices along her smooth slit and down one trembling thigh.

Standing at the helm, His strong hands on the spokes of the boat's wheel, He looked like any other boater out for a day cruise on the Gulf, buttressed against the chilly March winds by soft burgundy sweats. A black stocking cap concealed His shaved head, and only the sun's reflection off the discreet silver stud in His left ear hinted that He might be other than a plain-vanilla businessman, doctor, or lawyer out playing with His toy.

Actually, Sandra thought, He was out playing with His toy. Her. And that thought made her hotter and wetter. His collar chafed her chin when she turned her head to get a better look at a sailboat in the distance.

"Don't worry. They're too far away to see us," Rocky said, pointing to the deck beneath his feet. "Kneel here."

No one would mistake the glittering lust in His dark eyes for plain-vanilla anything. He projected dark desire, sexual control…and something more. Something she feared.

Her old master had only wanted her body for his pleasure, her pain. He hadn't loved her—and he'd expected the sort of subservient commitment that was physical, superficial, never asking her to engage any deeper emotions. She wasn't certain he'd possessed any emotions other than that carefully disciplined sadism that had once excited her so.

Perhaps that's why she'd accepted her old master's desire for degradation as part of her subservience. He'd satisfied her sexually without demanding her heart.

She feared Rocky wanted to own not only her body, but also her soul. And she was very much afraid that if she gave in to His demands there would be nothing left of Sandra Giancone because He would be so easy to surrender to without reserve. To love.

She dared not surrender all. Yet her cunt spasmed and her clit swelled and hardened against His ring, demanding that she accept Him and immerse her whole being in the pleasure only He could give.

Steeling herself not to give in to any demands beyond those of His sex and hers, she sank to her knees and clasped her hands behind her back, lowering her gaze to His scuffed deck shoes while she awaited His further orders.

"Look at me."

Damn it, she wanted to obey Him. Wanted to be not only his sex submissive but His total slave. Yet she needed to maintain some control...some say in how she lived her life, some say in deciding what she would and wouldn't relinquish in order to accede to His domination—His mastery.

His callused fingers clasped her chin, tilted her head

back until she had no choice but to look Him in the eye. "I'm going to talk. You're going to listen. You may look at me or amuse yourself by tickling me with this."

Glittering in the morning sunshine, a silver vibrating tongue ring lay in His big hand. Something she'd never tried...but which make her mouth water in anticipation of using it. Using it on His cock, she'd set up a vibration in His cockhead by tangling it with His PA ring. She imagined the sensation would drive them both wild.

She wanted to...she thought she felt her tongue swelling with anticipation. "May I please lick Your cock and balls, Master?"

"Give me your tongue."

Keeping eye contact with Him, she stuck out her tongue, enjoying the slight pressure of His fingers on its sensitive tip as He replaced her barbell with His tiny electronic toy and set it in motion. Then He slid His hand inside the fly of His sweat pants and drew out His jewels.

Already half-erect, His cock beckoned her and she rose to pay it homage, but now she wanted to taste His satiny scrotum. She tongued it with long, slow strokes, pausing every now and then to suck His testicles into her mouth and play with them one at the time. Strange yet pleasantly arousing, the vibrations from the tongue ring spread to her nipples and clit and deep inside her ass and cunt even as they apparently stimulated Him to full, mouthwatering arousal. In her excitement she nearly lost her balance, but she dared not move her hands from behind her back. It surprised her when He very gently steadied her.

"Because you wear my collar, it's my duty to serve you as fully as it's your job to serve me," He said, His tone implying a mild rebuke. "You don't have to ask if you need something. And you don't need to maintain that posture if it's making you uncomfortable. Steady your hands on my legs or ass, whichever is more comfortable for you."

Hesitating for a moment, for she feared He might have been playing mind games the way her old Master used to do sometimes, she unclasped her hands and brought her arms around. She made a special effort to keep her head still and continue swirling her vibrating tongue over His balls while grasping His muscular thighs through the soft cotton of His sweats.

Half-expecting a sharp yank on her hair or a painful swat on some sensitive spot, she raised her head further and began to lick the long, hard column of His shaft. The slight pressure of His hand tunneling into her hair and stroking the sensitive hollow at the nape of her neck shocked her with its tenderness…aroused her even more than the vibrating stimuli in her tongue and cunt.

When He spoke, His deep, quiet voice poured over her like honey. "I'm a dom. A master. I like being in control, giving you everything you need in the way of sexual pleasure. But baby, I'll never harm you. And I'll never lift a hand to you in anger. I'll never hurt you at all unless you beg me to.

"But I'm forty-two years old. I discovered not too long ago that I want more now than wild, kinky sex with a woman who's into submission. I want a woman I can care for. Love. I want you. Hell, I've wanted you before I dreamed you'd ever let me fuck you, much less that you'd be hiding the soul of a slave under that armor of control you wear. Sandy, I want you twenty-four, seven. Always. I want the right to come in your office and kiss you in front of Harper Wells and everybody who works there. Damn it,

I don't want what's between us to be just this." Suddenly He lifted her head until she had no choice but to look into His eyes.

What she saw there terrified her. Excited her. Made her want to jump overboard and swim for her freedom and long to beg Him never to let her go.

"What do you say, slave? I don't care if you wear my collar when we're not alone. But I want you to wear my ring."

"I–I do. Already." The delicious tingling in her clit reminded her of the little ring that now dangled between her inner labia.

He laughed. "The one I'm talking about is about as vanilla as it comes. It goes on your finger, where everyone can see."

When *"yes"* threatened to spill from her open mouth she clamped it closed over the bulging head of His cock and manipulated His PA ring with her tongue. Oh, how she wanted Him. But the idea of becoming His slave in every facet of her life terrified her.

As she had more than once in the nearly twenty years since she'd figured out that she needed a man with the balls to force her to subservience in her sexual relationships, Sandra forced herself to remember her childhood. She pictured her cowed, timid mother who never had dared even plan a meal without taking her dad's preferences into consideration. And she renewed the vow she'd made so long ago to take her sexual pleasure where she found it without handing over her whole being to a dictator—however benevolent he might be.

"Well?"

From Rocky's tone Sandra guessed His lust apparently was building with every vibration her tongue carried onto His swollen flesh. She also gathered He expected more of a response than her enthusiastic licking and sucking of that flesh when He reached down and gave a not too gentle tug to her hair.

"You want us to..." She dared not even mouth the word *marriage*, but that was what a ring seemed to imply. "...live together?"

"What I want is for us to get married, but I'll settle for living together. For now. We were good friends before yesterday, and we're sure as hell sexually compatible." Rocky slipped his hands inside her robe, lifted her, and cupped her breasts. "I can hardly wait for your pretty clit to heal so I can suck on it and drive you as crazy as you're making me now. Say yes, baby."

God help her. She didn't know.

Rocky was her Master. Her friend. The most exciting lover she'd ever had. In her heart, she wanted to say yes, and every cell in her sensitized cunt emphatically agreed. But then she remembered how her mom and dad had lived and her own vow. A little voice in her head screamed no, that she might be a man's slave, but she'd never become his doormat.

"I don't..." Damn it, why couldn't He just order her to do his bidding now? After all, He forced her to fuck and suck and service Him and—and He made her come over and over again, harder and hotter than she'd ever come before.

"Can't make up your mind, baby?"

"I...I—no. No, Master," she amended, bracing herself for the punishment she'd earned by that omission.

"I told you I'll never hurt you. Your only punishment if you don't say yes will be losing this." He pulled her close, nudged her with his steely erection.

"You mean—you mean you don't want to keep me as your slave if we don't live together all the time?"

"I want you. As my friend and lover all the time. As my sex slave when we make love because that turns you on as much as it does me. And believe me when I say I get off by turning you on." He lowered one hand, sampled the hot throbbing dampness of her pussy. "You can't deny it. You're on fire now, just thinking about getting back on your knees and sucking me dry. Or spreading those pretty legs and wringing my cock out with your tight, wet cunt."

No, she couldn't deny that. Not when every cell in her body demanded His cock and a steady stream of her love juice kept slithering down her inner thigh. And not while her nipples ached to feel the pain and pleasure His teeth and tongue could provide.

"N-no, Master," she said, hating her body's weakness, her inability to say either yes or no. "You know I'm your willing sex slave—but as to a full-time relationship, I need time to think."

"Three weeks. You've got three weeks to make up your mind. But remember, if your answer's no, we're through. After today, you won't see me again until your time's up. I want you to think about what we've got here…" He stroked her swollen clit ever so gently. "And what we'll both be missing if your answer's no."

A reprieve. Three weeks to think. To hold onto her control and steel herself to give up the incredible pleasures Rocky coaxed from her reluctant body. "Thank you, Master," Sandra murmured, lowering her gaze to His still-rampant cock. "May I take You in my mouth again, please?"

"Oh, yeah. Feel free, baby. Anything that makes you feel good." Rocky had a few hours left with her, and he intended to make the most of them. After all, he'd just committed himself to three long weeks of celibacy, gambling that she'd miss the sex too much to turn down the rest. "Just let me anchor the boat away from the shipping channel, and we'll make this a mutual fuckfest."

* * * * *

He'd explored every inch of her, nibbled her toes and fingers and made her sample every nook and cranny of His smooth, hard-muscled body. The sensual feel of Him rubbing his tongue on the back of her knees had damn near made her come and shocked her with the wildly erotic sensation that simple act aroused.

Her hair, a tool her old master had used to control her, became an instrument of sensual pleasure when He dug His fingers through it and caressed erogenous zones on her scalp that she'd never before realized were there. His purr of apparent bliss when she'd returned the favor made her want to be bare there, too, so she might experience that ultimate delight.

She'd sucked His balls, soothed the raw spots left by His jockstrap with her tongue. His huge cock had filled her mouth, her ass, even her cunt—though He'd been ever so gentle there as if he'd feared hurting her newly pierced clit.

He'd come and she'd come, and they'd come together more times than Sandra could count. And this time He hadn't inflicted the slightest bit of pain.

It had definitely been a fuckfest meant to hold them both for three long weeks. Still pleasantly aroused two weeks and five days after Rocky had docked *Neptune's Dungeon* and driven her back to her lonely condo, Sandra's greedy pussy throbbed with the agony of wanting Him.

Wanting to acknowledge His ownership—their relationship—yet not quite believing she could take Him as Master in every way without losing her personal identity altogether, she'd spent twenty-one long nights debating the issues with herself.

Maybe she'd read Mom and Dad's relationship wrong. The more she'd considered that, the more Sandra came to believe it was simply her mother's tentative personality that had made her defer to Dad—not fear that if she hadn't, Dad would have taken any sort of retribution. She couldn't imagine Rocky wanting to dictate what they'd eat or where they'd go, unless the food or trip in question had some sexual connotation.

She hadn't slept for wanting to submit to Rocky's hard body, His monster cock. More important, she'd spent her days hoping for a glimpse of His smiling face and missing the easy companionship they'd enjoyed before becoming lovers. Sandra didn't just want her Master. She loved Him.

Maybe. No, not maybe. Sandra had gone and fallen in love with her Master, so deeply she was ready to risk losing herself if that's what it took to be His slave.

His wife? That, too, if marriage was what He really wanted. Sandra shut off the computer on her desk and lifted the phone. She'd let Rocky know, end the misery of being separated from Him.

Suddenly she felt queasy, so she set the phone down. For the past few days her stomach had been rebelling every afternoon about this time, yet another phenomenon she attributed to the turmoil He'd set off in her mind. She'd call Rocky later. Now she needed to calm her stomach.

Andi would be here any minute to discuss the order

they'd be calling witnesses for the Barnes trial next week. Maybe, if Sandra sat very still, she could avoid…

No such luck. She barely made it to the ladies' room before heaving her guts out. When there was finally nothing left to come out and she emerged from the stall, there was Andi, looking concerned.

"Are you okay? You damn near ran me over in the hallway outside your office."

"It's nothing," Sandra said weakly. "Just a touch of stomach flu."

The younger woman looked unconvinced. "Have you been to the doctor?"

"No need. It'll pass."

"If you say so. We can put off going over the witness list—"

Sandra must have looked even worse than she felt to merit such concern from her colleague, so she glanced in the wavy mirror. "I do look green, don't I? I'll be okay now, though. This seems to come on about the same time every day. I throw up, and then I feel fine until the next day. Strange."

"Not strange if you're pregnant. The first couple of months I was carrying Brett, I got sick like clockwork, ten o'clock in the morning, every morning."

"I'm not pregnant," Sandra said. "Come on back to my office and let's get those witnesses sorted out so we can enjoy the weekend."

* * * * *

Pregnant. How freaking ridiculous could Andi be? Sandra thought as she drove home from work that night.

But was she? She recalled her gynecologist taking her off the Pill six months ago and fitting her for the diaphragm she'd inserted three weeks earlier at her Master's command. Thinking back beyond the incredible sex they'd shared, she tried to remember. Had Rocky used a condom that first time? She thought He had. Every other time they made love she'd had the diaphragm in place.

Then she remembered his PA ring. It certainly couldn't have split her diaphragm. Could it?

No. Sandra told herself she couldn't be pregnant from one weekend of sex, no matter how hot the sex had been. She'd even replaced the spermicide after every bout of fucking.

Once is all it takes, Sandy. Besides, good girls save their cherry for their husbands. Her mother's long-ago warnings, repeated so many times they'd stuck in her head for more than twenty years, rang out in Sandra's ears. It was that first admonition that reverberated—the second one she'd tossed out as female subjugation propaganda years ago.

"Oh, hell." There was one way to put that unlikely conclusion as to her sudden nausea to rest. Braking carefully, Sandra pulled in at the neighborhood supermarket and picked up an early pregnancy test along with her milk and bread.

Waste of money, she decided once she got home and dragged the little box into the bathroom. She'd wait, and unless she got sick again tomorrow, she'd return it to the store unopened.

The following afternoon she sat at the vanity in her bathroom, the bitter taste of vomit still in her mouth as she stared at the shockingly clear pale blue lines on all three pregnancy tests. Those lines indicated, according to the instructions on the box with the cute baby face on it, that she was about to become a mother—an unwed mother at that—at the advanced age of thirty-eight.

Could the test be wrong? Yes. That was it. She'd call her gynecologist and… Oh, shit. No way was she going to show off her shaved pussy and Rocky's clit ring that even now had her creaming her panties every time she wiggled her butt on the vanity chair. Not when this test's accuracy rate was touted as close to a hundred percent. And not when three of them had come up with the same alarming results.

Idiot! You'll have to bare your pussy to the doctor soon enough. Get tests and vitamins and maybe something to stop the damn throwing up. But Sandra didn't have to do that immediately. What she had to do now was make up her mind. No, she had to tell Rocky that He'd made her pregnant.

Pregnancy. According to her old master, it was the sure cure for an overactive sex drive and a word he'd ordered her never to utter in his presence. He'd told her once that if she ever got knocked up, she'd get rid of it unless she wanted to get rid of him.

Rocky might feel the same. But somehow Sandra didn't think He'd demand she get rid of the baby. She wouldn't do that even if He ordered her to, she realized as she stared at the picture of the smiling infant on the box.

Oh God, Sandra didn't want to lose Him now, when she realized how much she loved Him. But she didn't want to lose this miracle child she'd never expected, either. She couldn't even consider destroying His baby. Padding across her bedroom, she sat gingerly on the bed and picked up the phone.

"Rocky, I'm…" Damn, she couldn't tell him on the phone. "…I need you. Please, Master."

"I'll be right over, baby."

Sandra figured she had ten minutes, tops, to transform herself from a heap of quivering Jello to the calm, collected, together woman she wanted Him to see.

Chapter Six

His cock throbbing with anticipation, Rocky clutched the bouquet of red roses that had set him back forty bucks at the neighborhood supermarket and used his free hand to lift the brass knocker on Sandy's door. Anybody who saw him would certainly have laughed at the silly grin he knew must have been splitting his ugly mug from ear to ear.

Sandy needed him. So much she'd broken down and called him a day before her time was up. So much it sounded as if she'd been about to lose it when she called.

But seeing the solemn, wary look on her face when she let him in sent chills down his spine. Her expression carried no joy, no excitement—no anticipation of the hot lovemaking he'd planned to seal a forever promise.

"What's wrong, baby?" he asked when she led him not to her bedroom but into the untouched and untouchable living room he'd hated from the moment she let him in her private space. Not even the brilliant red of the roses or the bright green florist wrap around their stems lent much cheer to the sterile looking end table where he'd laid them down.

She stared out the window, her rigid back to him. "I'm pregnant. I didn't intend to be, but y-You have the right to know." She paused, as if to catch her breath before more words tumbled from her mouth, faster than before. "Of course You don't have to do anything…I don't expect You to. I'll take care of it, but I won't get an abortion."

Abortion? The very thought that she thought he'd want her to get one snapped him out of what admittedly had been a fine case of initial shock. "Hold on a minute. What the hell makes you think I'd ask you to do that?"

She turned, her posture like that of a soldier at parade rest. "We didn't plan this. It's not as if a baby fits in with our—Your—lifestyle."

"If your lifestyle has to change, baby, mine will, too. Because we're in this together. You can forget any idea you may have gotten about ditching me. Go dry your eyes and put some going-out clothes on. You're about to go meet my mom and dad, because I've got my grandma's ring at their house and I want to put it on your finger."

"Wait. I didn't say I'd—"

"You don't have to. My kid's inside you, and he's going to have two parents who're together for him—and for each other." Reaching out, Rocky grasped Sandra's arms and drew her close. "Feel my cock. It's already hard and throbbing to make you come. Feel how much I need you. Don't you love me just a little?"

She buried her face against his shoulder, and he thought he felt her tension easing. "Damn it. I love you a lot. I'm just afraid--afraid there won't be anything left of me. Don't want to end up like my mom, too cowed to buy a roast instead of a Christmas turkey unless Daddy gives his blessing."

"The only place I want your unconditional submission is in bed. Or on the boat, or in the shower, or wherever we get the urge to get it on. Whatever you do about your job is up to you, and I couldn't care less what you serve me to eat as long as you give me free access to your gorgeous mouth and breasts and pussy."

* * * * *

They'd had to stay for dinner with his parents after he put his grandmother's old-fashioned diamond ring on her finger, and Rocky had insisted on stopping by to give her family their news in person. Sandra's cheeks grew warm when she remembered her mother's shock at Rocky's announcement that they'd be providing the family with another grandchild before too long.

You're old enough to know better, girl. Too old to be having a baby, too.

Her mother had quickly recovered after making those hurtful pronouncements and offered her good wishes–but the initial reaction had stung and Mom's words still rang in Sandra's ears.

"What's going through that clever mind of yours?" Rocky asked once they'd done the family thing and returned to her condo—and the bedroom where they'd revealed their respective needs and made love for the first time.

She couldn't begin to sum up all the conflicting emotions bubbling around in her brain—love and desire, certainty and doubt. Abject fear that this dream match would turn into a nightmare. All she could do was shake her head and try to smile, hoping He was right and that they could build on friendship and the lust that had them both locked in its steely grip.

The lust was stronger than ever, it seemed, because her clit tingled when she sat on the bed and started taking off her clothes, reminding her how she'd been dreaming of Him playing with the jewel he'd had put there. "I'm thinking You might want to check out the other ring You gave me, Master. And that You might allow Your personal sex slave to play with Yours."

"Undress and lie on the bed," He said, watching her comply while he dispensed with his shirt. Her mouth watered at the sight of His hard, powerful chest and abs, as tanned and glowing and satiny smooth as the skin covering His perfectly shaped skull. The single stud in his ear glittered in the lamplight, calling her attention to His strong jaw...and dark eyes soft with desire when He met her gaze.

He was a beautiful man, a strong, dominant male. Dark like her, yet with features that needed nothing to enhance them. "If you let your hair grow—"

"It would be black, like yours," He said, good humor in His tone. "What little there'd be of it." With that He shoved His jeans down, revealing His hard, huge cock and satiny ball sac, thick, muscular thighs and calves, and big feet with high arches and neatly trimmed toenails.

Sandra smiled. "I hope our baby looks like you," she told Him when He came down on the bed and dragged her arms above her head.

"I want her to look like you. Don't move now."

Wasn't He going to tie her? Apparently not, she decided when He made no move to get a set of restraints from the drawer but bent instead to place open-mouthed kisses along her jaw, her throat, her belly—everywhere but on her taut nipples and her sopping cunt.

Restrained only by His order, she lay still, concentrating on the rasp of His jaw against her tender skin, the moist heat of His breath, the increasingly ragged sound of His breathing and her own. Her clit throbbed against His ring with every swipe his satiny tongue made around her navel and over her mons, and her cunt contracted, spilling out slick hot juice that dribbled down her slit and pooled around the opening to her anus.

She'd never felt hotter, more mastered, even when He'd had her tied and blindfolded and helpless to His desire. His softly spoken order restrained her as well as any silken cord or leather cuffs.

When she whimpered, He bent and caught her clit ring between his teeth. The sensation stole her breath, swept away her reason. Arching her hips, she gave Him better access to her swollen clit, her cunt. Anything He wanted, she wanted to give. With every swipe of His tongue along her slit, her cunt spilled more nectar to feed His voracious appetite.

"Fuck me, Master," she begged, desperate for Him now. "Please fuck me. I need Your big, hot cock in my cunt. So-oooo much." Her belly tightened as He slid up her body to take her mouth.

"Hold me, baby," He said, dragging her hands to his mouth and kissing them before balancing His weight on one arm and feeding His big cock to her cunt with infuriating care. "God, but you're hot and wet. I love feeling you with nothing between us. Love you, baby."

"I...love You, too. Oh, Master, don't stop...may I... Ooh, yessss, Master, I'm coming."

Rocky reached a hand between them, stroking her clit and tugging gently on the tiny ring while he tempered the strength of his thrusts, wanting to prolong her orgasm. But it had been three weeks. Three long weeks. His balls felt as though they were going to burst. Before her ecstatic spasms slowed, he let go the control he couldn't maintain any longer and exploded in her.

At least he had the presence of thought to roll them onto their sides before giving in to the satiated exhaustion that had him weak as a kitten in her arms.

Epilogue

Seven months later

A Cadillac of a stroller held a giant teddy bear from Rocky's detectives. A top-of-the-line playpen was doing double duty as a container for the blue sheets and blankets and little outfits that Sandy's coworkers had brought to the surprise shower at Andi's bungalow in Old Hyde Park. Rocky figured he'd have one hell of a time wrestling all of it into his SUV.

At least there were a few guys here among all the women. Maybe he could commandeer a couple of them to help load up the loot.

Their baby boy had received a hell of a lot of it. So much he wondered where they'd stash it all in the nursery off the master bedroom of their new house. But Sandy would find a way. He'd never run across a woman before who was so damn organized.

And so much fun to love.

Even now, when she was big as a barn and he was scared shitless that he'd hurt her or their unborn son, she still wanted him when he imagined most women as pregnant as she was would as soon cut off the guilty party's cock as suck it.

Yeah. Rocky was one lucky SOB.

"Congratulations, Detective. I hear you're the lucky father?"

Rocky turned and held out his hand. "Yeah. Thanks. What are you doing at a gathering of cops and prosecutors, Landry?" he asked the defense lawyer he figured he ought to thank for having rattled Sandy's cool enough to send her straight into his own bed.

"Pursuing Kristine Granger."

Visually scanning the room, Rocky picked out the young attorney who Sandy mentioned had tried her first case a few weeks ago—and lost. "Nice," he murmured, though the patrician-looking blonde didn't do it for him. "Sandra liked working with her."

"Past tense?"

"Yeah. She's decided she wants to be a full-time mom, at least for a while. Maybe later she'll get bored. Hell, maybe later she'll even try working from your side of the courtroom."

Landry grinned. "Tell her to come see me if she wants a job. Winston Roe can always use another kick-ass defense lawyer. The way you guys do your job, there's never a shortage of defendants."

"And the way you do yours, there always seem to be plenty tossed back on the streets so we can catch 'em and you can defend 'em again," Rocky replied, too mellow tonight to get into a serious debate about the merits of *innocent until proven guilty.*

"Uh-huh. Keeps the fees rolling in, keeps my partners happy. Take care, man. I'm going to try to extricate Kristine and escape."

Watching Tony Landry drape an arm possessively over Kristine's shoulder, Rocky wished them well. Life was good, and he couldn't even begrudge happiness to Landry, whose skill at getting criminals—accused criminals, he amended—back on the streets made his job more difficult that it had to be.

It was about time, he guessed when others started leaving, so he headed for Sandy. "You're tired, baby," he said, bending to nibble on her earlobe. "Let's thank Andi for the party, find a couple of guys to help load up your presents, and head on home."

"I'm not *that* tired..." She lowered her voice to a whisper... "Master."

Yeah. Rocky was damn sure a lucky man. Master...and mastered by the luscious woman who was his wife.

About the author

Multipublished in both romantica and mainstream romance, award-winning author Ann Jacobs believes in the power of passion and love to resolve even the deepest conflicts and lead the way to happily ever after. A full time author since her first sale in 1996, Ann lives on the Florida Suncoast with her husband and children.

Ann Jacobs welcomes mail from readers. You can write to them c/o Ellora's Cave Publishing at P.O. Box 787, Hudson, Ohio 44236-0787.

Also by Ann Jacobs:

- A Mutual Favor
- Awakenings
- Black Gold series
    - Another Love
    - Firestorm
    - Love Slave
- The Color of Magic
- He Calls Her Jasmine
- Lawyers In Love series
    - In His Own Defense
    - Bittersweet Homecoming
- Love Magic
- Anthologies
    - Mystic Visions
    - Captured

A CHOICE OF MASTERS

WRITTEN BY

JOEY W. HILL

"By the Holy Mother —"

"For shame, Sir Thomas," the priestess chuckled, her voice as seductive a pull on his cock as the acolyte kneeling before him, sucking on it. "Blaspheming the Virgin's name."

He jerked, his powerful muscles flexing as his grip tightened on the arms of the wooden chair. The rough surface digging into his palms was no distraction from the warm, relentless heat and wetness of the mouth serving him.

The young woman kneeling before his feet was all he could desire. Small, elegant, pure. The priestess had told him she was a virgin, and she was sucking a man's rod for the very first time, those dainty lips never before stretched by a man's brutal need. Her blue eyes lifted to his, reflecting joy in each groan she wrung out of him. Innocence and carnal seduction. The priestess had found his every weakness.

"My lord, you have taken your eyes from her again."

He grunted. Sweat ran down his broad back as he fought for control. He lowered his gaze to the sprite. She balanced herself with a graceful hand gripping his thigh. He started to tremble, gritting his teeth.

"Watch her soft, moist lips pull on your shaft. You have a thick and powerful staff, my lord. It tickles the back of her delicate throat, and stretches her lips so wide she will never smile again without thinking of you. See how she sucks you in, so slow. Hear the noises she makes, feel the glide of her tongue on the underside of your cock."

He moaned, a plea or threat, and his fingers clenched into fists, pulling against the chair. That was the wrong thing to do, because it created a resistance the girl was not expecting. Her tiny mouth slithered down his cock like a thin velvet glove pulling away.

"Celeste, slide your gown up to your waist, and fasten the train so our visitor is able to see the outline of your pretty round bottom. Sir Thomas, don't make me tell you again to keep your eyes on her."

The priestess's fingers grazed his back, using her nails. Thomas's testicles tightened in pleasure at her touch. He looked down as Celeste braced one hand on the floor, and gathered up the train of her gown in the other. She kept on his cock, working it in her mouth, her tongue performing slow, tiny licks, head and body rocking like a lamb suckling its mother's teat. The gown was adjusted and he saw the shape of a perfect white arse, and the fragile bumps of her spinal column. Sweet Christ, the girl didn't even have any scars to mar her perfect skin. Her soft buttocks quivered as she renewed her pumping motion on his organ.

He could do this. He would not go over. He tried to find the sharp edge of that cliff in the passionate haze of his subconscious. He needed to achieve stasis there, give himself more time to understand what thoughts and emotions assaulted a person on the verge of cataclysmic sensation. The High Priestess Helene had dedicated herself to teaching him that control, for nearly thirty days now.

He was far from the man he had been when he entered the doors of this temple. Followers of the Old Way, these priestesses drew their considerable powers from carnal pleasures. No Christian priest or monk dared come near the place, for fear of being ensnared by the sensual delights that were promised behind these walls.

Thomas had thought he understood the sins of the flesh. He had come here for help, but a detached help was what he had wanted. A set of simple instructions that answered his questions and would allow him to be on his way, his contempt toward willfully unchaste women, masked as self-righteous courtesy, intact.

*****

He had been brought to Helene's chamber, the High Priestess of Ashteroth. She sat in a chair, regal as a queen, wearing a sheer tunic that showed him her full breasts through its fine sheen. Her nipples were rouged to a dark red, and the down between her legs was as raven black as her hair.

"You seek to free Lilith," she said, in soft tones that slid down his spine, arousing and soothing, evoking a peculiar image of whore and mother at once.

He snapped his spine straight inside his armor, shoving the thought away with anger for his weakness.

He made a bow. "Yes, m'lady. You know the nature of the spell laid upon her, as do we all. I am pledged to rescue her, but I must know how it can be done. It has come to me, through fasting and penance, that you have the information I seek."

"I dreamed of you, too, beautiful man," she said, "and knew you would be coming to ask this of me. But why do you pledge yourself to this quest? Do you seek the glory of defeating a mighty wizard, and earning your spot at an imaginary Round Table that has not existed for centuries, if it ever did?"

Thomas flushed. "You know nothing of my mind."

"To know your mind, I need only watch your cock. It points to her. It is her you want. You want her to call you Master, and yet you want to cherish her with your soul and body. You lie to yourself about your own reasons. I will not help you."

She rose and the woman who had escorted him moved forward to lead him from the temple.

"No," he said. "No."

Helene stepped down from her throne, and passed him, her expression indifferent. The diaphanous cloth of her robe slid along the calf of his armor. It did not catch on the joints, as he would have expected it to do. It moved over him like the wind, like her. Able to touch him with a welcome cool breeze in the cruelest heat, or blast him without mercy. His desperation rose in him, and he spun around as she reached the stone archway.

"No!"

Helene stopped, looked back at him, and said nothing. She gazed at him out of violet gray eyes, so pale he thought of clouds on a day when the sun and rain warred for dominance.

"I dream of her. Nearly every night now, she is there." Thomas took a deep breath, assuaging the pain in his chest. "I pray for your mercy, Lady. You must help me."

* * * * *

His dreams of Lilith were vivid, and seemed longer than the night itself, as if time stopped while he was with her. He yearned for his nightly plunge into unconsciousness.

It would start in darkness. He would first be aware of

her perfume. She was the flower with an elusive scent, that bud or blossom unseen by a knight traveling through the deep forest. It touched his nose with a haunting fragrance meant to be experienced only a moment, and remembered forever.

Her hair would brush his arm. He would realize that he was standing in this world of darkness in nothing but the flesh God had given him. Her hair was so long that, as she passed, the strands slid over his forearm, feathered across his ribcage, caressed his hip.

He reached out, closed his hand on it. It was like the mane of a steed in a king's stable, so lustrous in weight and health he could feel its beauty through his fingertips. He curled his fist in it and tightened his grip, capturing her. He felt how much stronger he was, how delicate and female she was. She turned into him, rolled herself up against his body in a motion like a languorous summer afternoon. There was a meeting of bare skin. Her slender feet stood on his, her toes stretching to give her extra height. Her hands settled on his shoulders for balance.

Hours of practice had made his shoulders broad and strong, and battle had given them scars. No woman's hand had ever felt this good upon him, not his first tumble, not even the gentle touch of his mother. It was a touch that held everything he wanted, everything he wanted to prove, everything that made him who he was. It almost brought him to tears, and surely the taste of salt on one's lips was not usual in a dream.

Her thighs slid down either side of his erect lance, her heat anointing him with a dew as rich as honey. She was ready for a man, ready for him.

She trembled, and he felt the quiver of her breasts, nipples swollen and tight against the coarse brown hair of his chest. His cock had hardened to an impossible rigidity, rivaling the steel of his sword. His staff bumped up between her legs, the length pressed against her cunt, the ridged head rubbing in the sensitive channel of her arse just beyond the seam of her thighs. Her breathing was rapid, her fingers clutched on his shoulders. He put his hand up and spread his fingers so he covered the side of her neck and cheek, pressing her head to his chest. The pose was as intimate as it was carnal, and he longed to possess her in ways that went far beyond the couplings of flesh.

"Protect me," she whispered into his heart. "Help me. Come to me, my lord. Make me yours."

Moonlight filtered into the dream, bringing light. He looked down at the auburn silk wrapped around his hand, his tether holding her to him. He wanted to see her face. He tugged her head back and the spiral of sensation in his gut tightened in pain and lust at once.

Looking upon her countenance brought him the humility and stillness of a sacred moment, and yet he was harder than he had ever been in his life. He ached to have his hands on her breasts, to bend her over and thrust his cock into the slippery mystery of her womb, making her his, and his alone. He wanted to be all things to her, lover, husband, lord, God to her Goddess. Protector, comforter, seducer.

God help him, he should throw himself to the cold floor of a church to beg forgiveness for the unforgivable sacrilege of such thoughts.

Instead his hands were on her bare waist, his fingers spreading and sliding forward to take hold of her arse. He squeezed the two halves, one in each palm.

"I will always protect you, cherish you, love you," he

muttered. "Always."

Her lips parted, lips he wanted to kiss, bite and suck, and from which he wished to bring helpless moans, just as he wished to bring forth a helpless gushing from between her legs.

"Tell me you will be my lady," he demanded.

"I am," she said. "Why else would I be in your dreams?"

The long hair waved around a face as fragile and strokable as the newly opened petals of a white rose. Lips, soft and pink, a bit moist, so that he could not help but think of that other place, just as inviting to kiss with its musky mysteries.

Her eyes were a dark liquid brown like a forest animal. He thought if he lost himself in those eyes, wrapped himself in that auburn hair, it would be like being in the earth, surrounded by her, cradled by her, her child and consort all at once. It was a dream, and he could not stop such pagan thoughts.

Her hands rose to his face, and he kissed her palm, kissed both her palms, kissed every tear from her face.

"Make me yours, my lord," she whispered, her hands sliding to his neck, her body closing in on his.

He lifted her and she gasped as she sunk to the hilt of his jutting cock. It was like being swallowed by velvet and heat, those lips parting to let him in. He felt her contract as she slid down, accommodating his size with shuddering ripples.

Suddenly, instead of being naked, he wore full battle armor, scarred and nicked. His loins were bare, his cock free and erect, and buried in her as before.

She was sweet oil inside, and his rod thickened and

lengthened inside her as she rode him. The pump of her hips upon him was as relentless as the stride of his stallion beneath his weight.

"You must bring me, my lord," she rasped, her fingers tightening on his neck, cutting herself on the collar of his armor. "You want to, you have never wanted anything so much as to bugger me."

Thomas reared back to see her face. Her eyes were wild and teeth bared. Her hair came forward in snarled tangles with each stroke to hide her face from him, as if her hair curtained her soul from his scrutiny.

"Lilith, stop." Each upward stroke smacked the vulnerable curve of her stomach against the base of his armor, wounding her flesh.

"No, my lady, do not —" he cried. He tried to stop her motions by banding his arms around her, but she squirmed and her slick cunt milked him, driving him higher. Blood, her blood, was running down his testicles and his thighs. She was screaming in anguish, but she would not stop, and he could not stop her, or himself.

His seed exploded into her body as she wailed in pain, her face a horrifying mixture of lust lost to the madness of suffering, each emotion struggling for dominance. He could not get her to release him. Her legs bound tight around him, her hands gripping his armor as she stared at him with feral eyes. A drop of blood slid from her bitten lip and splashed on the top of her breast.

He awoke, shuddering, covered in cold sweat and his own semen.

* * * * *

"The priest recommended prayer vigils, fasting,

flagellation, hairshirt, penance in all shapes and forms." Thomas managed to bring his voice back to an even pitch. The priestess stood, still expressionless, her attendant a shadow at her elbow.

"All of this I tried, because he said she was a demon to be cast out. But it makes her so sad. She cries in my dreams when I try to shut her out, when I treat her this way. I know I will do anything to make her smile, to make her mine. It is not what I have known chivalry to be, this wish to possess her, and yet it is. I want to be her Master, yet I also want to be her protector. My soul is torn between lust and devotion and I am going mad."

Helene remained silent. Thomas bared his soul further, casting aside his earlier strategy to hold himself aloof.

"No knight has undertaken the quest to rescue her. They wish the glory of taking from the wizard what is his, but they care naught for her. They see her as his minion and so the prize is not great enough to tempt them. I must help her. I cannot fail, or I shall die at the thought of failing her. Will you help me or not?"

This last, more belligerent than he intended, but he was angry that she had drawn it from him, with her steady stare and calm acceptance of his story that he could not match.

"You do not know if the girl prefers mutton to fowl, if she worries more about our borders or the ribbons she will wear from day to day in her hair. If she is educated, or a simpering fool." Helene raised a brow. "These are important things, my lord."

"It does not matter. In my dream, I know her. She is part of me. I will love her, no matter what she is, or what she is not."

"A man of great discipline, torn between his doubt and what he knows in his heart." Helene pursed her lips. "Yes. I will help you. You are not a true liar." A corner of her mouth twitched. "You were just lying to me, not to yourself. You must stay with me a month to know the way to go about it. Longer, if you can."

"I cannot stay a month."

"It must be a month, or nothing. You obey me in all things for that month, and learn the control you must possess to save her. You will need every moment. You have much armor to shed, Sir Thomas."

* * * * *

So here he was, while an innocent licked him with the flames of hell in her tongue. He was stripped of all his clothes, as well as his armor. He had not worn clothes for most of these four weeks. He had walked among the dressed priestesses this way, open to their admiring glances and caresses, as they tested his resolve and his flesh in ways he could not have imagined.

He kept his attention upon Celeste as the priestess had commanded, knowing it would finish him to see the small head bobbing, the soft line of her cheek, the tender wrinkle of her lips as she handled his cock. Still he hoped. He fought it. He tried to think of the cold flagstones of a church in the dead of winter, the scourge taking flesh off his back.

Thomas snarled as Celeste's teeth lightly scored his engorged head. She started making wet, slurping noises of enjoyment, underscoring every lash of her tongue and slide of her lips on him, as if his nerve endings needed the additional help of his hearing to increase his agony.

Her tongue flicked, once, twice, three times along the slender vein that pulsed from scrotum to head, and the vision of scourge and flagstones was consumed by a purifying fire that roared over and through him.

He groaned, the guttural cry of a wild male animal, and he bucked hard, stretching that dainty mouth, plunging into her, wanting her to take all of him deep within her, knowing it was beyond her capacity and not caring. He would bruise her if he needed to, mark her with his power.

He felt the back of her throat and was surprised she did not gag, only lifted her small hands and dug her fingers into his arse, pressing him in further. The mewling noise she made vibrated along his throbbing head.

She took every drop of him. As he emptied, her touch eased and soothed his shuddering skin. As his seed drained, so did his passion, and he stared down at her, filled with shame and fury at himself. She looked up at him, innocent as a doe, and wiped her mouth with the back of her hand, not like a fishwife, but a deliberate movement, as if she was handling a sacrament.

"Leave us, Celeste."

The young woman rose, readjusting her gown and rebelting it. She curtsied to Thomas and her lady, and left them as ordered.

His knees were weak, and it further humiliated him that he could not stand in courtesy to the priestess as he should at this moment. Helene slid a hip onto the arm of the chair, and put a gentle hand on his shoulder.

"You did well that time," Helene said in a neutral voice. "Three hours and the mouths of four of my priestesses to bring forth your seed. Your physical discipline is commendable, Sir Thomas."

He laid his head back and closed his eyes. "Now, who is the liar?" Her fingers stroked his hair, the color of burnished copper, away from his sweaty neck. "I continue to fail."

"No, not in the sense you think. Your physical discipline is perfect, Sir Thomas."

"And yet my body betrays me. Why?"

"My lord," she admonished, "this is not sword fighting, or breaking a lance. Has it ever occurred to you that the secret is not clenching your fist, but opening your fingers and marveling at the shape of your hand, made so by no will of your own?"

"Damn it all, woman, do you always talk in riddles?"

Her low chuckle warmed him, despite his weariness.

"This is a spiritual test for you, my lord, not a physical one." Her violet-gray eyes were serious. "It has been a long life for you," she said. "Has it not? Longer than the years of your face reveal."

He closed his eyes, not denying the truth that burned in his throat to hear it spoken.

Her voice was a mist in his mind. "You are a long way from the time of Arthur, and yet you have served his ideals well. You have forgotten what magic is, because you are tired." She hesitated. "And so lonely."

"I wanted the way to free her to be a way without magic."

"Ah, my lord, you must realize that the power of the body's response, it is a magic all of its own. When the heart becomes involved, it is potent. It is in fact the most real thing on this earth, and the joining of bodies can render all other magics insignificant."

"I saw Lilith once, when she was a young girl in her

uncle's court," he admitted. "I did not feel this way about her then. Now she invades my dreams as the grown woman I have never seen, and it is as if I will be unable to breathe if I try to contemplate a life without her in it. I would call it sorcery, but it is not. I have seen enough to know the difference. It is something my heart hungers for as much as my mind."

The priestess's hand traced his damp forehead. "The gods who know our destinies are sometimes kind, sometimes cruel," she clicked a nail over one of the scratches she had made on his back. "Soulmates may pass each other, strangers in this life. It is not time for them to join. In another life, one will recognize the connection and the other will not, leading to heartache. The gods know why, but there are painful lessons we all must learn to achieve our destiny.

"Then," she continued, "there is the blessed life, when they are aware of each other. Suddenly what each feels so deeply in his or her heart is enhanced beyond their imaginings by feeling it together."

"Will she, do you think - "

"I cannot say, Thomas." She tugged on his hair. "I tested your body not only to reacquaint you with sensual pleasures, but to help you understand what it is to hover in that moment where control and the bliss of oblivion are equally beyond your reach. Suspended pleasure is excruciating in its intensity. To decide to stay there of your own volition requires perfect love and perfect trust of the one asking it of you. It is a pleasure of its own.

"However," her expression darkened, "to be forced to stay there is a cruelty beyond measure, because you are completely vulnerable, your spirit as well as your body. Can you imagine feeling like that for five years, Sir

Thomas? Everything laid bare, like an animal skinned alive, exposing the complex wonder created by God and Goddess, but unable to bear even the touch of the air? That has been Lilith's life."

He swallowed, the muscles tensing in his shoulders as if he could draw a weapon and spare his lady that suffering. Helene's hand touched him.

"In her dreams, she knows you, and that, I will venture to say, is a good sign. The ritual I will show you will let her reach through the horror of her current existence, pull the curtain back and see you clearly. From there, the choice is hers. If she turns away, out of fear or denial, then you will have lost her in this life. I know Zorac's power, and there is none to equal him, save the Lord and Lady Themselves, or the Christian God, whichever face you prefer to give Divinity. Love is the closest kin to Divinity, so only the pull of a soulmate can wrest her from Zorac's grasp."

"A soulmate she has never met," he murmured.

"But a soulmate nevertheless," she reminded him. "Whether or not you have ever met in this life does not matter, not if the connection is a true one." She molded her hand over his slick shoulder, leaned forward so her breasts pressed against his bare arm, and laid her cool cheek against his. It was a touch of comfort, and power, and he sat still beneath it. "You are a strong man, Thomas. Lilith will respond to the hand of the man who has her heart. You are her Master."

"Will she acknowledge it from the beginning, you think?"

"No. She will be more like the nightmare part of your dream. The wizard has corrupted that within her which is sacred. Her ability to express her love with her body, enjoy her body, and choose to submit to a Master, the man she loves."

He grimaced and turned his face away, but she caught his jaw, made him look into her stern violet eyes.

"You must accept the duality of your nature. You can love Lilith, protect her, and still want to push her to her back, spread her thighs and conquer her. Lust and love together is not a sin, because one balances the other. You are a strong, virile man, a forceful one, and by all appearances," she smiled, "a very determined one. You may love a woman, but you will also want to dominate her physically, have her acknowledge that dominance, submit to you. That is part of your nature. It does not lessen your regard for her. The difference between you and the wizard is you want to win your lady's favor, her desire for you to be her Master, not take that choice from her."

"I was not fair to you, when I came here," he said at last.

"I have grown more attached to you as well, Sir Thomas," her eyes crinkled. "So." She settled back. "I am not what you thought I was. Experience can change the scope of your morality. It can make that scope greater, and, at the same time, focus you on what the most important moral principles are. There are actually only a very few, but they are so important, the fate of every soul rests upon them."

Lilith's fate. It lay unsaid between them.

"Arthur once said,…" Thomas hesitated. The priestess looked at him with that opaque gaze she had mastered. "…To love someone with all your heart, you must believe in her strength and be there at that moment she needs you most, no matter your own fears or weaknesses. Magic, he said, lies in this unconditional gift. At least," he added, shifting, "it is believed he said that."

"You do remember some things," she said softly, a smile crossing her face.

"In my dreams, I remember everything," he said. Exhaustion closed his eyes again, giving him the temporary peace of darkness. "The nightmare as well as the beauty. Like him, all I want now is to hold the woman I love in my arms and know peace."

She smiled. "You have discovered the greatest miracle, in a world of many miracles."

He nodded, and found the strength to raise her hand to his lips. "It is the only one I seek now."

* * * * *

When the moon rose full in the sky, he took his leave of the women of Ashteroth. He hoped he had the weapons he needed to succeed in his task. He was certain he would give all his strength, his life if necessary. He could tarry no longer with the priestesses, no matter the value of their counsel. He was driven by the call of a dream, the woman of his dreams, who had captured his soul in a way more powerful than sorcery, and who needed him.

A week later, Thomas reined in his horse on the rise just below Zorac's castle. His palms beneath his gauntlets were sweating, and his heart pounded hard against his chest, like a sword relentlessly striking the breast plate of his armor during a battle.

It was not Zorac making him feel thus. Surprisingly, and perhaps foolishly, he felt no anxiety about the wizard. His reaction was all about Lilith. What would she think of him? Would he measure up to her expectations, would he be equal to the task of rescuing her? He prayed it was so. A knight's faith was what saw him through every fight, and he would not shirk it here.

He spurred his mount forward, and the powerful stallion responded, cantering up the approach.

He had spoken to the tenants of the wizard's lands as he traveled across them, and found people who were well fed and protected from harm, content with their overlord. As a soldier, he assessed the castle before him. It was a sturdy structure with walls eight feet high, a gatehouse and round towers. However, its lord apparently relied on magic wardings to protect his holdings. The drawbridge was lowered to allow crossings over a purely decorative sparkling brook, versus a stagnant moat or steep ditch, and the portcullis was open.

There were only shadows to indicate the movement of a few retainers along the curtain walls. The horse snorted at the unusual quiet, his hooves clopping across the boards of the drawbridge. Thomas raised his gaze and brought his mount to a halt several strides back from the portcullis. A man stood on the wall above it.

Thomas twitched the reins on the horse's neck. The horse bent a leg forward and Thomas matched the motion by dipping his own head.

"Greetings, Lord Zorac," Sir Thomas said.

He had no doubt this was the wizard overlord of this place, though it surprised Thomas to see him there, meeting him alone.

The knight had no preconceptions about wizards. He had seen them in many forms. However, Zorac had the bearing of a king. Tall and broad-shouldered like a knight, with golden hair past his shoulders. He was clean-shaven, like Thomas, and his eyes were a transparent pale blue, like water. Despite a handsome mien, he did not appear to be a vain man. His hair was combed and held back with two braided outer strands. He eschewed colors and wore a dark tunic of fine wool with silver trim at the hem, matching dark hose and a fine woven cloak. The right shoulder of the cloak bore an embroidered representation of the crescent moon and a cluster of stars.

Thomas studied the man's face. That Zorac had great power, he knew. He looked for evidence of danger, the tell tale sign of friend or foe, and found it in the wizard's lips. They were thin, sensual, and had a tension to them that suggested his ability to be cruel.

"Greetings to you, noble knight," the wizard replied in a tone that was no more than courteous. "What brings you to my domain?"

Thomas straightened from the bow. "I bring you greetings and regards from the High Priestess Helene, and a challenge from myself."

"The one gains you entrance, and the other piques my interest," the wizard replied, his attention moving carefully over every aspect of Thomas's appearance. "You wear mail. Have the roads to my home become so dangerous?"

"Nay, my lord." Thomas looked down at his hauberk. "A knight is always prepared to defend the honor of the innocent."

"Or the not-so-innocent." Zorac cocked his head at Thomas's sudden still expression. "The wind carries many tales to me, Sir Thomas. I have some knowledge of why you are here. It will amuse me to hear why you waste your time. Come in and share my table, and your challenge."

Thomas inclined his head. "My lord."

He passed under the grate into the gatehouse and a

stable lad was there in the open courtyard to take his horse. The boy put his hand on the horse's neck. "I shall take good care of him, my lord. Does he have any special needs?"

Thomas dismounted. "He's ridden far. Just see he's groomed and well fed and given a dry stall. I'm sure he'd appreciate any further coddling you're willing to give to him."

The boy smiled. One eye was closed, the other gone, the mark of the weapon that had taken it making a diagonal scar from his forehead to his cheek. "Aye, my lord," he said.

"What happened to your face, boy?"

"Raids on the border, my lord. My family was killed and Lord Zorac took me in. He said losing my sight was a small matter, because at times it is best if you do not see too much of this world."

"My lord?"

His heart leaped into his throat, but even as it did, he knew the voice did not belong to Lilith. Thomas turned, and a lovely girl in a blue surcoat with a white cotte beneath stood before him.

"I am Asneth," she curtsied. "Please follow me."

She brought him to a well-appointed bedchamber where a manservant waited with towels and a basin of warm water to help him wash the dirt of the road from his body.

"Are you Lord Zorac's kin, my lady?" Thomas asked courteously, as a male servant began to help him remove his heavy hauberk and chausses.

"No, my lord. My father sold me to a man who peddles flesh to men who wish to defile virgins. My lord

Zorac bought me, untouched, and brought me here to educate me, teach me to run his household and care for his guests until I choose a husband of whom he approves. He says he may be someone I love," she considered him with a frank interest that was young and appealing, and Thomas could not help smiling.

"And are you supposed to allow his guests to take liberties with you?" he asked, shrugging out of the russet gambeson.

"Oh no, my lord." She raised her mischievous gaze to him. "My lord Zorac has warded my body. The man who attempts to handle me in an unchivalrous manner receives burned fingers." She placed her hand in the palm of his, as if to demonstrate, but he thought it might just be to test the fit of his palm and fingers around hers.

"Suitably biblical," Thomas murmured.

"Lilith services the guests in the manner in which you refer. She is my lord Zorac's Great Whore."

She flinched at his grip. He withdrew his touch.

"My pardon, lady. You startled me. Why is she made to do this?"

"She is being punished. My lord Zorac said her fate is divine justice to women who refuse to be satisfied by any man."

"Asneth," the manservant said. "Lord Zorac awaits his guest. We must prepare him."

"Of course," she curtsied to Thomas. "I leave you with John to help you bathe and change. I hope to see you again, Sir Thomas." She smiled at him, her innocence and hope for a suitor as fresh on her as dew on a leaf.

* * * * *

Thomas had a well-made hunter green tunic which he chose to wear over a natural linen shirt. He belted the tunic over tan hose that clung to his muscular thighs. Asneth returned, once he was attired, to brush out his hair and scrub the lingering grime of the road from beneath his nails and the crevices of his knuckles.

He was not a vain man, and normally he would have waved away such additional measures to make him more than adequately presentable. However, he wanted to look his best for his lady, no matter her state, and so he sat and allowed Asneth to comb out his hair. It lay just past his shoulders and she claimed it picked up the same color and shine of the copper threads embroidered along the edge of his tunic. She compared his eyes to the amber in a lion's gaze and made him smile with her earnest flirting. After the harsh training of the past few weeks, her youth was like the touch of sunshine, balancing the dark intensity of what lay ahead of him. The manservant laced up his thigh high velvet boots, and then Thomas followed Asneth to Zorac's great hall.

It was a small gathering that awaited him there. Zorac sat alone at the head of a polished long table that was embellished in an unusual manner. As he drew closer, Thomas saw a trained trellis of interwoven rose branches bordered the table's edge. It was approaching summer, so there were buds of a soft pink color preparing to burst forth among the thorns.

"It is an enchanting spell, sir," Thomas touched one of the unopened flowers.

"Nothing but the magic of the Goddess and the sweat of my gardener," Zorac said. "The man sanded the edge of the table, to give the runners a rough edge for their roots." Asneth stood close to the wizard's shoulder and he reached up and took her hand, making her smile when he pressed it to his lips. Thomas watched, intrigued, as the girl stroked his hair with adoration and the wizard accepted her touch with affection.

"The idea was Asneth's," Zorac explained. "She easily sees ways to turn the world around her as beautiful as her soul. And," the wizard added dryly, "it is a pretty way to inspire good manners. If you do not respect their beauty enough to keep from slumping on the table, the thorns you respect. It is an interesting exercise, to see which lesson my guests require to maintain their posture at dinner. But I have spoiled the test for you."

"I suspect there are other, more serious, tests you have in store for me," Thomas said.

Zorac chuckled and beckoned a servant forward to offer his guest wine. "Go from here, Asneth, and take supper with the servant women."

She curtsied, smiled again at Thomas, and took her leave.

At another table, several of the guardsmen ate their meal and spoke quietly amongst themselves, though now and then they cast an interested eye upon Thomas. The stable lad was there, and an older man, perhaps the gardener Zorac spoke about. The knight and the wizard were alone at the large table.

"You do not keep a large company here, my lord."

"I share my home with those humans whose company I can tolerate. That number is few."

"Your reputation beyond your borders is far more sinister than within them, sir," Thomas observed, taking a seat to Zorac's right at his gesture of invitation. "Your people seem well content with your rule."

"You and I both know that a man with powers that seem beyond a normal man's grasp is often feared, Sir Thomas."

Thomas held the wizard's keen gaze. "I know that often there is reason to fear a man with such power, for a man is still a man."

"Perhaps. How came you to be so serious of eye, Sir Thomas, with so few years upon you? You are not thirty, I'll wager. And yet I have heard of some of your courageous exploits."

"I was charged with the duties of a knight at a young age," Thomas replied.

"There is a legend," Zorac considered him with that same penetrating gaze, "that Arthur knighted a child, a mere peasant lad, before he went into the battle of Camlann."

"I have heard that legend as well, my lord."

"It was long ago, of course. Centuries. The legends say that this last knighting was special. The boy was blessed by that deed, and he aged more slowly than most, in order that he could make sure the tale of Arthur was known and never forgotten, that he could live his life as an enduring example of Arthur's dream."

"All power comes from God, my lord."

"Mmm. If the story is true, I suspect that would be a lonely life."

"To spread the word of a dream can compensate for many things, my lord."

"Not as the years continue to pass and men grow deaf. Then there is just loneliness."

Thomas took a casual swallow of wine. "Indeed, my lord. Do you find yourself lonely in the path you have chosen, that you would dwell on the loneliness of a legend?"

The wizard's power was a wash of heat, even without a flash of annoyance spiking it. Thomas held his posture, the wine to his lips, even as the table beyond them stilled, the men sensing the irritation of their master.

Zorac's gaze shifted from Thomas. "Enough of word games," he said abruptly. "Lady Lilith. Do not stand at the door like a shy maiden, for you are far from that. Come in and meet your guest."

Thomas's breath caught in his throat. He placed the goblet back on the table and turned, straddling the bench, so his face was averted from Zorac's scrutiny.

She was his dream. He knew she was more than his imagination, but to see her in the flesh, confirmation that his visions had been true, knocked his senses down, and rolled over them. The soul and body he craved were here before him now, within a few strides. He felt as if the air for his lungs would from this moment on be dependent on her very presence.

He smelled that sweet scent to the air, the scent from the dream, but in this reality, there was more to it. It had a woman's sexual secrets beneath it, her secrets. The fist holding his heart squeezed mercilessly.

She had auburn hair, the browns and reds glinting in the torchlight as she moved across the room. It was piled on her head, rather than free on her shoulders in the way of unmarried women. He wondered the weight of it did not bow that slender pale nape. She was one of those women with such fair skin that a faint freckling sprinkled her throat and the curve of her shoulders he could see. Rather than marring her, it added to the tapestry of her beauty.

She was small to have dominated so much of his dreams. All delicate bones, her wrists like works of porcelain. Her breasts were firm apples pressing against her bodice. Even the soft glide of her slippered feet on the fresh rushes aroused his senses.

The dress she wore was like nothing he had seen before. Her gown was black lace over an undergarment of sheer white fabric that showed the pale color of her skin through it. Her nipples were clearly visible to him, the deep blush aureoles drawing the eye as much as the prominent points sculpted by the fabric.

The black lace molded her bosom and waist, but was cut in ribbons at the skirt so it fluttered away from her as she walked. She wore no hose or undergarments, and so her dress exposed the body beneath, giving it only the modesty afforded by shadows of the hall's torchlight. With each step, he saw a length of thigh and calf, and the gates of paradise, the burnished curls over the opening of her tight cunt. For he knew from his dreams she would be the tightest of gloves, into which he would eagerly ease his fingers to test its warmth and fit. She had wide, generous hips that swayed as she moved, the pendulum swing enhanced by the fact her upper body seemed curiously immobile. Her walk was an undulation of sensual movement, as if she felt the stroke of a man's stiff cock with every step.

"No man can look at her and not want to bugger her arse," Zorac said flatly.

Thomas's gaze snapped to him, the crudity out of character with the demeanor of his host. The comment produced a coarse bark of laughter from the table of guardsmen. From their openly appreciative glances at Lilith, it was obvious they had been given that privilege often.

Thomas fought for calm, and watched as his lady's lips curved in the practiced suggestiveness of a whore, mocking their response. He knew as if it was his own reaction that she raised this shield against them, a challenging taunt to the wizard that held her captive. Thomas wondered if he were the only one who could see the cold and desperate quality to it, like the wounded soldier who thrust up from the ground for one more engagement, even as his life's strength waned from him.

He wanted her out of here. Away from them. Now. He forced himself to sit still, and impassive, and simply watch her, but he could not remember any challenge that had been harder for him.

"Come to me, first," Zorac commanded.

She passed the table of guardsmen. One reached out, stroked her breast, another her thigh, a quick fingering of her cunt through the clothes. She stopped at that touch, her facial features tightening in rigid reaction, and a soft gasp escaped her. The man chuckled, pushed her on her way with a sharp slap to her arse.

As difficult as it was for him to do so, Thomas turned his gaze from her to study his adversary. Zorac's face had gone flat and hard, not as if he saw a beautiful woman moving toward him, but something he detested with all his being, its very presence to be loathed.

As for Lilith, as she drew closer, Thomas saw her lips and jaw were taut and her dark eyes glassy, as if polished by a daily wash of tears. The skin stretched thin over her prominent cheekbones was like white stone polished to a soft satin luster by the constant flow of a waterfall.

Thomas noticed her fingers twitched in agitation at her sides. She wet her lips, and her eyes darted to Thomas and away, at least a dozen times as she crossed the hall. Her throat worked in nervous swallows. By the time she reached Zorac's side, her breath was coming in shallow pants.

"Ah, you like that we have a guest tonight, don't you, my lady Lilith?"

She shook her head, and Zorac chuckled, but Thomas saw nothing he would have called humor in the man's expression. "Sir Thomas, this is the Lady Lilith, who is, in fact, very pleased by your presence among us tonight. Let me show you."

The wizard reached out and drew back the lace cover. The threads of the sheer underdress that had rubbed between her thighs as she walked now shimmered with her honey.

Lilith made a soft noise of protest, frantic eyes shifting to Thomas's face.

"My lord, she is in pain," Thomas said.

"If she was, she would deserve it, but she is not, good sir, you may believe me, or believe the evidence of your nostrils. She is *in pleasure*."

"But her arms," Thomas gestured. Lilith's arms had not risen from her sides during her walk across the room, nor now, when Zorac held her dress up, exposing her honeyed thatch to the view of Sir Thomas and the other interested men.

"They are capable of movement, at my command," Zorac explained. "Lilith does nothing except at my command. Is that not right, my little whore?"

Lilith's lips drew back from teeth wet with saliva. "Yes, my lord." Her voice was like air glinting with the soft gold of early morning. Her gaze was full of hate and lust at once.

"My lord," Thomas sat back, though his hands itched to do creative forms of violence. "You are making me very uncomfortable with your unkind treatment of this woman. I believe in courtly behavior toward women of all classes."

"Women like this make victims out of men like you," Zorac said, his eyes suddenly dangerous fire. Lilith made an abrupt noise of protest.

"It gets worse when I'm angered, doesn't it?" Zorac murmured. He took his hands away from her. She continued to stand beside him, shivering, but the wizard shifted his gaze to Thomas, ignoring her.

"There is a whimsical spell, Sir Thomas. It involves the resilient thread of the spider's web, which can hold its prey immobile until the spider decides to feed its hunger. And a strand of the lady's hair in question." His palm pressed the side of Lilith's fair cheek, his fingers caressing. She made an inconsolable noise, like a bereft soul faced with the hopelessness of hell, and turned her face into the wizard's hand. She bit him with passion, sucking on his skin. Her cheeks were flushed and she made a desperate noise of protest when he withdrew his hand and wiped it distastefully on his napkin. She looked away from Thomas's intent regard, her eyes filled with shame and uncontrolled hunger.

"Then, regretfully," Zorac continued, as if he had been interrupted by a dog begging for scraps at his elbow, "the spider, too, must go into the spell. For a true and strong binding always requires blood. What comes from this potion is a fabric, transparent like that web, so you cannot see it. That means you do not obscure from view that which you bind. My lady Lilith wears this spell on her arms, from elbows to wrists, binding their movement to her sides in the way you see. You can remove her clothes without disturbing it," Zorac leaned forward. With a sharp jerk, he pulled the soft fabric of her dress, from where it rested on the points of her shoulders, down to her waist. "So you need not be denied in any way."

Her breasts would be perfect in his palms, like fresh oranges. Thomas could well imagine the firm flesh giving way beneath his touch, quivering as she gasped, a bit breathless from his gentle kneading, the brush of his thumbs over those incredibly plump nipples. He had seen grapes in Italy like them, a deep burgundy color, begging to be taken into the mouth for the juices to come forth and fill every sense, not just stroke the taste buds.

She stood there, helpless to do anything but be exposed to the appreciative glance of every man in the room, including himself.

Thomas was shamed that even in this moment he felt such desire for her. Aye, he was hard as the stone bench on which he sat. However, unlike the other men, he desired to plunge himself into the hot wetness of her soul, penetrate and fuck that, until it shuddered around him and surrendered.

"The spell has many advantages, as you can imagine," Zorac took a sip of wine, never glancing at those perfect breasts, "but some drawbacks. While she wears the binding, Lilith is dependent on my hand for food and water, lest she cares to drink and eat from the floor with the dogs.

"At first, she spurned my hand, until she was so hungry she did scrounge for scraps with the dogs. The depths of her pride surprised me. She relented when I decreed that, if she would act like a dog, then she'd be fucked like one. It is something you do not often see," the wizard's impassive gaze shifted to Lilith, whose expression revealed nothing but her hunger. "A woman desperate to fulfil two needs at once, gulping down food from the floor as fast as she can, choking out moans between bites because a man is hammering her cunt from behind."

Thomas rose, his face hard. Zorac remained motionless, watching him. Lilith's dark, hopeless eyes studied the knight.

"What crime has this woman committed, my lord, that you feel she deserves to be shamed in this fashion?" the knight asked.

"This is not the public square, my lord Thomas, where sentences must be read aloud. Suffice it to say she has committed a sin for which this punishment is not nearly severe enough."

"You are God, then, to judge her so?"

Zorac leaned forward, his pale blue eyes glittering like ice in the longest days of winter. His lips curled back in a snarl. "In all things concerning her, I am. Hell's justice is slow, Sir Thomas. At time, Lucifer needs a hand to carry out God's sentences. And since I am God in this place, I think we shall now find out more about what brings you to us."

Thomas turned quickly as a guard came forward and dropped his saddlebags before the wizard.

"You usually go through your guest's belongings, sir?" Thomas asked coldly.

"I protect my interests, Sir Thomas." The wizard opened the flap of the saddlebag and peered in at the contents, but did not remove them. After a moment, he replaced the flap and sat back, considering the knight. "So your challenge *is* for the Lady Lilith, as I suspected," he said.

"It is." Thomas gauged in his mind the position of the guards in the room, and what he might have to do to defend himself or his lady. "And I would have told you that honestly, in our conversation tonight. I bring no intention of subterfuge, my lord. I am here for Lilith. I do not intend to leave without her."

Lilith's attention darted between the two of them, confusion altering her tense features.

"I see. You have brought tools to perform the ritual of awakening," Zorac said thoughtfully. "The High Priestess Helene has given some thought to what might overturn my spell, without offending me." He chuckled, startling Thomas with his sudden affability. "It is clever, I give her that. However, Helene overlooked one thing." The wizard's lips pulled back into a smile that enhanced the cruelty Thomas had suspected there. "There is no way this worthless whore can survive the ritual of awakening. There is nothing in her soul to awaken. It will destroy her hollow mind and you will leave here with less than the hope with which you came. Knowing that, I can afford to be a gracious host, and offer you something for your trouble. Show him your wiles, Lilith. Take off the dress."

"I do not require—"

"Do not make it worse on her," Zorac said, his voice sharp. Lilith's breath caught in her throat and her body shuddered. Her head dropped back on her shoulders and her fingers closed into fists. "Let me proceed, Sir Thomas, unless you enjoy seeing her torment heightened."

The muscles in Thomas's jaw flexed and he gave a bare nod. It was obvious the task of taking off the dress would not be an easy one for a woman with her arms bound. Thomas supposed that was the point, to humiliate her further by making her do the crude maneuvers before them all.

With a steel glance at the wizard, he stepped upon the table, and down to stand before her. Now he was within touching distance, nothing between them but air. Despite his objection to their surroundings for their first face-to-face meeting, he felt as though his emotions would burst from him like his seed. She was so small, the top of her head just at his collarbone. Her breasts swayed with her uneven breaths.

"I will help you, my lady," he said.

She looked up at him, her eyes like the depths of a man's soul. Thomas was conscious of Zorac watching them, but the wizard made no protest, which was fortunate for him. This close to her, feeling her pain, smelling the scent of her arousal, Thomas would have cheerfully drawn his sword and gutted him for defiling what was his.

For she was his. He had known it in his dreams, but now, here, this close to her, it was as plain and miraculous a fact as the color of her hair. She was his, whatever her imperfections or mysteries. She was his heart. He could feel it beat faster in his breast as it recognized her.

He went to one knee and set his hands to her bare rib cage. Heat. Her skin was so warm to be so fair. At his touch, her lips parted and moistened, a flush spreading across her throat and fair shoulders. Thomas reached around her, bringing her a step closer to him inside the span of his arms, in order to ease the back lacing of the gown and take the full ensemble down over her hips. Her breasts were no more than a finger width from his face, and he saw the blue veins just below the milky skin.

The bare curves of her buttocks molded into his palms

as he brought the fabric down over them. As he guided the dress to her ankles, his thumbs curved over her thighs and he touched wetness. He slid his fingers forward and found that there was a track of moisture trickling from her. He smelled her arousal like an exotic musk wafting from an infidel's tent, offering forbidden pleasures. The visible area of her cunt was a red full rose, slick with a dew that only the heat of a man's lips, like the sun, could absorb.

"You see, my lord," Zorac spoke. "I told you true. She is not in pain, but frozen in pleasure. She cannot go forward, or back. I have perfected the spell which keeps a woman on the cusp of that *petite morte*, never quite there, but not able to withdraw from its heights, so she is always off balance, teetering on the edge of a cliff from which she can neither leap nor retreat."

"Pleasure meets pain, and —"

"The two never separate. It is the reality which most of us choose not to face. Lilith bears the lesson every day. Let me show you how pleasure can bring agony." Zorac motioned to one of his guardsmen.

"I need no such demonstration," Thomas said, though he knew his words to be cursedly untrue. Helene had counseled him.

It will be difficult, my lord, to see her thus, but that is why I have taught you to discipline your most primitive of instincts, including aggression. Before you begin the ritual, you must be sure you understand fully the type of spell she is under.

He wished a dire curse on all priestesses and wizards, but called on the discipline of a lifetime to stay where he was and say no more. *Forgive me, my lady.*

Her eyes were glazed, and she was leaning forward awkwardly, without the balance of her arms, as if the throbbing between her legs were making it impossible for her to straighten. Thomas steadied her, closing his hands on her shoulders, and she pressed her forehead into his shoulder.

The guardsman Zorac had called over was a burly fellow of mature years, with a stern but not unkind air about him. A captain of the guard, perhaps. He stood behind Lilith and looked down into Thomas's dangerous expression.

He shifted his glance to Zorac, and the wizard nodded. "It is fine, Cullen. The knight will not interfere, not if he values his lady."

Cullen did not look as if he feared a fight. "My lord Zorac knows the ways to mete out justice and mercy, sir," the guardsman said, addressing Thomas. "His actions may seem harsh, but he has been just to me. I would not serve him otherwise."

Thomas did not speak, his expression reflecting his barely contained fury. Cullen shrugged, and his eyes went to the tempting bare arse offered before him. The combination of that and the wizard's encouragement overcame his concerns with Thomas. He pulled aside his woolen hose and braies, and thrust his erect and impressively-sized cock into Lilith from behind.

The jerk of her body against his hands was like a mortal blow to Thomas's chest. In his travels, he had been forced to witness things he wished he had not seen, participate in things he wished he could have avoided. Even before Helene's regimen, he had mastered the art of keeping his emotions chained down in order to learn from what he saw, and act to prevent even greater suffering when he could.

This should be no different, except it was his lady

being dishonored while he stood and allowed it for the sake of her ultimate freedom. It was a bitter taste in his mouth, like the blood that spilled onto his tongue, from his teeth grinding into the meat of his cheek.

The man's hand spread over Lilith's bare back, her ridge of spine, and pushed her down further to make the entry smoother. Her forehead now pressed against Thomas's chest.

He held her as the man grunted and thrust. Her legs spread to accommodate him. She threw her head up, her teeth bared. She moaned, a long, lonely cry of passion that would stir the loins of any man.

Please—" she gasped. "Please—"

"No, my lady," Zorac said, devoid of mercy. "Feel Cullen's cock in your cunt, feel yourself hanging on that precipice, like a man on the gallows just a moment from the gates of Paradise. Know that the pleasure will just build and build, and there will be no release, just pleasure that becomes the greatest of agonies to bear."

"Hold,...my...me..." she managed, her eyes on Thomas, tearing.

Thomas collared her throat with one hand to keep her balanced, and caught the fingers of her left hand, bound to her side, in his own. Her grip was spasmodic, but the intimate link made her eyes close. The tears spilled free, marking her cheeks, even as her cries became more guttural, a woman trembling on the edge of climax.

She surged forward, her mouth devouring Thomas's, her tongue wet and sweet in his mouth.

"Sweet Blood of Christ, but she's always so tight," Cullen managed. His thighs slapped hard and loud against her arse, as if he rode the body of a galloping mare. He groaned, long and low, the sound of a man releasing his seed, his fingers clutching her hips in a bruising grip.

Lilith wailed, not in pleasure but in frustration. He finished and pulled out of her, as matter of fact as a man finished relieving himself against a tree. She would have jerked around, but Thomas held her as the man withdrew.

"No, no..." her other hand strained toward herself but of course could not reach. The man adjusted himself, did a half bow to Zorac, and resumed his place at the nearby table. Thomas noticed, despite his professed loyalty to the wizard, that Cullen did not meet anyone's eyes.

"No, no..." her lips and teeth sought Thomas's face, neck and ears as she thrashed like an animal in a trap in his grasp. Her hair had come down, and with her teeth bared, she looked like a forest sprite on a rampage for a man's blood and virility both.

"She will calm down in a few moments," Zorac assured Thomas. "She has gotten very good at controlling herself. I used to spread her out on the floor and manacle her to keep her from doing harm to herself. Her scent perfumed our meal and reminded my men of the delights of the night to come. Of course, they had to take her there, on the flagstones, because the spell gets worse with every man who takes her. She can become quite dangerous, more wild than any wounded animal I have ever seen."

Thomas rose to his feet, holding Lilith against his side.

There was a scramble of activity, steel being pulled. The guardsmen were there, and Cullen stood at his lord's shoulder, his sword out. Thomas wondered if Zorac had called to them in their minds, or if his expression alone had warned them he was a breath away from taking their lord's head.

"Would you strike me down, Sir Thomas," Zorac said, his expression as dangerous as that of a falcon sighting a lone fox kit, "if you thought it would free her?"

Thomas did not blink. Every muscle of his body was tight with restrained power screaming to be unleashed.

"If I thought that was the answer to this," he said in measured tones, "to save my lady from a wretched fate such as you have designed for her, yes, I would. You would not rise from that chair again, no matter what men or magic you have to command."

The guards shifted, muttering, but Thomas's attention did not waver from the man before him. "But it is not the answer," he said, after a charged silence. "The answer lies in her heart, and yours. I cannot influence yours. Hers I can win."

"You are foolish, sir," Zorac scoffed at him. "I am not isolated here. I know the few knights who still pursue quests of honor whisper of her, and wonder if they should embrace the challenge of defeating an evil wizard such as myself to win one of the most beautiful women in our world, though she is only of basic noble birth. But in the end, they realize there is no real glory or wealth in it, just some fleeting notoriety and a well-used whore. So they think of it, but do not come.

"You have come," he cocked his golden head, "and with the endorsement of the mysterious Lady Helene. However, I wonder if, by morning, you will decide Lilith is a prize not worth winning and simply ride away. I have patience, and am willing to wait and see."

"Then, sir, I would prefer to take the lady to bed now," Thomas said. "I demand the spell be removed from her wrists. It gives me no advantage with the ritual, and you know it."

"I know that, but the binding stays, Sir Thomas. Do not presume on my hospitality any further than you have.

Your challenge intrigues me, that is all. At this moment, you, and your arrogance, endure on my sufferance."

The two men locked gazes for several more tense moments, and then Thomas inclined his head. "My lord."

It was as much permission as he would seek. He lifted Lilith in his arms. She was far too light, and it further infuriated him that Zorac had not nourished her as he should. He stepped around the table, his contemptuous gaze raking the guardsmen before he exited the room. Lilith's damp cheek pressed against his heart.

* * * * *

His chambers had been attended while he was gone. The servants had left a tub of water by the fire for morning washing, and some bread and cheese on a board for late evening appetites. The bed was made up with a heavy mound of covers.

Lilith had begun struggling in his arms halfway up the stairs, attempting to rub herself against him, making little mewling cries. Thomas set her on her feet in the chamber, holding her away from him. She fought him, but he was much stronger, and simply waited until she raised angry, agonized eyes to his.

"No," he said softly. "You cannot do anything for yourself that way, lady. You know that. Be calm and strong, as you have taught yourself to be. Be calm."

He kept his hands still, so as not to add to her agitation, though he ached to stroke her hair away from her face, touch those lips, give her the comfort and protection of his body.

Her eyes squeezed shut as he held her. In a few moments, her writhing became a rhythmic rock against his grip, like a metronome settling to a slower pace. At length, she stopped moving and opened her eyes, gazing at him.

"It feels like almost dying or almost being born," she said, surprising him with her sudden coherence. "Not quite finished, trapped between world and dust, or womb and world. I am afraid one day I will be torn in two and yet still live." Her attention roamed from his eyes, and she looked at his hair, his forehead, the slope of his shoulder. "I dreamed of you," she said. "You disappeared in the mist."

"I will not do so again, milady," Thomas said, his throat tight at her lost eyes and trembling, roused body. "Come lie down for me, on the bed."

She stared at him, as if she might refuse, but then she shrugged and turned, bringing a peculiar grace to the action, since she had to move slowly to balance herself without the use of her hands. The bend of her knee to take the mattress and the turn of her hips showed him the deep pink folds of her damp cunt, the sway of her breasts, the nipples tight from cool hallways and bespelled arousal.

"Lie back and open your legs to me," he said.

She tossed her head, another tendril of red hair sliding free of its bindings. Her hair was more than half undone by the rough fucking she had received and her own struggles. As she turned on her hip, and began to lay back, he moved forward. He caught her head in the palms of both of his hands, arresting her body in mid-recline. She trembled, her torso parallel with the diagonal tilt of his own, less than a handspan between the meeting of their hips, stomachs, chests, and lips. Thomas cradled the back of her skull in one hand and freed her hair.

Ribbons came loose, and he flicked pins away so fire spread over his fingers. He eased her back and his palms came forward, tumbling her thick mane over her shoulders and covering her breasts. She was freshly fallen snow before his gaze, with a swirl of fire at her center, like the color of her hair.

"Open your legs, Lilith," he repeated. "Show yourself to me."

"You are not my Master. I am not yours to command," she said, but her voice was weak.

"I am your Master. You know it, or you would not try to refuse me. You would be as you are to all the others, indifferent to them, while your body is desperately compliant. You are my lady."

His hands were on her thighs, and he eased them open. They shivered, like the lean bodies of two soft white rabbits, unmoving under human touch but remarkably feral in their shuddering response, so there was no doubt that he touched something wild and untamed. How often had he seen kings and lords keep ferocious animals in chains or cages in their halls? They wanted that exotic beauty within touching distance, they wanted the animal's wildness. They put the animal in a cage, making him dependent on scraps. He went mad or listless, only a shadow of the wild creature he once was. The captor sucked away the animal's wildness, and became the beast instead.

His wild creature was spread for him now, her whole body shuddering in a way that made him want to cover her, surround her, feel her fragile thighs and breasts against him. He wanted to warm them with his heat and protection, fill her tight channel with his cock, lock them together as one being.

There was a glitter at her nipples he had not noticed in the hall. He bent and looked closer. "What are these?" he asked. He grazed his fingers over the slim silver circlet around her full left nipple.

She writhed at his touch, but managed an answer. "They make them more aroused, larger. It pleases my lord for me to wear them."

"Lilith," Thomas sat on the edge of the bed. He bent, his breath hovering over one engorged nipple. "You will not call Zorac 'my lord' any longer. He is not your Master. I am."

Her brow furrowed, and she began to shake her head in denial. He laid his lips over the tip of the right nipple and pulled it and much of the breast around it into his mouth. Lilith arched off the bed, crying out, her fingers straightening at her sides, as if extending all the digits would make up for her helpless vulnerability to all he could do to her.

His act had a very functional purpose, though suckling her sweet tits and feeling her moan beneath his touch swelled his cock to a painful thickness that made him lightheaded. His rage, lust and desire had all fueled the erection. He wanted to use it as a weapon, and he fully intended to do so.

There was not much difference between him and Zorac in that regard. Helene was right. Thomas wanted to free Lilith from Zorac, but not make her free. She was his. However, he wanted to claim her rightfully.

She would fight him, he knew, for he had to prove himself worthy of being her Master. Thomas's lips curved into an unexpected smile on the fleshy curve of her breast. Goosebumps rose under his lips as the cool air mixed with the heated flow of his breath. It was as Arthur had been known to say. Might is not right; might should be used *for* right.

This was right.

He had both tiny circlets in his mouth, slick with his saliva, and he spat them out onto the floor. "You will not need such things to stay roused for me, my lady," he said. "You will experience full pleasure tonight at my command, I promise you."

If he did the cursed ritual right. Fighting a border war was far easier than this.

Thomas rose, moved down the bed and spread her legs wider. He attached them to the cuffs Zorac had left at the corner posts, apparently to contain Lilith for his guests' pleasure. He did not wish to use them, but knew he must. They were tools and he must not give them any more significance than that. Thomas shut out the misery of their immediate surroundings, the ways Zorac had tortured her, his fury with the wizard. He had found her, they were together, he must make this work. It was that simple. The room was a room anywhere, with the comforts any man who had served in battle could appreciate.

"My Lord Thomas," she murmured, and the words nearly brought him to his knees.

"My lady."

"I do not know if I can bear more pleasure. It is something about you that...opens me, inside. I am afraid I cannot bear it."

"It will be all right, Lilith. Do not fear."

He turned, a basin and a wet cloth now in his hand, and studied her in the flickering light. Her body twitched, little ripples of movement, a press of hips into the bed, a thrust of breasts upward, a restless toss of her head, all movements of a woman wanting a man upon her, inside her, movements she could not control. Artificial cravings Zorac had instilled in her.

He came to her, and her gaze centered on the empty basin in his hand.

"I want you to relieve yourself in this, my lady," Thomas said, sliding his hand under her back and lifting her so she was upon it.

Her cheeks stained with color. "My lord, I am noble born, and will not—"

"Be still, and obey me, lady. There is no shame here. I will not have you suffer the smell of another man's seed forced upon your lovely cunt. Relieve yourself and I will wash you. His eyes burned down into hers. "No man, other then me, will ever have you again."

She swallowed, her lips tight. She closed her eyes, averted her face, and a moment later he heard the trickle in the basin as she purged herself of Cullen's issue.

He set the basin aside and set to work on her with the cloth. Her thighs tensed at his gentle ministrations, and her back arched at the pleasure of his touch.

"It is such a small thing," he said, dropping to one knee. He was tall, so she could still see him. "You see?"

She gasped, as he laid his thumb on that bud of sensitive flesh just above her warm and moist opening. It was the barest of touches, but it stayed there, a light, immobile pressure that transformed her small movements into hard spasms.

"A tiny thing, smaller than my thumb pad, but it is so much of what you are, Lilith. It has such power, for you, from you. It is the center, your power and your vulnerability at once. But it is not your heart. Only your heart can tell you what Master's hand you will choose to welcome within." He exerted a small pressure and she cried out, her fingers clutching the folds of blankets beneath her.

"You must give me your heart with your sweet cunt," he slid his thumb down, and teased the slippery folds as she writhed, her teeth clenched against his emotional and physical assault. "Call me Master and renounce Zorac's hold on you."

"I am under his spell," she managed. "I can do nothing."

"You can do everything, you simply must choose," he said.

He left her to think on that, disposed of the contents of the basin. He took the amulet he wore from his neck, left it by the fire, and then brought another basin, this one filled with clean warm water.

Lilith looked up at him, her lips parted. He indulged himself, leaning down to cover that mouth with his own. She murmured against him, incoherent, urgent noises. He cupped his hand behind her neck, holding her firmly, feeling the stroke and dart of her tongue against his own, painting her with the wetness of his mouth, letting her get to know him as he was getting to know her. He pulled back. He could not smile at her protesting whimper, as he would have if she was truly free to make the choice to be bound to him. There was too much animal desperation in her face, a feral need that was beyond the pleasures of sexual teasing.

Zorac had lied. He had not introduced her to a marriage of pleasure and pain, but the mutation of pleasure into pain, a pain she embraced because of her body's unnaturally heightened response. It filled Thomas with hard anger anew. She could do harm to herself in this state, allow a man to fuck her with the dagger he used to cut his meat as readily as his cock. He wondered at the "pleasures" Zorac's guests might have tested against the spell.

Would she be able to survive what had been done to her, even if he broke the spell? Maybe, if she made the choice, and let Thomas be the Master who stood by her side to help her heal.

He had to put such thoughts aside for now. You must pretend you are a surgeon in the battle field, Helene had said. You must amputate and bleed the patient without letting your emotions interfere. He wondered how a surgeon would feel if the one coming under the knife was his lady, his heart and soul.

Thomas settled down beside her thigh and stroked the curve of her waist. "You are beautiful in every way, Lilith," he said, his voice a rumble against the muted pop and crackle of the fire.

She swallowed, fighting visibly for some control over the roar of her body. God knew she must have enough practice doing so.

"I am not, my lord. My beauty is only in my skin. My heart and soul are far too black for the purity of yours."

Thomas glanced sharply at her. Up until now, her voice had held frustration and not a little anger. This was resigned despair. She believed her words.

"Zorac is an evil man who enjoys having a woman with your beauty under his thrall."

"You do not believe that."

Thomas lifted a brow. "He has done you harm, Lilith. For that alone, I would take his life."

"You have seen Elias, the stable boy. Cullen, Asneth. They are here as the acts of a man who desires to save and preserve innocence that has been lost, and protect the wounded. Why would Zorac punish me, if there was not a blackness in my soul deserving of punishment? You would do better to leave here and —"

He laid his fingers on her lips. They parted beneath his touch and he stroked them, one at a time. Her tongue came out and kissed his skin, just a slight curl of the wet tip against the sensitive skin between his knuckles.

Thomas turned from her, and brought the amulet he had left by the fire. The disk was now heated by the flame.

"This is a coin I found at Camlann. It is from Arthur's time, from that battle."

Lilith's face revealed the effort it took her to focus on his words.

"You were lucky to find it, my lord. So much has been looted from that place, or carried away as relics."

"Indeed." He held it up to the light, a simple dented piece of silver strung on a much more expensive chain of beaten silver. A cross was still faintly visible in the center of the coin. "I look at it and think it perhaps fell out of some man's pouch or pocket while he fought. Perhaps he would have used the money for an ale, or to buy a lady a trinket. I kept it, to remind myself how close death and life are to one another, and how the quiet of peace is only a breath away from the rage of battle. Love and hate are the two sides to this coin. Light and dark are in us all, Lady Lilith, and they are both necessary to make us complete."

He stroked the heated metal over the blood-filled petals of her sex, eliciting a soft cry from his lady's throat. He dipped the amulet in the basin of water and lifted it, allowing the water from it to drip into his palm.

Thomas moved his wet hand over her hips, turning his fingers downward. A single drop slid from his palm to hang on the tip of his middle finger, centered so she stared down the length of her body at it as it hovered there, clinging to his skin. It grew fatter, as more water from his palm trickled down and joined it.

"This shall fall right on that tiny spot above your weeping cunt, my lady," Thomas said. "It shall feel like the press of a lover's tongue there. Watch it glisten, think of its impact as it—" the drop loosed from his finger, "...falls."

Lilith's thighs strained up against the manacles holding her legs open as the drop plunked against her, where he said it would.

"You will not argue with me, lady," Thomas said, continuing to hold his hand above her. Another drop gathered at the tip of his finger, gained size, sparkled in the firelight. "Or hide your thoughts from me. Will you?"

"No, my lord," she gasped as another fell, then another. Her hips thrust upward.

"Good. You must trust me, Lilith. Why does Zorac punish you?"

"I cannot..." Lilith's words caught in her throat as another drop hit. Thomas watched it melt on her hot folds. He watched the way the curve of her arse cheeks, visible between her open legs, flattened as she pushed her hips down into the pallet. He shifted, straddling her spread thighs with his own muscular ones, settling so he held her thighs down, immobilizing her hips. He dipped his amulet, let another drop fall. She made a strangled cry.

"My lord, you cannot...please do not torture me so,...I cannot..."

He cupped the water now in the shallow basin of his palm, and the drops falling off his fingers became a rapid tattoo of rainfall on her. Lilith moaned, her breasts swelling impossibly rounder before his eyes, the nipples turgid points. Her thighs were tight beneath his own as he kept her still, forcing all sensation to come from that one still point of her body. He was aware of the arched column of her throat, her gasping breaths, her pleas, the clench of her hands at her sides. Yet his eyes never left that small area of flesh, and he hit it every time, his aim unerring.

"Fire is first, because fire is, of all the elements, the most transitory," he murmured. "The sun may or may not shine down upon you from one day to the next, but you anticipate, you shiver, and the sun comes forth.

"Fire heats water, but water touches fire, and fire is vanquished. Fire and water, the east coming to vanquish the south, a circle turning backwards, ending what has been done. We will travel from the most mutable elements to the most immutable, and when you are one with that most immutable fifth element, which is the Spirit, you will decide for yourself whether to accept and choose."

He had thought when he began the ritual, the words he had been taught would be stilted on his tongue, but he looked upon his lady and felt the heat she generated, the sweat of her thighs trapped beneath him. The words came as natural to him as a battle cry.

"Let your waters vanquish the fire, lady," he urged, his voice a husky caress, affected by his own arousal. He felt no shame for it now. He would create a sacred place for the two of them in this wretched castle, and there would be no sin of lust. Lust was only a sin if it was a physical response with no spiritual basis, like eating too much meat or sweets and then having the desire to vomit, to cleanse oneself of the taint of excess. He could never have an excess of Lilith.

The priestess's words were in his mind, her wise, beautiful eyes. His lips moved, repeating the invocation to fire and water again. The air grew even warmer around them. Lilith's gaze rested on his cock, straining hard and prominent against his hose, over her eager opening.

"Not time for that yet," he said. "Not until you choose, lady. Then, if you choose rightly, I will bring you so many pleasures. I will bring you a comb for your hair. I will feed you tender meats from my own fingers. I will give you a hard ride on an early morning when you first wake. My stiff cock will penetrate your tight, slippery channel and remind you each day which Master you embrace."

"I have no such choice to make, my lord. Zorac—"

He was perspiring, and a drop from his forehead fell. The sweat of his brow struck at the same moment as the water from amulet to palm. Lilith's back bowed up against her restraints, and her face showed her shock.

Thomas watched, suspended in an agony of male arousal, his dripping fingers over her sex as the flesh quivered, rippled and then spasmed, a flush rushing outward across her hips and pale belly. As the drips slowed from one palm, he poured a full trickle of water upon her from the other, keeping the tattoo of sensation unrelenting, dragging her release from her body with grim force of will and the overwhelming power of water itself.

Lilith screamed, her fingers digging into her thighs, her heels thrusting into the bed. She strained hard beneath him, a rhythmic, primitive dance. The tidal wave came, and she was on it, riding it so powerfully that she choked on her own saliva and began to cough, her distress no deterrent to the strangled groans that the climax ripped from her throat.

"Sshh, sshh, easy, lady," Thomas leaned forward, as the first wave passed. He set the amulet aside, careful not to touch her soaked cunt with any part of his body. It was still contracting with the aftershocks of her hard orgasm. He soothed her brow with one hand, letting her suck on the fingertips of the other one by one, not like an aroused woman, but a nursing child seeking comfort. She suckled fervently.

"It will not last long, my lady," Thomas told her, stroking her working jawline. "Zorac's spell still holds sway over you, and the desire will come back quickly, but be comforted in the knowledge I will bring you pleasure at least one more time this night."

"How did you,…what did you…"

"It is not easy to explain, my lady, but I will bring forth your pleasure, using each of the four elements. It circumvents Zorac's spell, for he only thought to think of a man sating his lust for you with his body. Cock, hands or mouth. Though he had enough forethought to make sure he prevented you from taking your pleasure with your own hands."

She flushed.

"You must not have any shame with me," he admonished her with a stern look, and indulged his own pleasure, covering her still pulsing sex with his hand to let her know his touch, before Zorac's spell returned to her in full force. She was silk and velvet both, and he was hard pressed not to dip into her heat. He felt the folds of skin shiver beneath his fingers. "I will, once we are free of here, command you to make yourself come with your own touch while I watch. It is a true pleasure most men have not discovered, nor most women. Zorac's spell prevents such an act from doing anything now but inflaming you.

"The elements, however, are not from men. Once all four elements have served you, the circle will be closed around you, and there is a final test, one that neither Zorac nor I can fight. You must open that place you are so unwilling to open, let me in and accept me for what I truly am to you. You will be stubborn," he smiled at her confused face, "because you are, and because you are frightened. But I am here, Lilith. I will not leave you."

"It comes again, my lord," she said, and the desolation in her voice pained him. He knew, despite his words, she had hoped the moment of respite had heralded the end to her torture. He forced his voice to remain even.

"So it does. I must lift you out of the bed now and take off this damp coverlet, before it wets the covers beneath you."

He unfastened the manacles at her ankles and lifted her body in his arms. His erection pressed against her hip and he nearly groaned at the pleasure of the soft flesh against the hard.

"You may take me, my lord," she said quietly. "Ease your frustration."

It cost her much to say it, he was sure. He could feel Zorac's hold stealing back over her body, parting her lips, transforming her features with that hunger.

This woman is mine, he raged, the anger surging up in him, tightening his grip. It was the aggression of a dominant, responding to the infringement of another into his rightful territory.

It came to him then, that a sexual purge to his own tension would aid them both. It would steady his focus, release some of his anger. And it would give him an additional opportunity to undermine Zorac's hold on her. Not by magic, not by machinations of wizards or priestesses, but by an act of will. He removed the cover, set her on her feet and pressed her to her knees on the floor. He took a seat in the carved chair in front of her, by the fire.

"Zorac has made you into a dog in heat, seeking your

own pleasure." At her pained flush, he reached forward, cupped her face in a gentle hand. "But you have a will that stands separate from any magic I do or he does.

"I want you to accept my seed into your mouth, my lady, to give me pleasure, seeking none for yourself."

"I have not done this for any man," she said, her tone resentful, suspicious.

"It pleases me to see your spirit, lady. It is not an act of humiliation," he said. "You offer me a gift, as great an act of fealty as that of a knight who kneels to his liege lord. That fealty is a promise to serve the lord, as long as he lives by the principles in which the knight believes, and treats the knight honorably. Will you offer me that, my lady?"

"This ritual you are undertaking to free me, it will not work unless I do this?"

"It may work without it. This is a step, but not one that is required."

Her brow lowered, her eyes on the space between his booted feet.

"What do you prefer, lady, mutton or fowl?"

Her gaze snapped back to him. "Pardon, my lord?"

Thomas smiled, shook his head. "What does it feel like, his spell?" he asked, to distract her from the decision she faced. "Tell me true, lady. There need be no formality between us."

She hesitated, her glance shifting to the fire. "I will tell you, my lord, but you must do something to help me."

"Anything, my lady."

"Please put your hand over my eyes so I do not have to see you when I say the words."

He nodded, and cupped his hands over her eyes, pressing his callused palm against the soft skin of her cheeks and forehead, the brush of her lashes.

"It is as if a man's lance is always there, stroking," she said, in an embarrassed whisper. "I feel it there and in my other opening,...my arse, at the same time. There are mouths on my nipples, biting and sucking every moment. Hands stroke my hips, my stomach, my neck, and yet there is no one, as if this wall of pleasure separates me from all else. To walk, to eat, requires so much concentration. I sleep little, and when I do, my dreams are decadent, horrible pleasures."

Her mouth tightened, and Thomas brushed the side of his smallest finger over her top lip. "He sends me perverse dreams. I am with animals, with women, with two men at once who care naught for me, who hurt me, and I do not care..." her voice faltered. "Even...with children."

Thomas laid his other hand on her twitching shoulder and her head bowed, pressing into his palm. "Then you came into my dream. I knew it did not come from him, and for a time I could bear the other dreams, knowing you might be there, somewhere."

He took his hand from her face, leaned forward and gripped her hand down at her hip. Her palm sweated with her growing need. "You gave me some peace," she said, looking up at him, so close to her. "Though in my dream of you, I always became a monster at the end. Was it not so in your dream?"

"You succumbed to the spell at the end," he said. "But it was a dream, lady. Just a dream."

Her face crumpled. "Perhaps I am where I should be, my lord. You must at least consider that."

"You are a young woman, Lilith," Thomas said.

"Barely out of childhood. How much evil can you have spread in the world?"

"Once, a young man betrayed his friend for silver..." her voice trembled. "One unforgivable act."

"And yet he was forgiven," Thomas reminded her.

She laid her head down against him and he fondled her hair, his hand under it at her neck, soothing, though he regretted his touch would also incite her to a greater degree of arousal.

"You know, we met once, my lady," he said. "When I came back from a campaign, and delivered a message to your uncle's home." He looked down and saw she was listening, her eyes on the fire, perspiration beading on her top lip. "I passed you on the gallery. You wrinkled your nose, pointed, and said to your friends that knights who stunk like the pigs should stay in the stable area."

"And what did you do?" she managed, her cheek soft against his hand, her bosom lifting and falling quickly against his calf.

"I kept walking, and smiled at a spoiled child's ignorance. I thought how pretty she was, and how lovely a woman she would make, when time and experience had softened her edges."

"There is nothing soft about me now."

"I beg to differ, lady. You have many soft spaces, but you are strong. I cannot begin to imagine how you have kept from madness through five years of such torment."

She shook her head against his muscled thigh. "It was just survival, my lord. A coward's fear of death more than hell's torment. If I can bear this moment, I can survive the next moment, then the next, and then the day is done. That is all. Sometime, I just, became...apart."

"Like you were there, but not?"

She nodded, looking up at him with the question in her eyes.

"On the battlefield," he explained, "the horror and death, like men, stack up around you. Taking it moment by moment, not thinking back or forward from it, is one way to survive. As you hack into the flesh of another man and he screams and dies at your feet, you become something separate from yourself, in order that you can go to the next man and do the same thing."

He heard his voice become dispassionate, but knew the shadows of the horrors lay in his amber eyes for her to see. "You are much stronger than you realize, Lady Lilith."

She gazed at him for a long moment. "This thing you ask me to do, with my mouth. It will bring you pleasure, my lord?"

"It will, all the more because it will bring it to you."

She turned, bracing her shoulder on the inside of his thigh so she could be square in between his spread legs. "Then, my lord," she said, "let me attend to you."

Thomas nodded. He drew his tunic up so the curve of his groin in the snug hose was revealed. He pushed the cloth aside, along with the folds of his braies beneath.

His cock came free, hard and attentive, and her eyes widened.

"I have...I have never done this, my lord."

"Put your mouth on it, as far down as you can reach, and then you slide your lips and tongue up and down. If your hand was free," he took his own and wrapped his grip at the base, stifling a deep grunt at the sensation, "it would be here, and move the same way."

"And I...stay on my knees."

"Yes," he looked down at her, her uncertain mouth only a breath away from his aroused organ. "When I come, you will swallow my seed, taking it within your belly." He passed a thumb along her cheek, a caress and a sensual command. "Do not spill a drop."

Lilith looked at his engorged lance. Slowly, so slowly he thought he might die, she leaned forward, her arse hovering above her heels, and she took him into the hot cavern of her mouth.

He had not been paying her false flattery. He knew what suffering was, and had some understanding of what could happen to the mind and soul of a person forced to endure torment each day, year after year. She had a courage and strength that he had rarely encountered, in man or woman. And she was not even aware of it.

He touched her bare shoulder, gripped it in his fingers. He felt the fragile network of bones, traced the light scattering of pale freckles across paler skin. Watched her head move gracefully up and down, her lovely mouth stretched around the length of him, felt the slide of her tongue along the pulsing vein that ran along the bottom length of his shaft. He could have come in her mouth in an instant, but the priestesses had taught him better. He must give her time to experience the pleasure of servicing him, learn his taste, crave the challenge of drawing his seed forth to her and only her.

She began to suck as well as stroke and he let out a deep, uneven breath. His lady learned quickly and he shuddered as he heard her make a soft noise in the back of her throat, a tentative purr of pleasure to answer his gasp. Her dark eyes flicked up to look at him and he caressed her chin with his hand, light touches that did not interfere with her movement, but which kept her gaze on his face so she could see his joy in her, his absorption with only her.

He shifted his hips forward to rock in rhythm with her movements, pushing himself deeper into her mouth, a little harder, demanding more of her. She made a surprised noise, gagged a bit and then adjusted. He smelled her scent and knew the friction of her cunt moving against her calves was adding to her arousal, but he thought there might be more than frustrated desire from Zorac's curse coursing through her veins. Her expression reflected the change in his, the growing tension in his features.

His touch on her shoulder became a convulsive clutch that moved up to her neck, then he gave up on a caress entirely and his fist tightened ruthlessly in her hair. She made a growling sound deep in her throat, a challenge and invitation. Some of his milky substance slid out from beneath her lips and started down his shaft. It escaped only a moment before she slid back down, using it to oil him further.

Thomas could tell she was feeling it, something she had not had for so long, like the first touch of precious sugar on a child's tongue. Control. Self-direction. A sense of self. A sense of choice. What started out in her mind as serving his pleasure, had brought him under her dominion. When pleasure became excruciating like this, the dominant became the slave of the servant. At this moment he was more certain than ever that he would do anything for her.

"Soon, my lady, when the spell is broken," he managed in a ragged voice, "you will do this to prepare me, and I will thrust in you, a hard sword impaling you, and fill you with pleasure."

She moaned, and he pushed her speed with his hand

tangled in her hair, taxing her strength and the limits of her delicate jaw. He watched the soft flesh of her throat work as he strove to penetrate her as deeply as he could.

"Be ready, my lady," he rasped. He held her firm and his cock contracted. The room got hazy, narrowing to just her and that glorious mouth sucking on him, stroking furiously as he exploded, jetting hot streams of seed into the back of her throat, demanding she take him, accept him.

He held nothing back. He let her see the snarl of feral pleasure on his lips, in his eyes, hear the deep male groan of release, see his buttocks tighten up like drawn bows against the seat of the chair, his skin glowing with sweat from his movements in and out of her mouth.

She was choking, but holding her own. His seed came from the corners of her mouth, but she quickly swallowed and dove down another blessed stroke on painfully sensitive skin to collect every drop. It made desire sharpen in his belly again to see his lady attend him so well. He shoved down the sudden fear that he might fail in his task and not win her from this place.

When at last he was done, his grip did not immediately ease. "You are my lady," he said it out loud, giving power to the words, as if stating it could make it so. "I will not leave here without you."

She pressed her forehead to his inner thigh, and he felt her wet lashes against him, anointed by eyes that had teared from the strain of holding him.

"I cannot be yours, my lord, I have already told you so. I am Lord Zorac's."

"And I told you not to refer to him thus." He caught her face in gentle but firm fingers to show her his resolve. He saw hope fight with the desire raging through her and wanted it all to be for him. "You are eager for me to make your cunt weep again, are you not, milady?"

"Yes, my lord. It does so now."

"Is it me, or anyone who will do?" His fingers tightened, a warning to her tongue.

Lilith's dark eyes were a force of divine energy, so expressive and mysterious they were. "It is both, my lord. I cannot deny the need Zorac forces up in me, but I know, at this moment, if I have a choice, it is your touch alone I desire."

"Good." He rose, adjusting his clothes and controlling his dizziness from the force of his climax. She slid back awkwardly, giving him room, but remained on her knees, watching him with that tension in her face that told him she was again in the full grip of Zorac's pleasure-pain.

He squatted and lifted her in his arms. He carried her close, so he could feel her substance against his skin.

"You are too thin," he said softly. He brought her to the bed. When he had removed the damp brocade coverlet, he had exposed a pile of furs beneath. He saw bear, lion and wolf, all the predators, and a sheepskin. The lamb and the lion lay together in this bed. He saw a pelt he did not recognize, a pale soft fur, like a horse's winter coat, the color of glimmering moonlight and pale sun melting together. One edge was tasseled with a long silken mane, nearly a man's arm in length. It was as thick as Lilith's hair, but the threads were so fine it fell smooth like water and did not tangle where it lay on the bed.

He sat her upon that skin and gathered it on her shoulders. The long mane fell over her breasts, mixing with her own red locks, so she looked a creature of fire and moonlight. He went to the table to retrieve the bread, cheese and wine left for them.

"What is the animal that created such a coat?" He asked.

"It is a unicorn."

Thomas stopped in mid-motion, turned. "You are not jesting," he said.

She shook her head. She looked down at the skin, touched the soft fur. "Zorac used the horn to make a rare powder to protect the innocence of those he safeguards. It is how a man is pained if he touches Asneth wrongly, and how Elias never comes to harm, walking around in blindness."

He would sink to such vile behavior as to murder —"

"No, my lord," she spoke hastily. "I cannot allow you to believe that. My lord Zorac came upon the male unicorn, dying from a hunter's arrow. He had been lured by the touch of the hunter's virgin daughter. At the last minute the girl betrayed her father, overwhelmed by the good of the unicorn. She tried to warn the beast, to make him run from her, but an instant too late. The man wounded him mortally, but the unicorn fled into the woods, denying him his prize, and that is when Zorac found him."

Lilith stroked the fur curved around her hip. "Zorac stayed at the unicorn's side until he died, and told him he would take the horn and pelt to his home so no one else would take advantage of the creature's power. Their language is different from men, but the unicorn understood him, and Zorac could hear the beast's language in his heart.

"So you see," she said, "there is no evil in Zorac, except that which my actions have inspired."

It was as if the whole castle was a shrine to lost innocence, with his Great Whore trapped amid it all, taunted by what she could no longer be. Thomas swallowed his heated reaction to the sorrow in her voice and brought the bread and cheese to the bed. He put the wine on the floor and sat next to her.

She shrugged, attempting to wrest the coat off of her, and Thomas reached out and held it around her white shoulders, pressing it so that her arms pushed against her bare breasts, curving them together and lifting them for his appreciative gaze.

"Pure innocence is a lovely thing, my lady," he said. "But in men it only exists in untested form. And in that guise it is close kin to ignorance, and unintentional cruelty."

Something moved in her expression. Shock. Perhaps fear. Helene had taught him the virtues of patience. So rather than pressing the advantage, Thomas said simply, "Far safer for the unicorn to come lay its head in the lap of the man or woman who has learned the nature of suffering and regret. To my way of thinking, that is the more pure soul, even if less innocent."

"You will despise me in the end, my lord, and ride away as Zorac said."

She raised her face, her nostrils flaring as if she were taking in the scent of his heated skin, and her lips parted. It was an odd sensation, watching her body react so strongly to his, while so many thoughts, disconnected from the desire, apparently swirled in her mind.

"You are my lady. I embrace your darkness as well as your light. You belong to me, Lady Lilith," he tucked a hair behind her ear, smoothing over the shell shape. "Now, I want you on your stomach."

"You are commanding again, my lord."

"I am, and if you are wise, you will obey." There was a

hint of a smile in his voice that seemed to startle her, and he managed to keep it there, though it angered him deeply that she had been denied an understanding of such a simple thing as intimate, teasing loveplay.

She turned onto one hip, and his hand came under her to help her with the turn where her own hands could not. Her dexterity without their balance spoke of how often Zorac kept her thus, but some maneuvers would require even more than the lean leg and stomach muscles she had developed.

He stopped her and slid the five bed pillows under her. They were overstuffed, so he had to raise her up, then lower her. He adjusted her forward, so that her thighs were forced open by the back width of the top pillow. Her breasts hung over the front edge, loose and wobbling. Her knees did not quite reach the mattress now, and she trembled, awkward and helpless, her cheek pressed against the mattress, her neck at an uncomfortable angle while her arse was tilted high in the air.

He brought a small stool from by the fire and placed it at her head, so she could lay her cheek against it to support her neck. Her head and neck now sloped down only a handspan lower than her shoulders. It was a vulnerable position, but no longer physically uncomfortable.

He sat back on the bed and extended a bite of the bread and cheese in his fingers. "Eat from my hand, my lady, and I will strengthen you for what lies ahead."

"I am content to go forward, my lord. My body fair screams it is so."

"But your body must be nourished by more than my seed, lady," he said. "The desire for simple sustenance has been drowned out by the cries of your mind for lustful excess. You need to ground your body with the nourishment of food, to know what your body truly desires. Eat."

She took it from his fingers, her lips as gentle and tentative as a foal, and she chewed. "You keep speaking as if I have a choice, my lord, to simply walk away from Zorac."

"Your body may not be able to resist his spell, my lady, for flesh responds to the strongest influence. However, your mind, properly reinforced, may be able to assert its own desires."

"You make it sound as if I can transform these carnal pleasures into a sacred ritual."

"Indeed, lady. Another." Her tongue touched his fingertips this time and he thought he might never let her take a bite of food again unless it came from his hand, to feel the caress of those lips. "Your mind is still strong. I see it in the way you look at Zorac, and at me. True pleasure is still possible for you, even amongst the pain and the lust he forces upon you."

"Your voice is as arousing to me as your hands, my lord," she whispered, drawing one of his fingers all the way into her mouth with the bread. "Please…"

Food could fuel the strength of the spell, he knew, and it appeared to be doing so, rapidly.

"My lord…" she breathed.

"Yes, Lilith?"

"This,…it feels…I am so roused for you, but it is not as before. I feel Zorac's hand upon me, but these things you do to me, it is as if more than my…than the place between my legs is roused. It is as if you are catching my mind and soul on fire as well. I cannot bear it if you do not put your lance in me. I do not dread it. I need to be full of you, joined with you. I can bear the torture if you at least fill the empty part of me."

Her eyes raised to his, hungry and confused. "How is it I feel this way? Is this part of your spell?"

Thomas laid his palm on her temple. "I cannot yet, my lady. But it pleasures me deeply to hear your words. You begin to see me as your Master, instead of Zorac."

"But is not being your slave the same as being Zorac's, my lord?" Denied, her eyes flashed. "Why must I have a Master to free myself?"

"You mistake my meaning, lady, but perhaps soon you will understand it. I told you, a knight is purposeless without a liege lord to whom to pledge his sword. However, a knight sure of what he believes will choose his liege lord carefully. He chooses his master, and that is very important."

"But I am no knight. Why do I need a liege lord at all?"

He lifted the bread board by its thick wooden handle, brushing crumbs to the floor. "Because, my lady, you are mine. It is a simple truth, and you deny it only out of fear."

Lilith's eyes widened at the sight of the board, clutched like a weapon in his palm.

"My lord," her lips moistened as she pressed them together. "Surely you do not intend to beat me?"

"I do, my lady." He bent and gathered her hair in his hand, pushing its weight off her pale back and hips so the mass of it lay in a fiery tangle to the left of her shoulder. He felt her shiver beneath his touch. "What is more, you are going to like it."

He slid his hand down her back, over the smooth skin, the shallow channel of her spine.

"But, I...did I do something to displease you?"

"Not a thing, my lady. It is amazing, how a firm spanking focuses the mind on your Master, and brings forth the pleasure in you to serve him."

"You did not strike me as the type of man who enjoys abusing women," she said bitterly, turning her face away.

He knelt, turned her face back to him with an unrelenting hand. Their eyes were only inches apart, and his were steady and hot, certain that he was causing her breath to quicken for more reasons than Zorac's spell. "If you feel abused, lady," he said quietly, "when this is done, tell me so. I will allow you to do the same to me, on any part of my body you choose."

"I am afraid you will hurt me, my lord. You are a large man, and a strong one."

"Trust is what this is about, lady. There is a power to trust that can clarify your feelings more quickly than you expect." He stroked the broad end of the board against her rump and watched her fingers close into nervous fetal shapes. "You will feel pain, but the pleasure will be greater, I promise."

Lilith studied him from beneath her dark lashes. Her lips were pale pink and swollen from worrying them with her teeth, drawing the blood to them, the way he intended his words to draw the blood to the slick passages of her cunt.

"I trust you, my lord," she said at last. "But would you..." she stopped, her jaw tightening. Her eyes flashed with something like chagrin, mixed with embarrassment.

"What, my lady?" Thomas laid his hand along her neck, stretched out between the pillow and the stool. He could break it with a hard clasp of his hand, but he had learned that breaking precious things was terrifyingly easy. Creating, building and protecting were the things that took true strength. Of course, Zorac had not found it so easy to destroy Lilith. He had not reckoned on her resilience, which Thomas was counting on to save her.

"Will you…kiss me?"

He smiled. He bent forward, bracing the board on one luscious buttock. The kiss was an act of deep intimacy, much different from the most carnal act, and his lady had requested it from him. That made it, to him, their first true kiss. He stroked his fingers beneath her chin, fanned them out to frame her jaw and cheek, the tips just brushing the opening to her ear. She murmured, a soft whimper of pleasure. He went under the line of her hair, and it tickled his knuckles.

His lips touched hers and sensation shot through him, from mouth to chest to groin to feet and back again, a wild spiral so fast it shuddered across his skin like the wind upon a lake.

He parted her lips gently with his, touched her tongue with his own, traced her teeth, let the moisture from their two mouths join and excite. His grip slid to her throat and tightened there so he felt her pulse against his hand, as if he held a bird. A bird who could soar far above man and yet be crushed in a careless fist. Her helplessness was a deep pull in his stomach, the knowledge that she must simply experience what he could do to pleasure her.

He pulled back just a breath and stared into her eyes, his knuckles rubbing up and down the cord of her throat.

"One day, my lady, I will spend a full day doing just this, from your first sight of sunrise, to when your eyes fall shut against the onset of night." He rubbed his cheek against the flushed heat of hers. "I will wake you in the morning with kisses and I will kiss you all day. In our bed, at breakfast, in your garden, in your bath. Short, gentle kisses, just bare touches of your mouth with mine. Long, deep ones that will loosen your thighs because you will unconsciously desire to be fucked as deeply there as I am penetrating your mouth.

"But I will do naught but kiss you, even as you beg me to do more. I will make love only to your mouth in all the ways you wish me to make love to your body."

"My lord," she murmured, unable to stop her body from performing sinuous rolls at his words. He wanted to slake his thirst with the perspiration that covered her skin, rather than take another drink of water again. "Please."

"Please, what, lady?" he asked softly.

"Please, do as you said you will. I ache for your touch, even if it is only through the strike of this board."

"Your will is my desire, lady."

Thomas rose, shifted the paddle in his hand and lay his palm on her tense back. He admired the white curves propped high before him, like the perfect softness of pale yeast loaves pressed together in the hearth, and the line that divided them and concealed other mysterious places. The board whispered over her buttocks, and she made a soft sound.

He slapped her bottom, a light stroke with the wood. She jumped, but he could see the lack of pain relaxed her. He did it again, several times, getting her used to the sensation, and enjoying the way the slender back arched and shoulders tightened, the bite down on her bottom lip. She was widening her legs, raising herself to meet his stroke, exposing her wetness to him. Her breath became harsh.

He caught her, sliding a hand beneath her hips next time she raised them. He lifted her body above the pillows.

He brought the paddle down in earnest, and she cried out. His next stroke delivered a stinging blow to those sensitive blood-filled folds. Her sex looked like a dark red peach, running with juices.

She cried out again, but he kept on, watching fair snow turn to a rosy blush, and feeling his own reaction grow and swell to painful proportions. Her breath came in a sob now.

"My lord,…it is so much worse, please…"

Her cunt was indeed rippling in the near orgasm that Zorac permitted her. Thomas was heightening the sensations, driving her mad with unrelieved desire. He watched, fascinated despite himself, as the rippling became a continuous spasm. Lilith's head jerked and her teeth scraped the wood of the stool. She gnawed like an animal losing its mind from the pain of a trap. Her legs kicked out helplessly against Thomas's strength, and her arousal was as strong a scent as perfumed oil.

Forgive me, lady. But I must do this to you. I promise I shall make it up to you, if God makes me worthy enough to free you.

"Hold, my lady," he murmured, and lowered his paddle to the bed. He kept her in the air with his one arm.

"No…" she fought him like a berserker. She was unable to twist around with his hold on her, but still she tried, rearing up to try and flip herself over, too far gone to accept there was nothing such a motion would gain her.

He turned her over on her back, so she was stretched out on the pillows, her back arched, her breasts the highest part of her, like fertile hills down a smooth, sloping expanse of stomach. He spread and re-manacled her legs, and with her arms bound to her sides, she was unable to do more than rock herself back and forth, and keen in that soft, breathy voice that slid down his back like the touch of her hands.

He studied the soft curls between her legs and the columns of her thighs, a landscape he would be content to contemplate until the Earth her body invoked in his mind crumbled away and left them all adrift in the Mother's Womb once more.

She drew deep breaths, trying to calm herself, though her eyes on him were far from calm. They had the hunger of the succubus. He bent to his saddlebags, withdrew the carved box that had revealed his intent to Zorac, and opened it.

The phallus had been formed from the soft, sucking clay of a cave deep in the earth. It had been gathered by the hands of the faithful, priests and priestesses of the Old Ways. The clay had been molded over the cock of one of the priests and painted upon the breasts and mons of the High Priestess Helene. They had joined with each other thus, in the ritual that brought together the incarnation of the Goddess and the Horned One, lord of sun.

When the ritual was complete, the anointed clay had been carefully removed from each of them, molded, fired and glazed into the smooth and sacred object he held now, containing the fluids of their passion and Creation.

Thomas believed in God, had fought in the name of His Son, but after his time with the priestesses, he found no conflict in accepting the truths of the Old Ways as well. What was in his hands was holy, and he intended to use it for a sacred purpose.

He lifted the polished phallic object so Lilith could see it. "I roused you with fire and water, my lady. Earth and air will complete a circle about your soul. These four elements are greater than man or magician."

He cupped the side of her face in his hand. She turned into his touch, her eyes closing, her face rigid with the torment of her unreleased pleasure. He lifted the curved sculpture of earth. He found her opening with his thumb, stroked through the soaked lips as she cried out in anguish, and parted them with the head of the large, smooth phallus. He kept his thumb over that sweet jewel that guarded her gateway, preventing contact between it and the tool of the ritual.

The cock was larger than a normal man, but curved for her shape. He took his time. Her eyes opened again, this time showing a trace of uncertainty.

"You can take all of it, my lady," he murmured soothingly. "I know you can." He eased it in an inch, then two, stretching her, feeling her juices coat it, further lubricate it for entry.

The chains of the manacles could be adjusted to spread her legs wider, and Thomas did so now, one-handed, though Lilith protested in an incoherent moan.

"We go wider, lady," he commanded, with gentle sternness. "Spread yourself for me."

Her thighs slid away from each other, further exposing what lay between them. Thomas swallowed at the sight of the pink nether lips gripping the large organ, feeling a sympathetic strong contraction in his own. He growled when she lifted her hips and showed him the tracks of arousal on the inside of her legs. He kept his hands steady though his heart was not, and pushed the lance in half way. She whimpered and his gaze shifted in concern, but her head had fallen back on the pillows and her mouth was open, drawing in air, her teeth bared as she gasped. The tiny bud of flesh beneath his thumb throbbed and she screamed. He put his hand to the side of her head and her teeth sank hard into the callused Venus mound of his hand.

She convulsed, her hips jerking savagely for a release he was denying her. He slid the smooth brown cock all the way home.

He hated drawing out her anguish thus, but the priestess's instructions had been thorough and precise. By the blessed Virgin, he had never been so hard in his life and not come. He could feel his seed leaking against his belly beneath his clothes. Lilith's eyes were on his cock, straining against the fabric of his hose. Her nostrils flared as if she could smell it.

"I can bear no more,...my lord," she said. The plaintive whisper wrenched his heart as much as her tears, which were falling from her eyes to the pillows.

"It must stay thus, for just another moment, lady. You must submit to its presence inside you, accept it being there, before I can proceed to grant you release."

She choked. "It is inside me, my lord."

"It is not that which I mean. You must become still, accepting it as a wild mare accepts the bridle of her Master and stands, eager to run wild but awaiting his will. You must be still, my lady, to hear the will of more than your own flesh."

"It is easy for you to say, my lord," she said on a harsh gasp, "when you do not have to endure it."

"Aye, lady, so it is." He cupped his palm over her feverish temple, touching the fine hairs close to her scalp, even as he kept his other hand on the phallus, and his thumb in place. "But when a man is wounded on the battlefield, there is a moment that comes, long hours afterward. You move past the agonizing pain, into an acceptance of the abhorrent trauma to your flesh. All senses of the body become dull, and yet the things of the spirit, your desires and perceptions, become clearer than anything you have ever experienced. It is a terrible and yet miraculous thing, for it often heralds the end. For you, it will be the end of your life here. Not your death," he assured her. "I will not allow you to leave me."

"Where?" she asked. "Where did such a thing happen to you?"

He pulled aside the fabric of his tunic so she could see the scar, the long gash of a battle axe, embedded over his heart.

She startled him by lifting her upper body. He aided her with a hand beneath her shoulders. He was not sure of her intent, but then she pressed her lips to that scar. His heart hitched in his chest.

Though her body blazed with heat from her passion, her breasts heaving erratically against his chest, her thighs trembling, her kiss was a tender one. She kept her mouth on his scar, motionless, and her lips felt like the touch of feathers.

She stayed in that position for awhile, saying nothing, her jaw pressed against the skin revealed by the opening of his tunic, her lashes fanning her cheeks so he could not see her eyes. He held her against him with one arm, his other holding the phallus still within her. He wished he could hold her cradled in his lap.

Her body's jerks eased at length, and he watched as she once again exercised a control over the uncontrollable that astounded and humbled him.

"I could have lost you in that moment," she said, her eyes lifting to meet his.

"You did not."

She stared at him, tears leaking from her dark eyes like tiny crystallized souls fleeing the horror of the abyss.

"My lord,…if this does not work, I beg you, please, take my life. I care not if I go to dust and oblivion. I am so tired, it would be as much heaven as I could want, and more than I deserve, I am sure."

Thomas caught her tears on his fingertips. "I know you think of yourself at the end of your strength, Lilith," he said. "I have pushed you hard. I feel your body roused to pain beneath my hands. But you have strength, and the end is so close. Inside the circle I will form about you, you will find the answer to your freedom, know it in your heart. Trust me, as you trusted me just now, to understand the nature of pleasure and pain together."

"You do not know what crime I have committed. I may not be worthy of this ritual, and you may not want me if you knew."

"That does not matter," he rebuked her, holding her close to him, her bare breasts pushed up against his broad chest, her softness the only pillow he would ever desire again. "You look into my eyes and see the other part of you, as I see the other part of me. I have sought you in my dreams, whether it is on the cold, bloodsoaked ground of a fresh battlefield, or the comfort of my bed, which I desire to share with you. You are my quest, the quest of my life, Lilith. I came not for the glory of God, or the desire to make a name for myself. I came for you."

"But Zorac said,…you serve the cause of Arthur."

"I, like many before me, have served Arthur's cause, and will do so, always. But he knew men and women make their own choices. His love for his two closest friends destroyed him but it also resurrected him. He honored the love they bore him, and for each other, until the end. It will always be a hard world with hard choices, lady. Men will be selfish and cruel, except in the cause of love. That is the one charge for which they will sacrifice everything. That is the cause I serve, though it has taken me many years to understand that."

He straightened. "Now, my lady, no more tears. You have accepted this cock within your tight opening, and now there is more."

He eased her back to the pillows and took his hands away from her, leaving the phallus seated deep within her.

"You must hold it within you, my lady. That is my command."

From the same elaborately carved box, he withdrew a purple feather with tiny beaded tips. The beads were so light they did not weigh down the strand on which each rested. He fitted the stem of the feather into a tiny slot just beneath the curved handle of the phallus. Lilith stiffened as the slight draft in the room, and the act of seating the feather, stroked the tips against that tight nub of flesh his thumb no longer guarded.

Thomas moved so he stood at the foot of the bed, gazing down the loveliness of her body from between her knees.

She tried to lift her head from the slight downward slope of the stool, but he made a gesture and she settled back, looking at him awkwardly from beneath her lashes.

"In a minute, I shall open the window," he pointed just beyond him, "and the night breeze will come through. The feather will begin to do its gentle dance on you, and render you helpless before the power of the slightest touch of air. You will concentrate on nothing beyond the build of pleasure in your cunt. You will feel your juices rising and the power of the Earth growing within you."

"My lord —"

"No, no words now," he commanded softly. "Ride it, Lilith. Hold it as if it is my lance you grasp with your muscles of silk. I challenge you not to call my name as you explode with your release. You will not be able to stop yourself."

"And you fancy yourself a magician now, able to command my words," she spat, her body's ache spiraling her back to anger again.

"I am your Master, and your love, and your heart. Soon, you will not be able to deny the truth of it, no more than you will be able to resist squeezing the phallus with your own muscles, work it deeper within you. Your body has the strength to serve its own desires."

Her chin lifted, her eyes flashing defiance. The tremble of her lips clearly suggested the turmoil within. He loved her, loved watching her pride fight her desire.

He rose, his gaze never leaving her, and moved to the window. The latch turned easily, well-oiled and maintained by Zorac's staff. Zorac had obviously never feared she would take her own life. Or perhaps he had not cared. A shadow darkened Thomas's eyes as he considered that Zorac had hoped to drive her to a damnation of her soul. Then he would have been spared the energy of torturing her. He could simply have contemplated her burning in hell forever. Let the Devil do his work.

Thomas took a deep breath. Anger had no place in this moment. He pushed the window open and felt the night air touch his face. The moon was rising in the sky, and there were stars, so many that they were a blaze of jewels, a good omen. The breeze from the nearby sea pushed against his chest and he stepped aside, giving it its way.

It swept into the room, riffling the heavy tapestries on the walls. The fire leaped in a flickering pattern. He heard a soft gasp and turned his head toward the bed.

There were things of beauty in the world. He had seen many of them, some of them ironically in the most horrible of circumstances. But he could not think of anything more beautiful in all his travels than what he saw on the bed.

His lady, his beautiful Lilith, her body arched high atop a mountain of pillows, her thighs spread, the muscles within her cunt tight, keeping the lance deep within her. Her white stomach an expanse of milk and satin. The crease of flesh where the weight of her breasts lay on her ribs, the pale curves trembling with her erratic breathing. The column of her throat, arched back and exposed as she gasped for air. Her body jerked, small motions, as the wind caught hold of the feathers and swept their beaded tips over her drenched petals. The motion was like a soft rain, unpredictable in where the drops would fall, but relentless in their determination to soak the earth.

He moved softly, not wishing to distract her, not wanting to change the picture in any way unless it was her desire that changed it.

The earthen lance moved, and Thomas's mouth became dry as he saw her wet lips tighten on the shaft, pull it into herself slightly and then ease it back that same amount with the muscle release. She would not move it further than that, with her thighs spread so far open, but that small movement would focus the friction of the head on the place within her that the curved edge of the lance was designed to seat against. The priestess had told him it was a place of intense pleasure to a woman.

He wished her hands were free so he could bind them

in her soft hair, wrap the strands around her crossed wrists beneath her to arch her body up even further, displaying her more tautly to his pleasure. That would be a joy he would anticipate for another time.

He wanted to be close to her. He needed to touch her now more than he needed air, but he stayed where he was, just watching her, his heart pounding, aching, knowing the rest was up to her.

* * * * *

Lilith had thought, so many times that it became one of the mantras she used to keep from losing her mind, that if she ever freed herself, she would eschew bodily pleasures forever and commit herself to a convent.

She knew only the pain of unrelenting lust, its savage tearing, its debasing need. She had never felt a woman's desire, as Thomas called it, this physical desire coupled with emotional need, this strong, overwhelming need for intimacy with one man. The ability, not only to join with him, but to crawl inside of him and merge with his flesh.

She had discovered much about herself over the past five years. She had learned that almost anything could be endured, and that hatred could give the body strength to survive. She had cried her share of tears into the unicorn's pelt, but it had been some time since Zorac had won the privilege of seeing them.

Her body was being consumed by the elements Thomas had invoked. She felt every naked inch of her flesh, that creation of dust that became so much more with the spirit to animate it. Fire licked over her skin and she wondered if it had leaped from the hearth and covered her with rippling, silken fingers. Moisture covered her beneath the cloak of fire, and gathered between her legs, soaking the object that impaled her. Her muscles acted against her will, milking it within her, sliding it that small, excruciating bit, forward and back.

He was there, larger than life, a shadow in her consciousness. His intent stillness, his focus solely for her, stoked that fire.

She was used to the futile build to peak and dreaded hanging there, like Zorac had described it, a convict condemned to hang in a state of eternal suffocation. This was a different feeling.

The first time, with the water, it had taken her by surprise. Now, she knew that delicious feeling was coming again, but it was taking her higher than before, lifting her spirit as well as her body. The height was beginning to frighten her. Every muscle of her body was gathering, as if preparing for an impact it might not survive, and yet she was splayed open, so vulnerable, when everything in her screamed that she should shield herself.

When Zorac had brought her here, she had no experience, no understanding of the knife edge of arousal he had invoked within her. In her ignorance, there were no shields to protect her from her body's responses. She had no control. Zorac had allowed her free rein around the castle and she had flung herself upon guardsmen who were strangers. She had wrapped her legs around them and undulated shamelessly against their cocks while they laughed. As each guardsmen bore her to the rushes to thrust into her, it heightened her raw desire. When one man relieved his own need, the next took his place. In the end, she rolled on the dirty floor, half-mad, her hands seeking herself, rubbing herself furiously for something, she knew not what. Her hands were wrenched away. In those first days, she was often chained up on the table, like a rabid dog, to buck in a sensual display for the pleasure of the guardsmen. A gag silenced her wails of confusion and need. Zorac watched her ignorant distress with a look of grim satisfaction.

She had learned then what true hatred was, and that she had pride that existed beyond childish vanity and self-pity. She learned to suffer her body's torment in silence, to fight her desire to rub and fornicate every second until exhaustion granted her a few moments of sleep. She learned it was tolerable if she was able to be still. Movement of any kind made it worse. Walking, the rubbing together of one's thighs, sitting where one's privates were in contact with a cushion, all those were things to be avoided.

She grew paler and thinner, but she grew proportionately stronger in will. The fire of hatred that fueled her rose into her eyes and burned there, so the guardsmen, while not averse to fucking her, rarely met her gaze.

She found her shields. She could not stop the desire from wracking her body ceaselessly, but now Zorac had to go to extra efforts to reduce her to those levels. She had no illusions. He could do it. Sometimes he pushed her that far, just to show her he could, but he seemed satisfied knowing how much effort she had to devote to keeping the slightest amount of dignity for herself.

Zorac had thought to punish her further with Thomas, as he had punished her by using her for the entertainment of his guests in the past. But Thomas was different.

She could no longer hold her shields in place. It was as if the first climax had shattered them, cleansed her with those purifying elements of fire and water to prepare her for this, this plunge into the primitive grasp of dark earth and howling winds. Her body arched higher, and still her passions were stoked, the phallus rubbing her in tiny, sinuous circles on a place inside that would destroy her when it exploded. Her thighs spread wide, straining against the manacles, working it, and the earthen lance thrust in deeper, rasping against her silken walls. The wind rose outside, and she cried out, a guttural cry, as the feathers picked up their dance, every touch a diamond spark against quivering, sensitive flesh.

"Thomas, my lord," she gasped. "Thomas..."

His name gave her an anchor, and he was there, at her head, by her side, kneeling where she could see him. He was so beautiful. She wondered if he knew that, how his amber eyes and copper hair enhanced a strong, sensual face that no woman would ever forget. And as if that were not enough, he had been blessed with a lean, muscular body that seemed quite capable of serving a woman's every need, whether it be from her heart or body. And he was hers, wasn't he? Didn't he say so? Why did she resist the thought?

"We may not touch, my lady, not yet," he murmured. "Though I dearly wish to do so. But I am here. Do not be afraid. Let every shield fall, and give yourself to me."

How had he known? She suddenly, desperately wanted to reach out to him, could not bear it if he moved away. She was afraid to do this alone, without his touch. Her mind was no longer able to think of anything that had sustained her until now. Not pride, not hatred. All that was mutable, but there was Thomas. Thomas was somehow eternal. She could almost see the light of him shining through the earthly skin and bone as she spiraled higher. The body would wither away in time, but the light would remain, would always be there to warm her, guide her.

A gust of wind loosed the shutter and the hard clap, along with the burst of erratic air, stroked the feather across her gate. Her thighs yanked back against her chains as if she was about to give labor, driving the phallus hard into her.

The light from Thomas exploded, blinding her, consuming her. The climax rolled over her with the power of the ocean thundering just beyond the castle. She felt as if the energy detonating from within her could have called the sea to rise up over the diminutive structure of Zorac's castle, crash over and through it, drowning them all.

She suddenly could see herself through Thomas's eyes, her body immersed in sensuality, her breasts thrust up as rigid as mountains from the slopes of the earth herself, her hair spread like fire upon the unicorn's pelt. Her dark eyes were onyx embedded with amber, and her slim fingers clutched the pelts she wished were the secure anchor of his skin and muscle.

She was helpless as an infant, and she gave a cry of terror and loss.

I shall not survive this.

I am here, Lilith. I am here.

Her breasts were impossibly full. They would have spilled over the cup of Thomas's large palm, and she could imagine them there, caressed by his long fingers. Her cunt was spilling honey over the contours of the cock inside her, onto her thighs, soaking the fur beneath her.

The cry escalated into a scream, the movements of her hips pumping her impossibly higher. The feather licked her like a wet mouth, the wind its breath, playing in among the saturated fronds.

Her sweating body formed a bridge, rising up in a graceful arch from the pillows. She was still screaming. The pleasure was tearing her, taking her on a ride like a galloping horse, rushing for a cliff. The stallion flung itself into the air. It tumbled her into a glittering stillness of white light and final, powerful silence.

I can take no more.

I am here, my lady, my own...

Thomas, my lord...

* * * * *

She was floating in that whiteness. There was no form or shape to the world around her. It was peaceful, still, the whiteness given texture by drifts like clouds traveling through the air around her, touching her skin with the kiss of fog-like mist.

Had she died? No, she knew she could not be dead. Somehow the ritual had taken her here. Perhaps this was the sacred circle of which he had spoken. Perhaps she was unconscious and dreaming.

She heard laughter, unkind laughter coming from the throat of a girl she knew, and her heart stilled. She turned, and the mist lifted a few paces away, as if she had the front seat for a stage play.

She looked at herself as she had been five years before, a prettier version, with a voluptuous body and no lines of pain or dark shadows in those bright brown eyes.

Her younger self stood before a young man with a fall of blonde hair and an earnest, somewhat scholarly face. He knelt to her.

"What may I do for you, my lady, to prove my love?"

"No," Lilith whispered. She felt Thomas here, behind

her, and did not want him to see, but she could not turn, could do nothing but watch.

The girl looked at her hand, clasped in that of her suitor, and considered. She blushed modestly, but Lilith saw the bored annoyance beneath the flirtatious lashes. It was so obvious, she wondered the young man did not see it.

Many of the young men pursuing the ideal of courtly love had gotten more obsessed with their flowery phrases than the women they claimed inspired them. But if she had only known how to look, through the eyes of experience and wisdom, she would have seen that this boy meant them deeply, even if his passion obscured the mettle of the woman to whom he said them.

"Prove your love to me in arms, my lord. Take yourself far away, to the service of Christendom and our country, on the borders. Die with my name on your lips."

Her voice was so gentle in its mockery, he never heard the acid undertones. Lilith wanted to believe she hadn't meant it, but she knew the truth was worse than if she *had* meant it. She hadn't cared whether she meant it or not. She had simply wanted him gone.

He stood, keeping her hand. Lilith's fingers fluttered, remembering her desire to pull free, get away.

"Your wish, my lady, is my only desire. Grant me a token of yours to give me strength and to send back to you when I have proven my love to you."

She didn't care for the necklace she wore anyway. It was a gift from her aunt, who had the taste of a stable hand. This was a good way to be done with it. The young Lilith put it on his neck, accepted with barely contained impatience his fervent thanks, and turned away. She did not bother to watch him leave.

The older Lilith watched the young man. He pressed his lips to the garish medallion of her necklace, touched with wonder the skin of his neck where she had touched him when she placed it on him. He had been so young, but she realized he had likely had no more years than she had now. She felt centuries older than he had ever been.

Hot tears stung her eyes and she reached out a hand, but the boy was gone. She recoiled as another stepped through his melting apparition. Zorac, with the same blue eyes as his younger brother, only his eyes and mouth were hard with grief.

The wizard strode to the younger Lilith, where she played with her friends in the solar. He spoke his introduction and extended the necklace. "My brother sends this to you as proof of his love."

Lilith watched herself take it, visibly try to remember who this man's brother might be. She shrugged, assessed the value of the gift she also did not recognize, then laid it aside. She used the moment to assess the potential of the messenger beneath her lashes and found him to her liking. She smiled up at Zorac in practiced innocent flirtation. The expression died before the rage that swept over his grief-ravaged face.

The images wavered and dissipated in the mist, and Lilith stood, staring at where they had been. She had lived portions of those two scenes over in her mind so many times. This time it was so real, it allowed her no place to hide from any moment of it. She could offer no apologies, could not beg for forgiveness, for her crime had been so great, she did not have the right to do either.

"How may I prove my love to you, lady?"

Like a warm wave of tears that passed through her entire body, his voice spoke to her.

Lilith turned.

Thomas stood ten paces away, but in this dream reality, his words were against her ear.

He was naked, as she was, and she drew in her breath at the fineness of him. Strong limbs, thighs and arms covered by a light mat of hair that gleamed with the same copper highlights of his hair. His proud cock was aroused and thick. She looked at it and it was as if her eyes were intimately connected to all the nerves of her body, for she could feel what it would be like to have the broad shaft of that cock against her dripping sex. She could feel it push in between the walls of flesh and claim its sovereignty in that dark, moist castle.

She had never felt that way about any man, not under Zorac's spell, not ever. He was here, in her world of sorrow, stillness and shame. He did not come to condemn her, or exonerate her, but to stand at her side. His lips and eyes reflected his love and gentleness.

Perhaps it was the purifying steps of the ritual he had taken, perhaps it was some magic she did not understand. However, the pride he had roused in her to resist his claim melted away. She was here in this space, just Lilith, and she needed him in her life, more than she would ever need anything again.

"I am not worthy of your love," she said, her voice as small as she felt herself to be.

"That is for me to decide, lady. How may I prove my love to you?"

She faced him, two beings as bare and alone as the day Adam and Eve faced one another in Eden, God's presence a mist around them.

"Be my Master," she said, "and never leave me."

She moved then. It was ten steps to reach him, and when she got there, his arms were open. She moved into them and him, pressing all of herself against him. She choked on her emotions as she realized she could raise her arms, wrap them around his hard waist, and hold him as close as he was holding her.

"How will I prove myself to you, my lord?" She spoke into his chest.

"You need do nothing, my lady, but be who you are."

She could not dare to trust the simplicity of that, but in his arms, here, it felt possible. "Will you kiss me?" she asked, as she had before, on a more earthly plane. She was seized with the fear this was a dream, and she would wake and none of it would have happened.

"I will do much more than that, Lady," he said, his head bending to reach her upturned face. "It is time, now that you have accepted me, to make you mine in truth."

Before she could reply to that, his lips were upon hers, and all the hard urgency she had seen him bank within himself as he prepared her for the ritual now poured into that kiss.

His palms slid down her bare arms, cupping her elbows, drawing her in so her breasts were on his chest. His cock pressed in a hot and insistent way against her, almost comforting in its demand, the wet tip making a line of need across her skin. Her hands clutched his sides, tracing the bottom of his ribs, wondering which was the empty spot where God had given one from man to woman, to join them forever.

"Your mouth, lady," he murmured. "Open it to mine, as you will your moist cunt to my lance, in due time."

She obeyed, and his tongue found hers, stroked, thrust and made her open wider, press more tightly to him, and keen deep in her throat, her fingers digging into his skin.

Yes. More.

He broke the kiss, turned her with irresistible strength so her back was against him, and he could caress her at will, explore her body as she rested against him, secure in the circle of his arm, his cheek pressed against her hair.

He did not explore her in the way she expected, touching her in those places men were wont to touch. He molded his palms to her shoulders, feeling the structure of the bones pressing into his hands. He slid his grip down her arms, and she could feel the sensation, every inch, because of how slowly he did it, learning her, as she learned to accept his touch upon her. He curled his knuckles, followed the indentation of her ribs down to the flare of her hips.

He was destroying her with his soft caress. Everything inside her trembled, as if her heart itself was capable of tears. His thigh pressed against her buttock and leg and she turned her head, pressing her jaw against his chest as he continued his exploration. He moved his fingers forward, down the curve of her stomach. He lifted his touch from her, just a breath away, and raised the fine hairs of her flesh with the heated aura of his fingertips. Her hips lifted and he made a soothing noise in her ear to settle her down.

"This is difficult, my lord," she whispered against his skin as the white mist of this sacred plane curled around them. "It hurts." Her chest and stomach were aching with something that felt like a wound.

His lips brushed the back of her neck, and his arms came all the way around her, one across her chest, just above her breasts, the other about her waist, his fingers splayed out on the point of her shoulder and hip.

A quiet sob, like the sigh of a fawn in a hidden glade, escaped her lips. He held her like that in silence for awhile, letting her feel his heart beat against her shoulder blades, his cock pulse against the small of her back. The taut strength of his thighs, the heat of his chest and stomach against her skin, the movement of his breath against her neck and ear. She felt the white mist roll around them, a blanket shutting out everything but each other and that heart thudding against her. She was weeping, and she did not know why.

"You will have to choose once more, Lilith," his voice spoke through her. "You're almost free, but you must be willing to make a choice, believe you have the right to do so, in the world we have left."

She knew he was right, but did not want to face it yet, for she might make the wrong choice, and this would be the last moment of peace she might know again. She knew there was not another Thomas in the world for her.

As if he could read her thoughts, he pressed his lips to her throat, using a hint of teeth at first, and then deepening the bite. He did not break the skin but he pressed down hard, marking her in a way she felt tingle to the tips of her breasts and deep within her cunt. She swallowed, and made to turn, but he held her still, cupping her breasts, and ran his fingers over them like the touch of air.

"Speak your Master's name," he said, soft.

"Thomas,…my lord."

It came to her lips before she thought it. It was there, as easy to her as her own name. He had been right, what they were to each other. It made her so terribly afraid, the stark truths of this place where nothing could be hidden, against the reality of the world to which she must return, where her sanity depended on what she could hide.

It was one thing to obey Zorac by force, another to choose in this way. She realized how little she had given to the wizard. Her body and her hatred were such a little part of the person she was. He was her jailer, not her Master. A Master wanted what Thomas wanted. A total surrender, no secrets, no shields, nothing between them, spirit meeting spirit.

He turned her in his arms, his eyes intent and burning with the strong light of stars. "I see you still need convincing, my lady," he said. "Put your arms around my neck."

She obeyed, lifting arms that felt as weak as the day she was birthed to his shoulders, and curled them there as he eased her up to her toes, pulling her in to him. He lifted her. She gasped as he effortlessly, and with precision, sheathed his cock deep into her, his hand coming down to the plate of bone just above her buttocks to hold her firmly seated, the other arm around her back.

It was like the moment of Creation itself, an astounding sensation that catapulted her body's nerve centers into screaming ecstasy and curious stasis all at once. It was not the perilous edge Zorac had made her ride. This was a sudden sense of utter belonging, of wholeness, that could never lose its sense of wonder. Her senses had known chaos and instability for so long. Now those senses rushed to embrace this wholeness, bond to it in the desperate hope that it never be taken away again.

Dear God, he was right. He was her Master.

"Thomas." She said his name.

She lifted her head so they were eye to eye, and his lips brushed hers, his tongue tracing moisture on her dry lips. Her legs had accommodated his entry, wrapping around his hips, her heels brushing the tops of his muscular thighs, and now she thought she felt her heart beat in time with the throbbing organ impaling her.

"You are sweet, dear lady, so sweet," he said hoarsely. "It is like coming home to the Earth herself and finding rest and passion at once. I want to hear you scream my name."

He pressed his hand against her back, pushing her deeper onto him, and the reaction shot straight up into her chest.

He did it again, rocking his hips so she heard the wet, sucking noise of her eager sex gripping him as it had never gripped a man before. Its urgency came from its desire to be pleasured, and an equal desire to stay joined forever, as if her life and all its functions depended on it.

"Lilith," he murmured, and thrust again, the muscles of his powerful shoulders rippling beneath her fingers. "Lilith," he said, his voice becoming deeper, more primitive. And thrust again.

Surely there had to be magic in this place, for she was certain his movements were causing the walls of her cunt to erupt into flame. Lilith struggled, not sure why she was struggling. Each shove of his hips pressing her thighs wider and penetrating her was pushing her out of hell, into the sweet air of the world again. His grip on her was ruthless, holding her hips still, not allowing her any movement. She simply had to bear the rub of his broad shaft within and without her as he withdrew, pumped forward, withdrew, each stroke a slow building fire across the tinder of her quivering flesh.

"I like the way you breathe, my lady, when I am fucking you so hard and well," he grunted. "You gasp each time my lance stretches you wide and buries inside you. I will hear that scream, Lilith."

She squeezed her eyes shut and buried her moan into his shoulder. His hands shifted, gripping both cheeks of her buttocks and opening her. He showed no signs of tiring, a man who carried pounds of armor into battle. She drank in his smell, felt the heat of his skin on her lips, and the need he roused in her turned savage. If he would be her Master, he could earn it, for she would be no meek servant, but a match for his strength.

She latched her teeth onto his shoulder with a growl, her passion bringing flashes of light and color to the inside of her lids, and now his blood on her tongue, mingling with her own saliva. She dug her nails into him, feeling the tough skin give way before her claws, and still he showed no sign of flagging.

"Fight me all you want, lady," he said, "I will not be denied your scream."

"My lord, let me —"

"No, Lilith," his voice was a groan against her throat. "You may draw blood from me, but you will take all of me within yourself. Feel my cock, and know it has the right to your cunt, as much as you have the right to my blood. I will not let you go."

The double meaning was not lost on her, but the white world was swirling into color around them, mist driven back by fire that would surely consume them. Color would take them back to reality, and she was afraid.

Her nipples rasped against the rough hair of his chest each time he brought her body against his with a powerful smack of flesh, the friction unable to be contained. He made her body shake with the force of his assault, the long, torturous slide of his lance all the way out, and back in again. Her muscles clenched him, tried to keep him deep within her, but he would drive her insane with this slow build to a climax that eliminated all her resistance to the truth of who he was to her, no matter what plane they were on.

She could hold her grip on him no longer. She reared back, her fingers slipping away, but his strength held her up. His head plunged down, his hot mouth capturing her nipple and half of her breast, licking, chewing, suckling her.

Lilith shrieked, convulsing at the strike of sensation that shot from that aroused nipple to her wetness. Her reaction gushed from her, too violent to be satisfied with a slippery impression of dampness, the usual discreet evidence of the volcanic spiritual and physical eruption of a woman in climax.

His name was on her lips, there waiting to be spoken again, to call him to her, bind him to her, as much as it bound her to him. It felt like her chest was tearing in two. Her heart screamed what it knew, her fear battling it to silence. Then she turned and saw his eyes, no more than a breath from hers, and there was nothing left to fear or fight.

Say it, Lilith. His voice was just a whisper in her heart, when she expected a shout.

"Master," she said. Then she screamed it, an urgent sound of pain and release at once, a wound torn open. The infection poured out, exposing all her hopes, impurities and fears in one moment, in that one word.

He held her, his lance pounding into her like a siege ram. Knocking down every defense, resounding within the echoing walls of her spirit, filling it with a promise, a possession. She felt him explode, a hot stream that made her cry out anew, her voice blending with his in their mutual surrender to one another, and his ragged breath chanting her name against her ear.

The white and colors came together, merging into darkness, until there was just a tinge of rose, like the light of the sun behind closed eyelids.

* * * * *

It was light behind closed eyelids. Firelight. Lilith slowly opened her eyes.

She was on the bed. Thomas held her in one strong arm while he gently cleaned her with a washcloth with his other hand. She watched him for a few moments, cozening her as he would a child. His copper hair fell softly over his forehead and bare shoulders, and his amber eyes glowed with the colors of firelight. As her ability to use her faculties returned and her nerve endings untangled enough to feel his touch upon her, it hit her like a warm slap of the sun that she was feeling his touch in languorous enjoyment.

Languorous, sated enjoyment. Her body trembled under his touch, but it was an emotional response, not a physical one. She had been satisfied. She, just as any woman after coitus, lay quiet under her lover's touch, wanting to touch him for the sake of intimacy, the remembrance of passion, and in anticipation of it, not the immediate demand for it.

She wanted to touch him. Her hand jerked up awkwardly, because she expected the bindings, and there were none. She hesitated, her hand in mid-air, afraid to move it further.

"It is gone," she whispered.

"I know." His fingers parted the lips of her cunt as he rubbed the cloth against her. She made a soft noise.

"I thought it was,…only there, that you and I…"

"The ritual of awakening took our minds there. Inside this sacred circle, our bodies obeyed what our spirits did elsewhere, so strong was its pull."

She got the courage to move her hand then. She raised unsteady fingers to his face, and he turned his attention to her. Beautiful eyes he had, and her fingers pressed on his lips, feeling their texture.

"You are angry with me, my lord?"

His brows drew together. "No, my lady. Why would you think it so?"

"You are so…quiet," she ventured. "I thought, perhaps, I displeased you in some way."

Thomas smiled, easing her heart, and he kissed her fingers. Done with his cleaning, he kept the warmth of the cloth over her tender opening, the heel of his hand pressed firmly there between her open legs, as if reminding her of his claim to her as much as soothing the tenderness his entry had caused, reassuring her further. She noticed he wore his hose and nothing else, so she could see the hair on his chest, the gleaming line of his shoulders. She noticed the elegant lines of the muscles in his legs, the bulge of his genitals straining the snug fit of the cloth. She noticed because she, Lilith, *wanted* to notice these things.

"I once thought," she managed, "that I would convince my father to marry me to a malleable older man of wealth. I thought I would run his household and my life in my own way, and he would not trouble me overmuch, just be happy to have a young wife while I spent his money on the things I desired."

"I am not a wealthy man, lady," Thomas said, "but I am not a poor one. I will give you a fine home to run, but I am afraid no one has ever called me malleable. I will have my way, though I cannot think of much I would deny you." He slid his fingers within her, just a slight amount, and she found a shiver of desire could rouse itself even in a sated body. "But I shall make sure you will not be uncompensated for my stubborn spirit."

He sobered. He took his hand from her and slid his arms beneath her, lifting her up in his arms in a smooth movement. He took them to the chair by the fire and sat down, with her cradled in his lap. "We must face Zorac, Lilith. Very soon, he will send his guards for us, if they are not already on their way."

Lilith swallowed. "My lord, what if—" she began to struggle away, to get to her feet, but he held her. "No, my lady. We will face him together."

"But what if he can undo,...I cannot bear to go back to being under the spell. If I do, you must do as I begged you. If you love me truly, you will release me, even if it means my death—"

"Hush," he whispered fiercely, grasping her hair in his hands and tugging it, hard. "Lilith, look at me. Look at me, now."

When she did, he gentled his touch. "You made a choice, lady, and I am here. We stand together."

He rose, lowering her to her feet, and went to his saddlebags. She could only watch his handsome, powerful torso in mute panic as he bent and withdrew a package from the bag. He unwrapped and shook out a gown of fine deep blue fabric, edged with a silver lace at the sleeve points, hem and modest neckline. There was a silk cotte of a sky blue color to go beneath it.

"For you, my lady. While you are beautiful in anything," he swept his glance over her, clothed in nothing but her hair and the firelight, "I will not have you displayed immodestly to others any longer."

Her fingers closed over the fabric, her panic settling into something much deeper and more painful as he gently pulled it from her touch, lifted it over her head. He threaded her arms through, helped slide the cotte down her body, adjusted it over her hips, his hand lingering on her waist. Then he helped her drape the silver edged gown over it.

She swallowed. "It is the first time, in a very long time, that I have not felt,…so naked." She lowered her head, and the sorrow on her face was hidden by the firelight and shadows. "You are too good to me, my lord."

"I could never be too good to you, my lady." From the same bag he withdrew a comb of polished wood, with carvings of leaves and flowers along the spine. He picked up a brush from the chair by the fire and began to brush out her long hair, freeing it from snarls with his fingers so he did not tug on her scalp. Apparently, grooming his stallion's long tail had made him adept at rendering his lady's equally long mane into warm silk that poured over his fingers.

"You would put a lady's maid to shame, sir," she said quietly, watching him in the mirror with eyes full of thoughts.

"You will never have a lady's maid with me," he said. "I will help dress you and fix your hair each morning, for you are my pleasure to care for."

"I find you just as pleasing to me, my lord," she offered shyly.

"It is good to hear, my lady."

They said nothing else. He finished her hair and drew it up from her face, fitting the comb against the crown of her head to hold it in place. He turned her to face him. Thomas's brow drew down as he looked at her. "What is it, Lilith?" he asked.

"I am not worthy of your love, my lord," she said.

Thomas's hands tightened on her shoulders.

"Why are you not worthy, lady? Is there a crime you have not paid for here? Do you believe you have not suffered enough to deserve your freedom from Zorac?"

A rueful smile touched her soft lips, lips she felt were swollen from his kisses. "I notice you do not offer me freedom from yourself, my lord."

Thomas did not smile. "In that, I am a selfish man, my lady, and you shall just have to get used to it. You must answer me, my lady, when I ask you a question."

"How much punishment is enough to pay for the taking of an innocent life?" she asked, her face full of pain.

A mailed fist struck the door, and she jumped beneath his hands before he could answer.

"My lord!" Cullen's voice was harsh. "Lord Zorac requires your presence, and that of the Lady Lilith, in the Great Hall. Immediately."

* * * * *

Zorac was alone in the Hall. He bade Cullen and his guardsmen leave as soon as they brought Thomas and Lilith to him.

Thomas had donned his sword belt and dagger over his tunic. Cullen had not stopped him, had looked grimly amused. Thomas understood the message. Zorac had little to fear from weapons of steel.

The wizard sat now in his chair, watching them approach. His eyes were on Lilith. Thomas had made her place her hand on his, and so he escorted her as a knight would a lady, the gesture emphasizing that the spell was gone, and giving her cold fingers the warmth and reassurance of his own.

"So, my lord," Zorac's voice echoed in the empty hall. "You did it."

"No," Thomas shook his head. "Lady Lilith did it, my lord. She had the strength to win her own freedom. You know the tenets of this spell and you know it is so."

"Or perhaps Helene tricked me, and there was more to this spell. You think I am stupid, if you think I would believe that either of you has the power to overcome my magic. Seeing as you acted dishonorably, I am free to kill you both. Your victory is short-lived."

Lilith's eyes closed, her grip on Thomas's hand tightening. He felt her fear. It made Thomas furious.

"No," he stepped forward. "It is you who deceives, Zorac. You lie to yourself. Once, a long time ago, I saw a man go onto a battlefield, a man who represented all I believed was good and noble, who had all those qualities of the man I wished to be." His voice was hoarse with emotion, and he felt Lilith's hand on his arm. For the first time, he took comfort from his lady's touch. "When I next saw him, he was dead. I touched his body, pressed his blood to my lips, the last act of honor I could offer him then. I could have turned to hatred, but what would have happened if the disciples of Christ had done the same, my lord? What if they had chosen to turn their hands and minds to hate and destruction? You think you protect innocence, but are you not hoarding it here?"

He had the wizard's attention now, and perhaps his

fury, but Thomas pressed on.

"My lady made a cruel choice as a child, and she has paid for her crime. The hardship you imposed on her brought forth this woman, a much different person from that selfish young girl. As in all quests that are part of God's purpose, she has changed and become far better than she was."

"Her face is the same," the wizard scoffed, surging to his feet. "The same treacherous face that compelled my brother to his death."

"Is it my face that so offends you, my lord?" Lilith said, taking Thomas by surprise with the raw anger in her voice. "Is it that which cannot allow you to forgive me, or yourself, for not being able to stop your brother from being as foolish as a cruel, ignorant girl? Here then, I shall help you."

In one swift stroke, she reached up, dug the nails of both of her hands into her left and right cheek, and tore ten stripes of flesh from beneath her eyes to her chin.

"My lady," Thomas was on her in an instant. He pulled her hands away from herself and pulled her back against his chest, his hands locking down on her wrists, crossing them against her body. "You will cease. Cease," he pressed his lips to her shaking temple.

As he tried to contain her efforts, he did not take his attention from Zorac, who was vibrating with a culmination of fury and emotion too great to be held within the walls of this room. The fire built and licked against the outer stones of the hearth, bathing them all in heat and the shadows of hellfire.

Lilith became still of a sudden. "Please let me go, my lord," she said softly.

"I will not."

"Please, Thomas." His name was a soft caress. "I will do myself no more harm, but I must be free to say what I wish to say to him."

Thomas looked down at her. She stared at Zorac and he at her, two wild, unpredictable animals gazing at each other over the expanse of a field, trying to determine who was prey and who was predator.

Thomas slowly released her wrists, but stayed where he was. She knelt, and spread the train of her skirt over his feet, her hips finding support against his calves, his body a bulwark behind her.

She made no attempt to wipe the blood from her face. Instead, she rubbed her palm over one cheek and extended her hand, smeared with her blood, toward the wizard.

"There is no stronger binding than blood in a spell," she said softly. "You told me this, when you seized my palm that day in my father's court and cut it with a knife to complete the spell you worked on me. It felt so strange. I, who had never felt the workings of the body in lust, suddenly felt so out of control, so animal-like. But I learned. Each humiliation you forced me to endure," her voice shook, "every rape of my mind and soul and body, I learned what it is to suffer. It was no great effort to figure out, in the end, that it was not your brother's suffering I was being forced to understand. It was yours. Your brother went to his death believing in the purity of love, believing his life was worth its sacrifice. He died in a peace you and I will likely never know."

Zorac snarled and turned his back on her, pacing to the fire. Thomas stood, tense behind her, trying to anticipate the man's actions, knowing he could likely incinerate them both without even looking at them.

"I know I will never ease your suffering, Lord Zorac. I

know I will never make up for your loss. So if you must kill me, do so. That is now my choice. I simply pray you will do my lord no harm."

"No, my lady," Thomas snapped. "I forbid you to offer him your life."

"You call him 'my lord' now," Zorac said, his voice muffled by the fire.

"I do," she said. "I gave him that which you wished most from me, my heart and soul. He is my Master now, and you have no more claim on me, save that you may take my life."

Zorac stared at her. She stared back, but remained on her knees.

"What was my brother's name?" he asked, his voice faint, strange.

Lilith met his gaze without flinching. "I do not know, my lord. I forgot it, and you have never spoken his name to me, even when you brought me the necklace."

The wizard made an anguished roar, and his arm jerked out from his body as fast as the steel flashed from Thomas's scabbard. The knight leaped over her, and Lilith screamed his name.

The silver fire from the wizard crashed into the blade and wrapped around it, crackled down to the hand guard. The impact made Thomas stagger, took him to one knee, his profile still shielding his lady, knocking her with his shoulder so she tumbled back.

"Zorac, no!" she cried.

Thomas snarled and righted himself. The blade he held shimmered, a golden glow rising from the steel, rippling fingers of light that linked with the silver and bound the power of sun and moonlight together. He made it to his feet, still holding the sword upright. He met Zorac's hard gaze across twenty steps that separated life from death.

The golden light spread from the sword, over Thomas's hands, across his chest. The silver stayed firmly anchored to the blade. Zorac snarled, tried to loose his magic, but found it held fast in the golden grip.

Lilith scrambled to her knees, and the golden light washed over her, as if Thomas was becoming sunlight. She found herself surrounded by it, bathed in warmth. The short path to her lord had become a shifting, blinding path of diamonds, like the track the sun laid down upon the sea in the early mornings.

Come to me, my lady. His voice was in her head and she obeyed, pressing through that warmth until she was against the back of his calves. She curled her arms around his one leg, her fingers pressing into the hard muscle of his thigh, her cheek against the back of it.

Do not let him die. I can bear it all again, I truly can, but do not take him from me.

"Give way, my lord," Thomas said hoarsely. "Your vengeance is not worth this price to your soul. Give way, I say!"

With a snarl, Zorac loosed his hold on the barbed silver light and it crystallized and fell, shattering into pieces so there was a mirror of silver shards littering the golden pathway between him and Thomas.

The golden light became matter and slid over the silver, silver and gold embracing and becoming one. The light slid from Thomas's shoulders and cloaked Lilith entirely for a moment. The touch of such purity held simple forgiveness. She could forgive herself, and Zorac. She believed in the love Thomas offered her. She clung to his leg, weeping, until he lowered his sword and bent, lifting her gently to her feet, holding her close against his side with one arm.

The last of the light faded, but the floor was a mosaic of two colors that showed the path of power between the two men. A golden circle marked the floor around Thomas and Lilith, a silver disk around Zorac.

The wizard's face was haggard. "So you are a magician after all," he said.

Thomas shook his head, raised his sword arm to wipe at his face with the point of his wrist. "You know better than that, my lord. You could defeat me in time, for I do not control the power that comes to my defense."

"I could kill you," the wizard agreed. "But I would not defeat you."

Lilith cried out, seeing the blood on the hand Thomas had lowered to his side. Her hands sought his face, where blood ran from his nose and his right ear.

"Easy, lady, I am well," he bade her. "This Light, pure as its intentions are, is not always kind to poor mortal flesh."

"You will not let him hurt you," she insisted, her mouth tight and stubborn. "I will not allow you to die for me."

"So you are giving the orders now, are you?" he teased her in a soft murmur, but he would not let her put her arms around him and hold him with her slim body covering the most vital parts of his. He set her to his side, and held her there, his sword point now to the ground, but not sheathed.

Zorac had not moved during this time, but now he did, sitting heavily in his chair and staring at the new design of his floor.

"My lord," Thomas said after the silence drew out long, and his lady's hand trembled on his arm. "I thank you for your hospitality, and ask your leave to depart, the lady Lilith with me."

Zorac's gaze rose. His eyes burned deep in his head as if he were fevered, or in great pain. "Does it matter whether I give you leave or not?" he croaked.

"It matters, my lord," Thomas's attention did not waver. "Not to me, but to you. You must let her go."

"Your powers let you do as you will."

"They are not mine, my lord. They come when they desire and I am not privy to the why. They felt this woman was worth defending. So did I. Perhaps they felt she had earned her release from your spell. Or perhaps the light was defending you."

At Zorac's startled look, Thomas inclined his head. "Much of what I see tells me you are a good man, Lord Zorac. Perhaps the light was keeping you from traveling down an even darker road than you have already."

Zorac's eyes closed. "Take her from here," he managed, his voice the growl of a wounded animal.

Thomas nodded, took his lady's arm, and guided her to the door.

"Let them go," Zorac snapped, when Cullen peered in around them. "And close the cursed door. I do not wish to be disturbed until...until I say so."

The guardsman gave a hesitant nod. Thomas and Lilith moved past him. When Cullen and one of his men shut the heavy double doors, a man in pain howled behind it.

* * * * *

Thomas kept Lilith with him, taking her back to the rooms to collect his things, delivering a short order on the way to Elias to prepare his horse. The word spread quickly through the castle, and none barred their way. The stable boy was waiting, the mount saddled, when they came back to the bailey, and he appreciated the boy's responsiveness. He did not desire to linger. Zorac's sound of pain had bordered on savage, and he knew wounded animals were unpredictable.

"Lady," the stable lad reached out, touched Lilith's waist. She knelt, and to the boy's surprise as much as Thomas's, she hugged him close. The little arms crept around her as he obviously warred between suitable manly behavior and the motherly attention an orphan craved from a sweet-smelling lady with gentle hands.

"You will take care of Lord Zorac," she said. "He will need your goodness, and Asneth's."

She held onto him tightly and he patted her hair, touched her cheeks. She laughed, and then she was crying, so Thomas knelt and held her when the boy squirmed away and ran.

She shook her head when at last she could speak. "It has been five years since I have been able to touch a boy child without the agony of the curse. As awful as it was to feel that way, I cannot express the horror of feeling that way when a *child* touched me, my lord. I tried to believe it was not the intent of his spell, that it was something he overlooked, that he would not have condoned such an abomination as that. Today, I believe that to be true. But oh, it feels good to hold a child again."

Thomas kissed her, a light caress, and lifted her up onto the horse, his hands staying at her waist. "Perhaps I shall give you a boy child all your own to hold, my lady. What think you of that? Zorac's spell prevented you from being fertile. It is so no longer."

She was stunned, and then she felt a becoming pink flush crept into her cheeks. "I would love to hold your child in my arms, my lord," her eyes darkened and she reached down, sliding back full into his arms, so he held her off the ground as she kissed him urgently, then tenderly, framing his face in her hands.

"I am afraid it is not real, my lord. That the dream will become the nightmare again."

"You can choose in dreams as well as life, my lady," he said, holding her as close and as tightly as he could without crushing her with his strength. "You have chosen, and this particular dream will have no more nightmares to it."

The stallion threw up his head and snorted as a bundle fell to the ground beside them. Thomas tensed and she looked up, where Zorac stood above them on the archway overlooking the courtyard, the same on which he had stood and faced outward to greet Thomas only a short day before.

"A gift to take with you," he said. His gaze flicked to Lilith and then back to Thomas. "To remember, for good or bad, that all choices have consequences."

She bent and picked up the bundle, a strand of the unicorn's mane exposed by the fall and the hasty wrapping.

"Lord Zorac."

The wizard had been turning away from them. At her voice, he stopped. Lilith waited, feeling Thomas's tension next to her. The wizard finally settled his gaze upon her, his body as still as a statue upon the wall of his castle.

"I spoke true, when I said I did not remember his name," Lilith said softly. "But when I came here, and found I had to create a soul, to give myself a place to go to survive each day, I found it was not born empty within me. It was a place filled with things I should have noticed. I remembered he was good, and kind in his ways, and you shared the same smile. I hope..." her voice faltered and Thomas put a supportive hand on her back.

She flinched, then relief swept across her face as she realized anew that the most casual touch would not arouse her to the painful lust. In time, she knew Thomas would teach her to do nothing but welcome his touch. It was a lesson she could look forward to learning.

"If you ever find it in your heart to do so, please know...I beg your forgiveness for taking him from you."

* * * * *

The horse had no fear of the unicorn's skin, but Lilith asked Thomas to carry it in the saddlebags, preferring to ride cloaked only by him. She sat before him on the horse, her body close, pressed in against his chest, her bottom between his legs, her legs over one of his thighs. He rode with her cradled thus in his arms, his cloak pulled around them both. He had not taken time to don his mail. He did not wish to tarry, he knew the people of Zorac's land were peaceful, and, most importantly, he wanted to feel her against his body.

She did not speak much, and Thomas did not disturb her. He watched her take in the world around her, seeing it through eyes no longer distracted by unabated need pouring through her body. Each bird's movement, each ray of the setting sun that flickered past an opening made by a fluttering leaf in the forest canopy, held her attention.

At length, her body grew heavy and relaxed, and he pressed her jaw against her temple, comforting her as she slept, a deep easy rest.

He rode through the night, his horse not objecting since he set an easy pace, so as not to disturb his lady. His lady. The night was much like a dream itself, her softness in his arms, her sweet scent, the quiet of the forest, the routine of the creatures in it, unmolested by humans.

She was woken by the rays of the rising sun, and found herself still in his arms. They had stopped, standing on the edge of a clearing, where the meadow grass was as gold and rose as the sun rising above it.

"I dreamed of you, my lord," she breathed into his skin.

She felt his jaw move, and knew he smiled at the sound of her voice. She felt something move, deep within her. It was physical and emotional all at once. She tightened her hold around his waist and he responded in kind, surrounding her with his strength and warmth.

"And was the dream pleasurable, my lady?"

"Almost as pleasurable as waking up in your arms, my lord. I've no other desire beyond that, ever again, I think."

Thomas tipped her chin back and drank from her lips. They trembled beneath his and he deepened the kiss, until her hands were gripping his shirt in two fists.

His hand gently touched her cheek, where she had scored herself.

"You should not have done this," he murmured. "You must never hurt yourself, it displeases me greatly."

"And what of you?" she looked up, touched her hand to his ear, where the blood had dried to a brittle crimson crust yet to be sponged away by her cozening. "It displeases me to see you harmed, as well."

"You will take good care of me, I am sure, my lady, and be sure I do not displease you often."

"I am at a loss, my lord," she said softly. "It will be some time before I know my place in the world. I may be a poor mistress in your home."

"You are the only mistress for my home, and your place will always be with me," he asserted. "If you will still have me."

At her surprised look, he lifted a shoulder. "I told you, my lady, accepting me as your lord and Master is your choice, and it always will be. Though be fair warned," he gave her a look that tightened things low in her stomach and brought a flush to her cheeks, "I will never make it easy for you to choose otherwise."

His lips were upon hers again, and the kiss went from spiritual to ravenous in no more than a breath, leaving her gasping in his arms. He raised his head, cursing himself for the need for restraint, but his lady took care of his worries.

"Take me here, my lord, under the first light of this new day. I want to feel you within me, as it was in my dream. I want the stroke of your lance to burn away the touch of all others and leave me branded by you only."

"It is perhaps too soon, lady. I can certainly contain my desire and give you time."

"My lord," she looked up at him, those dark eyes alive with need, and a promise of the smile he knew he would coax from her when her heart had healed under his care. "I am asking my Master to fulfill my desires. Will he deny me? I need you, my lord," she added quietly. "What I experienced in Zorac's castle is no more like what I share with you than taking the sacrament is to spitting in the dirt. I feel I have been empty so long, I need you to fill my body to fill my heart. Please do not make me beg."

"Forgive me, lady," he swung down, a smile in his voice. He took her with him, carrying her in his arms. "I forgot. As your Master, my first task is always to serve your desires."

"Yes, my lord."

About the author

Joey W. Hill lives on the North Carolina coast with a wonderful husband (who keeps her believing in the magic of love), their dauntless 30 foot O'Day sailboat Shadowfax, and their eight four-footed children. She is further blessed with an amazing, indomitable mother (who isn't sure about all this fantasy stuff), and a brave, one-of-a-kind brother who is the original prototype for the crusty Bruce Willis-type anti-hero.

Joey writes fantasy and romance and enjoys feedback from her readers. In today's world, there is a great need for faith in magic and love, and there's no better place to rediscover them than through a book or short story. She invites you to try one of hers.

Joey Hill welcomes mail from readers. You can write to them c/o Ellora's Cave Publishing at P.O. Box 787, Hudson, Ohio 44236-0787.

Also by Joey Hill:

- Make Her Dreams Come True
- Holding The Cards

DEATH ROW: THE MASTERING

WRITTEN BY

JAID BLACK

"The rich rob the poor and the poor rob one another." — *Sojourner Truth*

Prologue

My Bella Nellie, I will return to you in a fortnight. Two more short weeks and my arms will be wrapped around you! I can scarcely wait. I miss you, my beloved. Do not let my absence these past six months cause you to think differently. I needed the solo adventure. I needed time to heal. When I received that virtual letter from you informing me of your father's death...

My wounds, I have realized, are cut quite deep. I had hoped staying gone from Federated Earth for a time would lessen the emotions I am experiencing as a result of Abdul's death. Your father was a monster. He was a demon amongst men...

But ah, glorious Kalast, how I loved him.

I shouldn't love him...I know as much. And Cyrus's truth, were Abdul Kan to miraculously rise from the grave tomorrow I would never return to him. I would fight him to my death before I'd allow him to return me to his harem bed. And yet...

ALWAYS, AS LONG AS I HAVE BREATH TO BREATHE, A PART OF ME WILL LOVE HIM.

I WILL SEE YOU IN A FORTNIGHT, DAUGHTER. KEEP THE VIRTUAL CANDLE BURNING IN THE WINDOW FOR MAMA.

NICOLETTA KAN
AUGUST 7, 2250

CHAPTER 1

October 1, 2225 A.D.

"My name is Nicoletta Isabella Carlotta Apollinaris," she whispered in a thick Italian accent, her dark chocolate gaze lowered. "I herald from the Greco-Roman biosphere. My talents are—"

"Raise yer voice, wench!" the chattel auctioneer bellowed.

Her heart began pounding in her chest, tiny beads of perspiration dotting her brow. As it was, she was a nervous wreck up on the stage. Sitting there naked, her hands chained high above her head against a wall, her legs chained wide open to bolts on the floor so the curious potential masters could see everything she had to offer them, the added embarrassment of being publicly yelled at felt nearly overwhelming.

She took a deep breath and slowly exhaled. *You can do this*, she staunchly told herself. *You have no choice.*

Nor did she wish for her seeming lack of finesse to cause the well-to-do males to overlook her. Nicoletta did not wish to end up the wife of a male low in the Hierarchy who could scarcely afford food let alone a wife. Such was the very reality her parents currently lived in, a reality they were hoping their daughter's exceptional good looks would keep her from repeating.

Not that every wench chained up on the stage wasn't exceptionally good-looking. All of them, every last one, were stunning beauties with large breasts, gorgeous faces, and curvy bodies. Hierarchy scientists had ensured long ago that no female child would ever again be born less than physically perfect. Any imperfection detected in the womb—from plain looks to pudginess to being overly thin—all of it was engineered out before the child was ever born. Disgusting, piggish, and a total abomination of all that was holy perhaps, but the unfortunate truth nevertheless.

You can do this! Now calm down and speak clearly.

There was little choice. Her looks were no better or worse than any of the other wenches on the marriage auction block this day. Nor could she claim any superior talents from the rest of them. The only rarity about Nicoletta was that she was still a virgin—an eighteen-year-old virgin who would lose her virginity this very eve to whichever male bought her as a wife.

Her heart raced impossibly faster. Sweet Kalast but she hoped her future husband would not be overly hard on the eyes! Male fetuses were not engineered like female fetuses were—a quick glance in the sea of wretched masculine faces confirmed that awful fact. So if fate decreed her bound for life to an ugly Master, she could at least hope for a husband who was semi-high within the Hierarchy.

"My name—" Nicoletta cleared her throat and began again, her voice audible if not loud this time. "My name is Nicoletta Isabella Carlotta Apollinaris." Her large breasts rose and fell with every breath she took, her nervousness waxing instead of waning. "And I herald from the Greco-Roman biosphere."

"State yer talents, wench," the chattel auctioneer mumbled.

She swallowed against the knot of cold fear in her throat. She decided she wouldn't be surprised if she fainted dead away before her turn was over. "My talents are in the areas of body massage and cock sucking."

Ah gods, she thought, her heart sinking, every wench in here was possessed of those talents. The sea of masculine faces looked heart-wrenchingly bored. She was doomed.

"I'm a virgin," Nicoletta said quickly.

The sea of bored faces perked up and paid attention.

Her chin notched up, her confidence restored enough to finish her rehearsed spiel. The others were just as pretty and were possessed of more talents, so she'd have to go with this one rarity she had. "I have never been vaginally or anally penetrated—only orally that I might perfect that skill for my future Master."

The chattel auctioneer inclined his head then turned to the next wench up for bid and repeated the process. He continued down the line until all ten chained-up females stated their names, origins, and talents. Only then, after the last of the chattel had spoken, did the inspection begin.

The inspection, Nicoletta thought, taking another calming breath. All ten of the brides up for bid had undergone genital waxings so that only a tiny inverted triangle of neatly groomed pubic hair showed on their bodies. They had also been bathed in exotic oils the eve prior that they might smell intoxicatingly arousing to the wealthier male bidders during the inspection period. Poorer males were given no inspection period—they made do with the leftovers the Hierarchy elite didn't deign to bid upon.

Please let me be bid upon!

Her thoughts drifted back to the tiny two-room quarters that had housed her family of seven for as long as Nicoletta could remember. She slept on a rough floor mat like a dog, begged for food in the airbus atriums in order to keep from starving... *Please!*

Everything, her entire future, all came down to the next hour in time. Sweet Kalast but she felt close to fainting! She could only pray to Cyrus her virginity would make at least a few well-to-do bidders curious enough to inspect her. She knew her parents would be gravely disappointed in her should she be auctioned off to a male of questionable means. They wanted her to marry well.

Not that she planned to stay married long, Nicoletta silently admitted, her heart drumming away like mad in her chest. Perhaps it was wrong to plan and plot against one's future husband before she even had a Master to speak of, but she simply wanted more out of her existence than...this.

This, Nicoletta sighed—cock-sucking, body massage, and breeding—*this* summed up the whole of a wench's value in Federated Earth. Given the fact that males outnumbered females five hundred to one, she supposed it was little wonder that females were thought of as creatures, as possessions to be haggled over and bought. And yet she wanted more than *this*, wanted more than to be some man's lowly chattel...

She wanted to be free.

It was a silly dream, Nicoletta realized, but nonetheless a dream she'd carried deep in her heart from as far back as she could remember. She'd heard rumors about some of the other planets out there—whispers about a woman-run planet called Kalast where wages were fair and a female was free to make her own choices. She didn't know if the place was truly a woman's utopia or if it had been idealized and romanticized by disgruntled Hierarchy wives, but she conceded one's lot in life could hardly be worse there than it was here.

Getting to Kalast would be no small feat. First off, she needed enough currency deposited in the yen chip in her brain to book the flight—such could not be done without access to a well-off person's virtual bank account. Secondly, she needed a successful escape plan. The law forbade Earthling females to leave the planet without being escorted by the male they belonged to. Thirdly, she—

Bah! Do not think on this! She was getting all worked up over how to execute her plan when she still hadn't managed to get past the first hurdle: acquiring a well-to-do husband. *Calm yourself...*

She needed a Master with ample means—not only so she had access to a prosperous virtual bank account, but also so she would not feel guilty when she ran from him. After all, the vast majority of the ugly masculine faces out there wanting to buy a bride this day had saved their yen for many, many years before they had enough to meet the minimum auction standards.

Most men of Federated Earth died having never known a wife. All of the males in the bidding crowd today, save the one percent Hierarchy elite, were the few fortunates who had been frugal enough—and lucky enough—over the years to acquire enough yen. Nicoletta did not wish to run from such a man knowing he'd saved and saved his entire life that he might further his genetic line. She wished to run from a man who could afford to replace her, a man who wouldn't feel devastated by the loss of her…

She needed to be purchased as chattel by a man in the one percent elite.

She took a deep breath and blew it out. She might as well wish to be named the Queen of all Kalast.

"Nice. Very plump and pretty."

Nicoletta blinked, her thoughts having been far away. She gazed up at the wealthy male standing before her, then lowered her thick, inky black eyelashes as he continued to tug at her nipples. Her breeding had not exactly been elite, yet she knew the way of things enough not to speak. Wenches are to be seen and not heard — she'd grown up hearing her sire utter that mantra over and over again lest his daughter forget when her day on the auction block came.

The elite male took his time fondling her large breasts. The stage the wenches had been lined up on and chained to rose about waist level on the average male that the Masters would not have to bend overly much to inspect their potential brides. Nicoletta suspected it was also symbolic: females bowed deferentially to males but never the reverse.

Her nipples hardened, elongating for the wealthy male, which seemed to please him. He made an appreciative sound in the back of his throat before lowering his mouth to her chest. He took his time tasting each one, sucking on them like a child's lollipop.

The sensation felt wondrous, Nicoletta conceded, her breath shuddering. So long as she kept her eyes closed and tried to forget about the fact that the wealthy potential Master was frail enough, and wrinkled enough, to be her grandfather.

She could only pray to Cyrus he decided to bid on

her. She would have no second thoughts at all about running from a male as old as this one. Besides, chances are she would not be his only chattel. It might be illegal in Federated Earth for a Master to own more than one wife, yet it was also widely known that most men of status within the Hierarchy purchased as many wives as they desired.

The elderly bidder's lips unlatched from around her nipple with a popping sound. Her teeth sank into her lower lip when he moved on to the next wench on the stage, hoping with everything she had in her that he would still choose to bid on her following the inspection period.

The next thirty minutes felt interminable to Nicoletta as not one, not two, but three potential Masters rubbed and kissed all over her body. They touched her where they wanted to, kneaded her big breasts like dough, massaged her stiff nipples, and played with her clit until she nearly climaxed…then walked away and inspected the next wench.

Her breathing grew labored as the hour of inspection for the elite males drew nearer and nearer to its finale. She had no way of knowing what any of them thought of her, or if a single one of the males would bid on her during the auction. All she did know was that any of them would do just fine for her purposes—a group of weaker, uglier, more spoiled men she had never seen.

"You have lovely dark hair," a masculine voice murmured, snagging Nicoletta's undivided attention.

Her face shot up. Her dark eyes widened just a bit before she thought better of it and attempted to conceal her reaction of surprise. But she was surprised—sweet Kalast was she ever! She knew this male—or knew of him was more to the point. She doubted a single person within the whole of Federated Earth wouldn't recognize the face of Abdul Kan, one of the wealthiest and most powerful men of the Hierarchy.

Not to mention one of the most handsome, she thought, her heartbeat accelerating. She tried to lower her eyelashes but couldn't seem to bring herself to look away from his intense, piercing green gaze. He wasn't handsome in a pretty way, but in a powerfully masculine way — in a way that separates a lion from a peacock.

"Thank you," she breathed out before she could stop herself. She quickly glanced away, her eyes widening as she realized she'd actually spoken to Master Kan. *Idiot! He shall never bid on a wench who can't remember to hold her tongue.*

But the more Nicoletta considered that, the better that reality sounded. She drew in a deep breath and slowly exhaled. Oh no, it would not do at all to be wed to such a man as that one. He was just a bit too wealthy, a bit too powerful, a bit too handsome...

And, she admitted on a heavy swallow as she took in the sight of him, a bit too dangerous. She'd heard the rumors about him — everyone had. Abdul Kan might have been born into wealth, but he had earned his own battle scars.

The wealthiest and most powerful of the Hierarchy's males tended toward the weak, soft side. Their bodyguards were the brawn, not the elite themselves. But this male...

Ah gods, Nicoletta thought, her heart racing, there was nothing weak or soft about him. The black silk tunic and matching black silk flowing trousers he wore — emblems of his status — did not conceal the muscles that rippled beneath them. Nor did the unreadable expression on his face mask the intensity, the knowing, in his jade gaze. It was as if he could see right through a wench, and right through Nicoletta's soul in particular. She found herself blushing, wondering if he'd guessed her thoughts.

"You are welcome," he murmured, his mouth unsmiling but his eyes blazing.

She stilled, not knowing if she should say more or keep quiet. She had expected Master Kan to grow angry with her foolishness in daring to speak directly to him. She had definitely not expected for him to seem even more intrigued by her for doing so.

His warm, callused hands found her breasts and began gently kneading them. She gasped, for some reason momentarily shocked by his touch.

"So very beautiful," Master Kan said thickly, his thumbs running over her distended pink nipples. She moaned just a bit, unable to suppress the reaction. "I've never seen a wench with such plump, juicy nipples as yours."

Her lashes shuttered as she gazed at him through heavy eyelids. "Thank you," she whispered, her breath hitching.

His right hand trailed down lower, over her flat belly, through the neatly groomed inverted triangle of black curls. Her nipples grew impossibly harder as she watched his left hand join the right and his fingers spread open her cunt lips.

"You are a virgin?" Abdul asked, his voice tinted with the smallest bit of hoarseness.

She swiped her tongue across dry lips. Her breasts heaved with every labored breath. "No," she whispered, not wanting him to bid on her.

One side of his mouth hitched up in a semi-smile. "You lie," he murmured. His gaze was intense—as dangerous if not more so than the rest of him. "Naughty girls who lie to their Master get spanked."

Her brown eyes rounded. With fear or arousal she didn't know. "You are not my Master."

He lowered his gaze and stared at her tight pussy for long moments. His tongue snaked out and made one long lick from the tiny hole all the way up to her clit. She whimpered, unable to suppress the reaction.

"But I will be, *ana wahid*," he said thickly, calling her by a name she didn't recognize in a language as foreign to her as his intimate kiss. "I will be," he murmured.

Nicoletta gasped as he took her clit into the heat of his mouth and suckled hard. She moaned a bit too loudly, having never felt a sensation like it. The mad desire to thread her fingers through his silky black hair and push his face closer against her flesh was nearly overwhelming, but she was thankfully saved from disgracing herself by the restraints that bound her.

She closed her eyes on a groan...oh glorious Kalast she was going to come so hard for him. She didn't want to, yet she couldn't help herself. "Please," Nicoletta gasped, her breath catching in the back of her throat. *"Ah gods."*

She came on a loud moan, her entire body convulsing as a violent orgasm exploded in her belly. He growled in the back of his throat as he lapped up her juices, the sound as deadly as it was aroused.

And then as quickly as she'd climaxed, it was all over. Nicoletta watched through dulled vision as the one elite male she had no desire to be bound to stood up and took his rightful place at the head of the bidding corral. His intense green eyes never wavered, never looked away from the frightened brown gaze stealing hesitant glances back at him.

Ten minutes later her fate was sealed. Ten minutes later the daughter of one of the world's poorest men became the second harem wife of one of the wealthiest.

Nicoletta's heart slammed against her breasts. She swallowed roughly as she watched her new Master stare at her. Those calculating, assessing eyes of his roamed up and down the length of her naked, oiled body as the chattel auctioneer unchained her hands and feet and handed Master Kan her leash.

"Get on yer knees, wench," the auctioneer reminded her with a frown.

Nicoletta came down on her knees before her Master and bent her head to kiss his feet. She went through all the motions expected of a bride during a marriage ceremony, her mind a fog as a ring was placed on either of her nipples and a chain threaded through them, symbolically binding her from the touch of any male but Abdul Kan.

"You will always be Mine," Abdul murmured, making her head dart up. "Always."

Her breathing stilled. Her eyes widened. It was as if he could guess her plans and was letting her know she'd never get away from him.

Never.

"Yes, Master," Nicoletta dutifully whispered. She lowered her lashes, concealing her gaze. "I will always belong to You."

CHAPTER 2
August 20, 2250 A.D.

(25 years later)

"...I said, would you care for a chalice of spirits, Mistress?"

Nicoletta Kan blinked, the serving droid's words finally registering. Lifting her gaze up to meet that of the naked silver female, she shook her head in the negative, too focused on memories to so much as consider imbibing a hallucinogen, even if it was but a mild label. She wanted her wits about her. "No thank you," she said, a polite smile enveloping her mouth. "I'm not thirsty."

The droid nodded and continued down the aisle to offer the next passenger on Federated Earth Aerolines flight 127 a cocktail. The star-carrier was filled to capacity, Nicoletta noted, so the serving wench had her work cut out for her.

Nicoletta turned her head and absently stared out the window. Since the star-carrier was currently in deep space, there was little to look at beyond the black abyss on the other side of the viewing portal. They'd been en route to planet Earth for over three days now. She imagined it would still be another hour before they broached the Milky Way. She could scarcely wait! Three hours after that and the aerocraft would touch down on homeland soil. And then a few hours later, Nicoletta thought with an excited grin, she'd be embracing her beloved daughter, Nellie. *Nellie...*

Oh how she missed her! She had wished to return to Federated Earth the very moment she'd learned of her daughter's pregnancy, but conversely, she'd been so overwhelmed with melancholia after learning of Abdul's death that she feared her presence would detract from the happy time Nellie and Kerick rightly deserved rather than add to it.

Abdul Kan—her dead husband. And what's more, she reminded herself with a tensed jaw, he was a dead husband whom she had no business grieving the loss of. She had run from him, had she not? Her nostrils flared. Yes, she had been on the run from her husband when death had claimed him. He might have been one of the wealthiest and most feared men within the Hierarchy, but the price of that power had come at the cost of so many dead and tortured lives.

He was evil. A demon in human skin. She herself had known as much for longer than she felt comfortable admitting.

It was Abdul who was responsible for Sinead's death—her beloved friend, his own first wife who had died at his atrocious hands. It was Abdul who was responsible for infecting countless voiceless prisoners. Those Hierarchy chattel had been infected with the most hideous disease imaginable for experimentation purposes. Those unfortunate men had became, at the whim of Abdul Kan...

Monsters.

She shivered. There was no better word for sub-humans, Nicoletta decided.

Monsters. Beasts. Abominations.

Her teeth sank into her lower lip as she recalled her last run-in with just such an infected creature. When first she had fled from Abdul, a sub-human male had absconded with her. It had carried her kicking and screaming into its den, then mounted her for two chilling days and nights.

After she escaped the beast-man and was reunited with Nellie, Nicoletta had worried for weeks that the creature's babe was growing in her womb. But thankfully, oh so thankfully, her blood cycle came upon her and she knew now that the abomination had not managed to breed her. And yet...

Still the creature haunted her. It was as if her soul belonged to both Abdul and the beast-man, for one commanded her dreams and the other her nightmares.

Despite her fears and the fact she hated to think back upon those two days and nights, she still felt a certain sorrow for the creature. It had, after all, been a man once upon a time. It had felt hope and despair and love and hate and joy and defeat and...

Her eyes narrowed. Once upon a time it had been a man. Abdul and his Hierarchy comrades had taken that humanity away to further their own sickening goals.

Nicoletta sighed as she stared out into the black abyss. She closed her eyes, deciding sleep was better than memories. She didn't wish to think about the beast-man. Nor did she wish to think about her dead husband.

Her eyes flew open. Her heart skipped a beat. Even in slumber Abdul was always there — *always*. She resisted the memories, rebelled against recalling anything at all wondrous about the years she'd spent in his harem. She fought and raged against it just as she'd always done with anything concerning Master Kan.

Twenty-five years ago Abdul had vowed she would always belong to him. While alive he had seen that promise through to the end. He might have been able to make that a reality during his life, but she'd be damned if he'd wield that power over her in his death.

Nicoletta agitatedly ran her hands through her long, dark hair. Maybe, just maybe, it would be easier to let go if she understood what it was that had changed him. She needed answers but didn't know where to look for them. She suspected the daughter of her heart, Nellie, knew...*something*...something she found difficult to speak of. And so Abdul's secrets, for all intent and purposes, had followed him to his grave.

Where had it all gone wrong? Nicoletta asked herself for at least the hundredth time in the twenty-five years she'd been wed to him. When Abdul had purchased her from the marriage auction block her hopes had been so high for a blissful married life, second wife or no. All youthful, idealistic thoughts of fleeing from him had been gone the moment their bodies had joined. That she had to share his heart and body with another wench had been difficult to accept at first, but from the moment she met Sinead she'd been too fond of her to let her spirits sink unduly.

At first it had seemed that her new husband might very well be that mythical, glorious, romantic lover all wenches dream will buy them. To be the chattel of such a male would make any wife swoon with happiness and Nicoletta had believed her husband to be just such a prince.

The first couple of months had been all she could dream for and more. He had been kind, attentive, and romantic—everything she'd ever wanted. And, of course, a wife could never ask for a better lover as Master.

Abdul had always been exceptionally lusty, Nicoletta recalled, settling deeper into her chair. She had found it little wonder he'd needed two wives to satiate his sexual appetite. He could make love for hours, spurting his seed left and right into Sinead and herself, his energy for the carnal seemingly endless.

But a few short months later, five years after Sinead gave birth to Nellie, everything began to change, including Abdul himself. A man who had always been dangerous became impossibly more so. A man who had once loved and cherished her — or so she'd thought — would turn on her in the blink of an eye.

She grew to hate him, to despise him, to detest the very presence of him. And yet...

Nicoletta sighed, her smile sad. And yet she had dared to hope. She had not run from him in the old days because she had dared to dream that Abdul would come back to her and once again be her Arabian prince, the knight in shining armor bespoken of in fairytales by the ancients.

But that had never come to pass. She had given him his beloved heir and son, Asad, and still it had not come to pass. Every day Abdul grew colder, every day he distanced himself from her more and more until she felt as though she was wed to a terrifying, volatile stranger.

The distancing continued. More wives were added into their family, bodies for Abdul to spurt into, bodies she suspected he'd purchased simply because he realized they didn't make him *feel* — precisely what he wanted.

By the time Nicoletta had been married seven years, the harem bed the Kan family slept in contained six: Abdul, Sinead, Nicoletta, and three more wives Abdul had bought, none of whom either Sinead or herself had ever taken to liking. Many years after Sinead's death Abdul had purchased yet another wife — another reason Nicoletta had run from him, though she conceded not the biggest.

Why, Abdul? she silently asked, her nostrils flaring. *I want to know why. Why did you force me to stay when you've loathed the very sight of me for years? Why!*

"Federated Earth Aeroflight 127 is preparing to broach the Milky Way galaxy," a cheerful, disembodied feminine voice announced, breaking Nicoletta from her thoughts. "All mastered and unprotected females are now required to remove their body décor. Thank you for choosing Federated Earth Aerolines."

Nicoletta stood up and removed the long, flowing robe she wore. She pulled it over her head and handed the body décor over to a passing by droid to store for her. Naked save her nipple rings and chain just as all mastered women of Federated Earth were required to be, she plopped back down in the seat.

That her husband was dead would not signify to the port authorities when they docked and had their virtual passports checked at the space station on the outermost cusp of the galaxy. Nicoletta's right buttock was branded with the sign of Abdul Kan. To them, whether dead or alive, she was and would always be his exclusive property. By law, no other male would ever be permitted to touch her. That didn't mean it wouldn't happen, only that it wasn't legal.

Nicoletta took a deep, drugging breath and slowly exhaled as she nestled back into her seat. Her eyelashes fluttered shut. To them, perhaps, she was still Abdul's property, but Nicoletta knew that she was free…

From now until forever, she thought, she would

always be free.

Nicoletta's heart sank as she watched Abdul finish making love to Sinead. His groan was long and loud as he spurted inside of her. It was long minutes before he removed himself from the harem bed so Nicoletta busied herself by pretending to fix her hair in front of the image map.

"It's you He loves, Nica," Sinead murmured, coming up behind her. Her smile was as gentle as her Irish lilt. "You know that, lass."

Nicoletta continued combing out her long dark hair in front of the three dimensional mirror. "That's not true," she whispered. She sighed, momentarily halting the combing. "I'm sorry for my jealousy, Sinead. I could not ask for a better friend nor confidante than you."

"But you want to be his only wife."

"I do." She closed her eyes briefly, pained by her own admission. To wish such a thing was to wish Sinead away and that she could not do. "Please understand this has nothing to do with my love for you. I just want…"

"The fairytale." Sinead nodded. Her gaze looked far away. "As did I in my own way," she murmured.

Nicoletta set the comb down then turned around and faced her. "I'm sorry, Sinead. Here I am feeling melancholy for myself," she contritely muttered as she reached out for her hand, "when you were the first wife. I can't imagine how upset you must have been when He married me."

"I wasn't," Sinead softly admitted. "I was happy for both of you." At Nicoletta's confused expression, she cryptically explained, "There is more to my relationship with the Master than you can know." She sighed, glancing away. "Just trust in me and in our love for each other when I say I wanted Abdul to find His happiness in you — happiness He will never find with *me."*

"I don't understand…"

"And I've already said too much." She shook her wine-red hair, then smiled and drew Nicoletta into her embrace. *"Just know that He loves you, Nica,"* she whispered. She ran her hands over Nicoletta's large breasts and gently massaged her nipples. Nicoletta's breathing hitched. *"As do I,"* Sinead said thickly.

Their tongue-kiss was intoxicating, just as all their kisses were. Sinead was the only female lover Nicoletta had ever known – the only female lover she would ever know. Her heart belonged as much to Sinead as it did to Abdul, though the love was different. She loved Sinead…

But she was in love with Abdul.

"I said stand up. Now, wench!"

Nicoletta blinked several times in rapid succession as a male she didn't recognize forced her up to her feet, jarring her awake from the deep sleep that had claimed her. *What's happening!* her mind screamed. *What do these males do here?*

Her mind was so foggy it was difficult to take in what was going on around her. Women were crying, men were bellowing. *What is going on!* She fought to rouse herself, to focus her eyes on her surroundings and to think without cobwebs muffling her brain.

Fifteen to twenty armed men were swarming the aeroplane, the expressions on their faces grim. A quick glance out the nearest portal confirmed that the star-carrier had crashed somewhere within the jungles of Federated Earth—where was anyone's guess. Another quick glance toward one of the star-carrier's four retractable wings revealed heavy damage...

Her breathing stilled. Reality slowly dawned.

They had been shot down. Sweet Kalast, she thought, her gaze wildly darting about, they had been overpowered by Outsider forces! But what did these bandits who dwelled below-ground want? What were they after?

She swallowed heavily as two rough male hands reached around her from behind and seized her large breasts. Frightened, she gasped as the lecher began tweaking her nipples, his erection poking against her back.

Ah gods, they wanted women, Nicoletta hysterically thought, her breathing growing labored. These Outsider males could not purchase wives legally since they dwelled outside the protection of the biospheres. They couldn't purchase wives, so they were stealing them. She had been freed from Abdul's harem bed for this? No...*no!*

Her heart pounding like mad in her chest, Nicoletta screamed as she tried to break away from the man holding her hostage. He fought with her, snaking her tightly against him so that she couldn't move.

"Let me go!" she raged, half hysterical and half venomous. This could not be happening. "I belong to another!"

"Stop it, wench," the man snarled. He bellowed when her teeth sank into his arm, drawing blood. "I said to cease," he gritted out, whirling Nicoletta around and forcing her to face him. Crimson stains showed in her mouth. "Who you might have belonged to before don't matter." His anger was a tangible thing. "The only thing matterin' to you now is who you *will* belong to."

Ah Cyrus, no, she thought, her eyes rounding. *Noooo!*

She opened her mouth to scream again, but was

brutally backhanded before a single sound escaped her lips. Moments later her attacker detained her by the shoulders as a second man held onto her flailing legs. Kicking and screaming, they carried her off the protection of the star-carrier and into the lair of the deadly jungle.

"Help me!" Nicoletta wailed. Nellie — Kerick — *somebody* must hear! *"Help meeee!"*

CHAPTER 3

Her heart pounded in her breasts as Abdul placed gentle kisses all over her face. They'd been making love a lot this past month without Sinead. Sinead seemed preoccupied as of late and Master Kan had not pressed the issue of returning her to the harem bed even though she had yet to bear him a male heir.

There were secrets between the two of them, secrets Nicoletta realized she was not privy to.

"I love you, **ana wahib***," Abdul murmured in the dark Arabian accent that had always left her knees weak.*

Ah gods, she loved him too — oh how she loved him! She thought to ask him the meaning of **ana wahib***, but his intense green gaze found hers as he again spoke.*

"I…" His nostrils flared, his expression pained as he looked away. "What have I done?" he asked hoarsely, as if to himself. His fingers threaded through her dark hair, holding on almost too tightly, as though she was his lifeline to sanity. "Cyrus — what have I done?"

Nicoletta's face scrunched up. "Abdul?" She grew alarmed, having never seen him lose his iron control before. Her eyes rounded. "Abdul, what is wrong?"

The mask was back, the raw emotions as though they had never been. "Nothing." He pulled himself up from between her legs and fell onto the harem bed beside her. His gaze was faraway, his expression so cold and remote it sent chills down her spine. "Nothing," he murmured.

She must have fallen asleep. How in the name of the ancient saints she had managed to do so under the present circumstances was beyond her, yet clearly she had. Always—*always*—Abdul haunted her dreams. Ordinarily Nicoletta hated that he wielded power over her in his death, yet even she conceded she'd rather return to her previous state of slumber, her mind busily recollecting days gone by in the harem, than to face this current, more frightening reality.

Bound, gagged, and naked, she had been dragged below ground into the catacombs, a series of dark, eerie tomb-like structures carved into the earth's belly where Outsiders made their homes. The thatched wood and mud place was lit only by torches on wall sconces. She shivered, goosebumps forming on her flesh from the chill in the air.

Her arms had been stretched high above her on the cold earthen floor and her legs had been hoisted apart at the thighs. Five men were all over her, their hands and mouths exploring all of her crevices. The Outsider rebels keeping her secured to the ground all looked to be brothers in their early twenties to thirties…and they also looked to be virgins.

They had never before mounted a real woman, she thought, her eyes rounding from over the gag. A droid perhaps, but never a human female.

Sweet Kalast, they'd be fucking her for days…

But they hadn't mounted her yet, she considered with much relief, wondering at that. Nobody was penetrating her now, only licking and fondling her various body parts. She felt no soreness between her legs either so she was fairly certain she hadn't been taken when she'd been asleep—or knocked out.

Yes, she *had* been knocked out. The memory was a threadbare one, but Nicoletta possessed the foggiest recollection of struggling with two men in the jungles…and then of a cloth that reeked of a chloroform-like substance called *sarsi* being wrenched over her nose and mouth until she knew no more.

She also suspected there had been illegal goings-on in the star-carrier itself. Like as not, the rebels had acquired help from the inside because only a gassing would account for being able to sleep through such a crash as that one.

Nicoletta swallowed roughly as she watched two males gaze hungrily at her nipples, nipples that were kept perpetually swollen and stiff from the rings she'd worn on them since the day Abdul had purchased her. She was not surprised when both of the men's mouths dove for a nipple, their lips latching around them and greedily sucking. The expressions on their faces were of bliss, of finally experiencing a wondrous sensation neither man had ever thought they would know.

Ah gods, Nicoletta thought, her breathing growing labored. *These males will not let me go without a fight. Perhaps to the death.*

She could only pray to Cyrus she was wrong and that these males had seen and been with real women before. If she was their first and last hope at obtaining a communal wife…

She briefly closed her eyes, terror lancing through her. If these five brothers wished to make her their communal wife, the consequence of that didn't bear dwelling upon. Escaping one husband had taken her twenty-five years. Escaping five? Sweet Cyrus, Nicoletta thought, her heart wrenching, she'd *never* be free.

"When'll the fuckin' Holyman get here?" one of the

brothers mumbled from around her clit. "I want inside her bad."

Nicoletta winced. Oh no...no, no, no! They *were* calling for an Officiator, for a male they believed to be sanctioned of Cyrus to perform the rite of marriage. In other words, they needed someone with knowledge of metals and brandings in order to remove the nipple rings she currently wore and replace them with their own — as well as to attempt to conceal the brand of Kan on her right buttock with the seal of their lineage.

"Dunno." One of the brothers with a nipple in his mouth let it pop out long enough to answer. "I already done paid twenty-five lizards to the Commune for her, though."

Nicoletta didn't know whether to laugh, cry, be insulted, or all of the above. Perversely, it was insult that won out. Her nostrils flared from above the gag as she considered the ugly truth that her worth this go-around was but twenty-five lizards. Twenty-five lizards! It was a far cry from the half-million yen Abdul had paid unto her sire. She cursed muffled Italian atrocities at the disgusting brothers from behind the gag, but they paid her no heed at all.

"I'll go see what's keepin' him," the youngest-looking of the brothers muttered as he stood up and stomped off. "Sweet Cyrus, my poker is hard. He best hurry up."

For the next fifteen minutes, the four remaining brothers took turns licking and sucking all over her intimate parts. Nicoletta felt disgusted by her traitorous body for responding, even realizing as she did that the unwanted arousal was a perfectly natural reaction to having her clit and nipples licked, kissed, and suckled. She knew as much, yet she still despised the dampness between her legs.

The eldest brother took her entire pussy into his mouth and sucked hard. Nicoletta whimpered from behind the gag, her already stiff nipples growing impossibly stiffer.

The brothers sucked harder. Her tits. Her cunt. A finger in her asshole. Their appreciative moans reverberated within the earthen chamber as they sucked harder, and harder, and —

Nicoletta groaned loudly from behind the gag, her body involuntarily bucking up as she came. Blood rushed to her face, heating it. Blood rushed to her nipples and clit, making them extraordinarily sensitive. She cried from behind the gag as they sucked even harder, the feeling painful with her body as sensitive as it was.

"Sweet Cyrus," one brother muttered. "I wanna poke her bad."

The brother sucking from her left nipple moaned his agreement. He released the pink nipple with a popping sound then flicked it around with his forefinger and stared at it, his elbow propping him up.

"He's on his way!" the fifth brother announced between pants as he ran back into the earthen chamber. "Cut her loose so he can work on them nipple rings!"

No — please no!

An ear-shattering growl reverberated throughout the Underground, the sound snaring everyone's undivided attention. The brothers stilled.

Something was coming, Nicoletta thought, terrified. Something with a growl eerily similar to that of a sub-human...

No! That wasn't possible. This wasn't the first

Underground catacomb she'd seen since fleeing from her now-deceased husband. The Outlaws always kept the series of tunnels and chambers sealed off from the predators that dwelled in the jungles. The two species lived as though they'd declared an unspoken, shared tenant: man ruled the caves, man-beast ruled the jungles. How would a sub-human break in? Why would one even try?

The growling sound grew closer, deadlier. She hysterically noted that none of the brothers were armed with flash-sticks. Ah gods, they'd all be made a meal of by the monster. They were all as good as dead!

The brothers cut her legs loose, her arms and mouth still bound, and jerked her up to her feet. "Let's go!" one of the brothers bellowed as he pushed Nicoletta out of the cavern and into the corridor opposite the one from the growling sound. "Move, wench!" he angrily warned when she struggled with him. He carried the ashen look of a man who knew death was coming. "Move or I leave you here to die," he rasped.

The attack came without warning—a gruesome bloodbath straight out of a nightmare. In shock, Nicoletta backed up, not stopping until the barrier of a muddy wall prevented further movement. Her heart pounded in her ears. Her haunted eyes stared unblinking as she watched the creature kill off its second victim.

Run! For the love of the ancient saints — run!

The beast whipped its head around. Its crimson-red gaze snared hers.

Nicoletta's eyes widened. Her face drained of color and her blood ran cold as she got her first good look at its face.

It had found her. That...that...*thing* that had

kidnapped her as she'd searched for Nellie—that thing that had dragged her into its jungle lair and mounted her body for two days and nights.

That thing that had done its damnedest to impregnate her.

It had come back…

For her.

Nicoletta opened her mouth to scream, only then recalling she was still gagged. *Run, you idiot! While its attention is turned on the brothers — sweet Kalast, Nica, run!*

Finally—finally—her feet cooperated. Ignoring the sickening sound of tortured death screams, Nicoletta fled from the catacombs as fast as her feet would carry her. *Faster!* she mentally prodded herself, fear feeding her adrenaline. She refused to look back, refused to know if the man-beast was closing in on her. Her naked breasts bobbed up and down as she ran—faster and faster and faster.

Faster! Faster! Faster!

Missing her footing, she fell to her knees, roughly scraping them. She ignored the fire that shot through them as she wrenched herself back up, her hands still bound before her, and continued running aimlessly through the jungle. Her heart pounded against her chest, perspiration soaked her forehead.

It was a solid hour before she stopped running, an hour before her body gave out and, exhausted, Nicoletta collapsed on the ground. *You must get up.* Her mouth and hands still bound, she attempted to force herself to her feet.

Ah gods she was so tired—too tired to stand up using only her leg muscles, she conceded between pants. But if she didn't find some sort of shelter she knew she was as good as dead. If *it* didn't find her, another sub-human would.

The fuck-doll of a demon or another one's meal. She didn't know which scenario she should hope for.

Her dark eyes narrowed as she spotted the entrance to a cave. She realized it might very well be the lair of a sub-human, but also knew there was a good chance it was not.

It's your only hope. Go, Nica…

With the last bit of energy she had left to expend, Nicoletta used her elbows to crawl into the cave. It was dark, it was cold, but it was also, thank the ancient saints, empty.

She whimpered as she fell back down. *Please, Nellie, find mama,* she silently begged. Her eyes slowly drifted close. *Please find me.*

CHAPTER 4

"You are never — never! — to look at another man, let alone flirt with one!"

His eyes were wild, frightening. The rage consuming him was unlike anything Nicoletta had ever seen. Ice-cold fear seized her as he forced her over his knee and spanked her hard.

"Do you hear Me?" he bellowed, his hand striking her bare ass over and over again.

"Stop!" she cried, the pain overwhelming as he struck her a fifth time. "Ah gods, Master — no more!"

"Do you hear Me?" he raged, smacking her impossibly harder.

She refused to answer. She lay there suspended over his knee, sobbing like a child as he repeatedly spanked her again and again.

"Stop," she gasped, feeling close to fainting from the pain of it. "Please…"

Abdul growled as he spanked her harder, his rage at a crescendo. When finally he was finished, he yanked her up from over his knee and jerked her to her feet.

"I asked you a question!" he bellowed, his jaw as tense as his eyes were wild. "You are never to flirt. Did you hear Me?" he howled.

Her nostrils flared as she struggled to stand. "No," she panted. Momentary fear showed in her eyes as he grabbed her by the shoulders, his fingers painfully digging in there, but she controlled it. "You took a third wife," she ground out, her anger as tangible as his. "How could You do that to me? How! I hate her!" she cried, tears welling up in her eyes. "And I hate You!"

"Thank the gods!" he raged back, shaking her by the shoulders. His fury was all-consuming, over-powering. "I don't want your love," he hissed as tears rolled down her cheeks. "Now get into the bed!"

"Never!" she cried, tears of heartbreak flowing freely.

She had prayed to Cyrus for a happy marriage. She had forsaken her plans to run from the moment they'd been joined because she'd foolishly believed Abdul's love for her was as powerful as her love for him. But that love didn't exist – it never had. And now, two years later, all she wanted was to leave him. She wanted to be free.

Nicoletta broke away from his hold, her eyes blazing with anger, with hatred, with hurt and betrayal. She straightened her shoulders as her gaze penetrated his.

"Force me if You must," she said icily, the venom in her voice barely controlled, "because I vow to You that I will never again willingly seek Your bed…" If looks were lethal, the god of death would have claimed him then and there. "Never."

She awoke to the sound of an eerily familiar growl, a low keening sound that reverberated throughout the cave as if to remind her she belonged to him…to *it*. Her heartbeat accelerating, Nicoletta shivered from where she lay naked on her belly. She was too afraid to turn her head and gaze upon the man-beast, though she knew it was there. She would recognize his growl and his scent anywhere.

She opened her mouth to scream, remembering when she couldn't she was still gagged. Her heart sank in her chest, resignation settling in. There was no point in screaming anyway—nobody would rescue her. And even if someone tried, it would only kill the unfortunate for daring to come near her.

Good Cyrus above, why was this happening? *Why!*

Still on her belly, her head came up and snaked around to gaze upon the creature. It was there, just as she knew it would be, standing upright over her body as if guarding her or preparing to possess her—

Or both.

It walked upright like a man, it gazed upon her with the carnal hunger of a man...

But it was no man.

The haunting red eyes were like a demon's, the heavy musculature like a superhuman's. The serrated teeth were like something out of a nightmare, the vampiric nail on each finger sent chills coursing down her spine.

The creature growled low in its throat, baring its dagger-like teeth. The gray, death-like pallor of its skin lightened a fraction as its muscles corded and tensed. It looked like it was preparing to kill her...it *should* have killed her, Nicoletta knew. That's what sub-humans did—it's all they did. They hunted prey and they killed it. Why was this one different?

Why was *she* different?

Nicoletta forced herself up from her belly and onto her buttocks. Her hands were still bound before her, her mouth still gagged, but nothing signified. All she could do was simply stare at the beast, every question she'd ever entertained there in her eyes for it to see.

Why do you want me? Why will you not leave me alone? Why do you not kill me!

One hand came toward her, the fingernails sharp enough to slice her to ribbons. She tensed, her breasts heaving up and down as her eyes widened from above the gag. It was going for the vicinity of her face...ah gods, her jugular perhaps? *No! No! No! No —*

She gasped as a single fingernail sliced through the gag, unbinding her mouth. She stilled, too surprised to so much as breathe. Wisely, though, the beast made no move to unbind her hands, as if it knew that would better enable her to flee from him.

Maybe it did know, she considered as she stared into its strangely hypnotic eyes. After all, this creature had once been a man...

Another atrocity she could lay at Abdul's feet. He had provided the human chattel Hierarchy scientists had experimented on. Had Master Kan not had an ample supply of prisoners to hand over like dogs in a madman's lab, there would have been no depraved experiments and sub-humans would not exist — this creature that thought it owned her would not exist.

"Why me?" she whispered, her gaze searching the beast's. Her heart pounded in her chest. Her breath caught. "I don't understand..."

It growled again, its razor-sharp teeth prominent. She should have been frightened it meant to kill her, the only sane conclusion in an insane world. But this time Nicoletta recognized the sound for what it was: territoriality, domination...

Possession.

Keep him calm, Nica. Sweet Cyrus she felt close to fainting! *Just keep him calm.*

The growl deepened, reverberated in its throat.

Keep him calm.

"This is what you want?" she whispered.

Lying down on her back, she stretched her bound hands above her head and stared at the creature from between two large breasts capped off with stiff pink nipples. Its crimson eyes tracked each nuance of movement. She slowly spread her thighs open as far as they could go. "This?" she murmured.

The growl continued as it slowly came down to its knees, its jaw tensed and serrated teeth bared as if preparing to deliver a death-bite. Perspiration dotted her forehead, her breathing rate accelerated. She had no idea if it meant to kill her or fuck her.

His thick, hard cock and heavy-lidded gaze suggested the latter. This time, strange though it was, she was hoping for the latter.

"I-It's all right," Nicoletta whispered, her assured tone at odds with the ever-present hysteria that threatened to envelope her. "I-It's all right." She wiggled her fingers from above her head, reminding him she was bound, showing the creature with superhuman strength she would offer it no resistance.

The growl deepened, though it was lower, less threatening. The man-beast sat before her splayed thighs, his crimson vision tracking the steady rise and fall of her breasts, then lower to her intimate offering.

A roughly callused gray hand palmed one large breast. He kneaded it then released it. She shivered as she watched a single vampiric-black fingernail trace the outline of one nipple ring. The action was done with such gentleness as to induce her forehead to wrinkle with confusion.

The fingernail gently scraped her stiff pink nipple. She

moaned, having no idea why a single touch could inflame her entire body.

It was just as it had been back in that cave when it had stolen her the last time. She hadn't understood it then. She didn't understand it now.

"What do you to me?" Nicoletta panted, her arousal heightening as the beast gently scraped at both breasts.

Forgetting that her hands were bound, she unthinkingly began lowering them, the instinct to shield herself fairly overwhelming. His answering snarl frightened her, made her jump.

"I-I'm sorry," she breathed out, blood pounding in her ears. She immediately placed her bound hands back above her head. The action made her breasts raise, the imagery of a submissive offering again complete. "I will not fight you."

Not that fighting would help, she thought, her tongue darting out to wet her parched upper lip. The sub-human male could kill her outside of a second.

"I give myself to you willingly."

She didn't know that it comprehended her words, yet its answering growl of dominance said that it comprehended her actions. Within moments, the sub-human was on her, sucking her nipples and making her moan with fear and arousal.

"What do you to me?" she gasped, her back arching and her eyes closing. "Ah gods..."

The beast palmed both breasts, gaining Nicoletta's undivided attention. Her gaze sought his. She watched the sub-human male stare at her through heavy-lidded eyes as it settled itself between her legs. Her breathing grew labored, remembering from their last run-in how sexually insatiable the creature was.

It hadn't managed to breed her the last time. Surely her scent told it as much. She swallowed heavily as she realized it knew — it *knew* — and perhaps this time it would make certain it impregnated her.

The beast surged inside her pussy on a loud, reverberating roar. Nicoletta gasped, having forgotten how long and thick its cock was. He slid all the way in, burying himself to the hilt, reminding her again and again with his growls of ownership just who her cunt belonged to.

Her legs splayed wide open, her hands submissively bound above her head...it wasn't difficult to remember she was his possession.

He took her hard, mercilessly, sinking in and out of her flesh in deep, branding strokes. Nicoletta moaned as it fucked her, her big tits jiggling with every thrust.

"Deeper," she gasped, deciding now was not the time to dwell on the fact she shouldn't encourage it. "Faster — ah gods — *like that.*"

The creature rode her harder, faster, fucking her as its low, steady growl continued. She could hear the sound of her pussy suctioning him back in with every outstroke, could smell the scent of her own arousal.

Palming both of her jiggling breasts, it lowered its face and took one stiff nipple between its serrated teeth. It gently scraped the nipple, back and forth, over and over, until Nicoletta was groaning, climax knotting in her belly. Drawing the entire nipple into its mouth, the man-beast sucked hard, hickey-kissing her areola while suckling her stiff nipple.

"I'm coming," Nicoletta moaned. *"I'm com — ohhhhh!"*

She screamed as an orgasm exploded in her belly, a violent euphoria that was as painful as it was pleasurable. The sub-human male's growl grew louder as her pussy began contracting around its cock, trying to milk him of seed. He covered her totally then, his vampire hands possessively holding her bound ones in place, as he fucked her.

Harder. Deeper. Faster.

Over and over.

Again and again.

Nicoletta threw her cunt back at her captor, gasping as her eyes closed and her head lulled back on her neck. "What do you to me?" she asked again, her breath catching.

He answered by fucking her harder, pitilessly. He rode her body like the animal he was, his sole focus on possessing her. Every warning growl told her she belonged to him, every branding stroke reaffirmed his dominance.

The sounds of flesh slapping flesh reached her ears, mingling with his growls of territorial arousal…

Harder. Deeper. Faster.

Over and over.

Again and again.

The beast came on a loud, reverberating roar, a deafening sound that echoed throughout the jungle cavern. The sub-human's entire musculature tensed and then convulsed, hot cum spurting like a geyser into her womb.

Her breathing had never been so ragged. Her confusion had never been so acute. She had encouraged her sub-human captor to take her — it might not have understood her words, but it definitely understood her body's actions.

The beast haunted her soul in a way none other but Abdul could rival. It had been six months since she'd fled from either of them, yet they both owned her in ways she could never put to words.

It was in the eyes. Something in the eyes pained her, beckoned to her.

Their eyes could almost make her believe they needed her.

It seemed like half of forever had gone by before either she or the creature moved. And then, surprising Nicoletta with a knowing she hadn't expected, her gaze widened as she watched one vampire-black nail cut through her binds, freeing her hands.

The creature moved off of her, taking to its side. But it was watching her, she noted. Its red gaze never left her.

It was waiting to see what she would do, she thought, her heartbeat accelerating. It was waiting to see if she would try to run or choose to stay.

Nicoletta rolled to her side too so that they faced each other. Her brown eyes were round, scared, her expression confused. Slowly, oh so slowly, one trembling hand reached for the sub-human's heart and rested there.

"What do you to me?" Nicoletta murmured. She closed her eyes briefly, dragging in a shaky breath. Her eyes flicked back open. "What do you to me?"

CHAPTER 5

"You set me up," Abdul hissed. "Why should I not kill you here and now? Give me but one reason!" he bellowed.

"B-Because you n-need me," Maxim Malifé sputtered, his fear a tangible thing. "I knew nothing of this. I was as shocked as you — I vow it!"

Abdul's nostrils flared. The man he had trusted to run Kan Technology in his absence was lying and he knew it. He had made Malifé a very wealthy man — so wealthy that he now held the fifth highest position in the Hierarchy of Federated Earth. Finding out how that had been accomplished made his stomach turn.

Abdul Kan thought Malifé had been handing over prisoners to Fathom Systems to put naught but bloody yen chips in their brains. He had no notion of the atrocities being committed, yet he felt himself responsible for every last one. He had handed those men over like lab rats to be experimented upon...

He had led them like pigs to the slaughterhouse.

"The scientists at Fathom Systems are so close," Maxim promised, his eyes blazing.

Abdul watched him, his gaze unblinking.

"A few more years, old friend, and immortality shall be ours." He waved a dismissive hand. "So a few men die. They were born dead. Nobody will miss them."

Abdul blinked, his expression incredulous. "You are mad."

Malifé laughed. "I prefer the word 'inventive'."

"Mad."

"It's done," Malifé replied. "The wheels are already in motion. And what's more, I act upon the will of the Hierarchy."

"Of which I sit higher on the apex than you," Abdul murmured, reminding him of his rank. "Nor do I believe for a second that a man such as Creagh O'Malley, a man whose position within the Hierarchy is superior to both of ours, would partake in such madness as this!"

Abdul wrenched him around to face him, grabbing his tunic at the neck and pulling it tightly. The slighter Malifé's eyes widened, his fear returning.

"I will have no part in this," Abdul hissed, his muscles clenching. "As of this moment your supply of prisoners is cut off."

"I don't need any more," he whispered. "We've infected hundreds already then released them outside the perimeter of the biospheres. All we do now is wait..." Malifé swallowed heavily, his eyes bulging. "And learn."

* * * * *

Three nights later

The gray-skinned creature followed her deeper into the cavern, careful not to let her get too far out of its line of vision as she made her way to a trickling stream that flowed from the top of the earthen lair like a small waterfall. For three days and nights it had fucked her practically non-stop. In her pussy, in her ass, in her mouth—it had taken her everywhere multiple times. She knew from experience her captor had to be tiring.

"Now where will I possibly run to?" Nicoletta asked

him without glancing back as she waded into the small pool the waterfall ran off into. "You are faster, stronger, you can see at night, and you've already caught me twice." She cocked her head and smiled slightly at the sub-human male from over her shoulder. "I think you can relax while I bathe."

She didn't know what was happening to her mind, yet she was alarmed it might have snapped. She no longer felt the fear that once consumed her. And, perversely, she was no longer wracking her brain for possible methods of escape.

"I feel guilty, you know," she told the creature as she stood in the cold pool and briskly rubbed her arms. The chill in the air made goosebumps form on her flesh and her already stiff nipples grow impossibly stiffer. "I've never been with any male save my Husband. Until you," she clarified.

She realized the creature probably did not understand her words. Somehow that made them easier to utter. "I've never stopped loving Him," Nicoletta whispered, her gaze faraway. Her breath caught. "I doubt I ever will."

She blinked, her gaze coming back to the present. "But it doesn't matter. You have no competition to speak of for He does not love me. And," she said quietly, "He is dead."

Nicoletta went down to her knees, the water of the pool not even deep enough to cover her lap. She kept her back to the beast as she washed herself, the curious sensation that it was staring at the sign of Abdul Kan laser-etched into her right buttock hard to dismiss. She glanced over her shoulder and confirmed that, indeed, it was staring at the brand. She wondered if the creature knew what it was. Or perhaps the symbol of ownership only triggered a memory from a former life.

"It means that I belong to another," she whispered, looking away from him. "I suspect you won't let that stop you, though."

And why should he—it? The sub-human desired her presence with a yearning Abdul never had.

She stilled, alarmed by the direction her thoughts had been heading. Perhaps Abdul's death *had* driven her mad. She couldn't stay with the beast-man. She couldn't even consider such a thing.

"It's the way you look at me," she admitted, comforted by the fact it couldn't possibly understand her words. "Your gaze is familiar to me and yet foreign. Familiar in a way I don't understand, foreign in a way I do." She smiled into the waterfall. "I always wanted Him to gaze upon me in the way you do," she murmured. "Every night I prayed to Cyrus, begging and pleading that my Master might love me." Her sigh was resigned. "But that never came to be. And now He is gone from this realm."

The sub-human seemed to be listening, a fact that made her shiver. She shook her head, grinning at the insanity of the situation—and at herself for thinking for even a moment the beast knew what it was she was saying.

She turned her head again, her grin fading as she took in the way it was staring at her. With yearning. With longing. With need.

"Did you love a woman once?" she whispered. "Before you were infected?"

The beast said nothing, only watched her, but then she had hardly expected a reply. She imagined she saw the answer in his eyes, though. They seemed to be absorbing her every whisper, drinking in the very sight of her.

"You did," she murmured. Her eyes gentled — with pity or shared pain she didn't know. "And I bet she loved you with her entire heart and soul."

It looked away and Nicoletta had the mad thought she had stirred something deep within him. She realized she was pinning human emotions onto an inhuman beast, a predatorial Neanderthal whose only instincts were to hunt, kill, and breed. And yet she found herself wanting to offer him solace.

She was definitely going mad.

Nicoletta was already on her knees so going down on all fours took but a second. She thrust her ass up high into the air, using her elbows for support as she spread her legs far apart.

"I need to be loved," she whispered. She glanced over her shoulder, wiggled her buttocks and smiled. "So do you."

The low growl began in his chest, a deep, deadly sound that she didn't fear in this moment in time. Later, she would question her sanity. Later, she would worry for tomorrow.

Two rough gray hands seized her hips from behind, making her gasp with a moment's fright. She had forgotten how quickly it moved, forgotten too the fatal strength the beast wielded.

Her sub-human captor sank his cock inside her cunt without preliminaries, his possessive roar making the tiny hairs at the nape of her neck fairly stand on end. She moaned as it began fucking her, his long, thick cock sinking into her pussy over and over, again and again.

She threw her hips back at him, sucking in her breath as she met him thrust for thrust. The creature's fingernails ran over the sign of her Master, its hand then palming the ass cheek it was branded into. Nicoletta's forehead wrinkled with a curious sense of déjà vu for Abdul had always done the same when mounting her from behind.

It fucked her harder, faster, its growl deepening.

"Yes," Nicoletta moaned, her tits jiggling beneath her as the beast rode her hard. The sound of cunt meeting cock permeated the cavern as the trickling waterfall flowed over them. She closed her eyes and let herself enjoy her approaching orgasm. "Yes, yes, *yessss.*"

It rode her pussy without mercy as her vaginal walls began contracting around his cock. Its right hand never once left the brand of Abdul Kan as she screamed out her climax, groaning into the night.

"*Harder, Master,*" she begged, unthinkingly calling him by the name of Abdul. Her teeth gritted as she gluttonously threw her hips at him, wanting fucked as deep and as hard as he could give it to her. Her nipples were so stiff with arousal they ached. "*I want it harder.*"

The possessive growl grew louder as the sub-human male fucked her harder. She gasped and moaned as his cock sank into her cunt, lightning-fast motions that were as deep as they were territorial.

She heard his breathing grow heavier, heard too the now familiar roar gurgling up from the depths of his throat. Nicoletta threw her pussy back at him as hard as she could, moaning with him as he convulsed and came inside her.

This time when it was over she knew the sub-human male would be seeking the rejuvenation of sleep. And, indeed, after picking her up with a warning growl and stumbling with her body toward a resting place, that's what the beast did.

Lying beside him, she watched his gray chest rise and

fall before her gaze flicked up to meet his. He was fighting the urge to sleep and he was losing.

Nicoletta stilled. She realized why her captor was fighting it, of course. This was precisely how she'd gotten away the last time. The slumber of a sub-human male is deep, all-consuming, as though in hibernation. It's the only chance prey has from escaping the one who hunts them.

There was resignation in its gaze, a knowing. The beast realized it was falling asleep, knew it could not stop her from running, yet at the same time wanted to hold on to every second it could with her.

"Sleep," she whispered, reaching a trembling hand out to stroke his brow. Her breath caught from somewhere in the vicinity of her heart. "Close your eyes and sleep."

CHAPTER 6

He wanted so badly to touch her, to hold her and tell her of his love for her just as he had when he'd first purchased her. But he couldn't — not without chancing that he'd hurt her. Once when they had been making love, his heart soaring with emotion, he had almost turned, had almost killed his beloved Nica. She made him feel...

The very thing he could not afford to do.

And so, not knowing what else could be done, but also realizing he had to keep her away from him until he could find enough answers to beat Fathom Systems and Maxim Malifé at their madman's game, Abdul had distanced himself from the wife he cherished. He had forced her to loathe him, to despise him, to detest the very sight of him...

Inevitably, sadly, it had worked.

"Do not touch me!" she snapped, pushing away from him. "Cage me, spank me, do what You must! But do not ever," she hissed, "touch me."

Her words were more devastating than a deathblow. He wanted to tell her that he loved her, that he would always love her. But her words made him feel, *damn it. It made the demon in him rise to the surface.*

Abdul plastered a twisted smile on his face. "You think I need you?" he taunted. "I've three new wives eager for My touch. I do not need you."

The look of unadulterated pain and betrayal on her face made his heart wrench. I do not mean this! *he wanted to say.*

Nica, you know I do not mean this!

"Well then," she whispered, her voice catching, her beautiful brown eyes filling with tears she was too proud to let fall, "You best go to them."

She smiled as she prepared to open her eyes, wondering what her captor would do when he saw that she hadn't run from him. Their eyes opened at the same time. Their gazes clashed.

Nicoletta's smile faded, her face draining of color. Her heart began pounding in her chest, slashing against it like a rock, making breathing difficult. She wrenched herself up from the ground and backed away from him.

"No," she choked out, stumbling until she hit a rocky wall barrier. Her naked breasts rose and fell with every forced breath. "This is not possible— *You* are not possible!"

He said nothing, only stared at her, as he slowly rose to his feet.

She was losing her mind, she decided. She had to be. There was no other explanation.

"Now you know My secret, Nica," he murmured, his intense jaguar gaze filled with such emotion she had to look away. "The secrets I did My damnedest to hide for twenty-five years that you might not look upon Me with revulsion." His sigh was long, weary, resigned. "And yet in order to keep it, I had to make you hate Me anyway."

She was going to faint. She was certain she was going to faint. Her heart was ringing in her ears it was pumping so violently.

"I-I…"

She swallowed against a dry throat, words deserting her as she stared at her husband—her allegedly dead husband who was very much alive. She had to be dreaming...or hallucinating. He and the creature—they were one and the same? No—*no*—it wasn't possible.

"Abdul?" she breathed out.

"I couldn't let you go," he said softly. "You deserve to be free—Cyrus knows you deserve to be. And yet..." He walked toward her slowly, not wanting to intimidate her. "I cannot let you go," he rasped.

His expression was guarded and yet she could see the misery and loneliness etched into his face. His stance was tense and yet forcibly relaxed, as if he was trying his damnedest not to appear threatening even though his first instinct where she was concerned had always been and would always be to pounce.

There was no way under Cyrus for Abdul Kan to appear non-threatening, Nicoletta thought. Her gaze flicked over his tanned, naked body, over the heavy muscles and battle scars. He was just as powerful and larger-than-life while a man as he was while a beast. Different and yet the same. Now she recognized what it was she'd saw in the creature—

Abdul.

His gaze found hers. "I love you, Nicoletta Isabella Carlotta Kan," he murmured.

She closed her eyes tightly to keep from crying. Her nostrils flared as tears streamed down her face anyway.

"I love you, *ana wahib.*"

Her heart painfully twisted. "Don't do this to me."

Nicoletta's eyes flew open, the anguish on her tear-streaked face plainly readable. "It took me twenty-five years to pull myself away from You," she gritted out. "Twenty-five brutal years where I begged and pleaded with the ancient saints and to every god under the sun that You might say those very words to me one day."

"Nica…" His voice caught, the first time Abdul had shown a weakness since that long ago night when they'd been making love. "I have always loved you."

She held up a palm. Her legs were trembling so fiercely she could scarcely stand. "It is too late, Abdul," she rasped out. "My love for You will always be, yet is there too much between us for anything to come of it."

His jaw tensed. "Can you not understand why I closed Myself off to you?" he growled, trying again to command the overwhelming urge he had to force her to stay. "If you had died at My hands I…" He sighed, his eyes closing briefly while he calmed himself. "I could not have bore it."

Silence.

Abdul's intense green eyes clashed with hers. "I will not force you to My side, Nica," he murmured. His smile was sad. "There was so much pain in you when first I bought you, years of poverty and neglect I wanted to erase from your memories as though they never were—"

Her eyes filled with renewed tears as she listened to him speak. She searched his haunted gaze, drank it in.

"—There was so much I wanted for us to share together. So damned much." He looked away as if lost in memories. "Yet all fate granted us before I became ill was a few short months."

"Abdul…"

"I love you," he murmured. His bloodshot eyes searched hers. "Even should you choose to walk away forever, I want you to know in your heart that there will never be another love for Me but you."

Silence.

He held out his hand but didn't approach her, letting Nicoletta make her own choice. Tears streamed down her face. There was so much emotion between them—there always had been, even when Abdul had wished it otherwise. And yet for all the emotion there was also much anguish...so much pain and so many years worth of loneliness and isolation.

Abdul.

Her first love. Her only love.

Nicoletta cried out as she reached for him, a guttural sound gurgling up from her throat. "I-I love You," she gasped, wrapping her arms around his middle and hugging him tightly. "I thought—" The tears were making it difficult to say the words. "I-I thought You were dead."

"I wanted to be when you ran from Me," he said hoarsely, his nostrils flaring as he hugged her just as fiercely. "I wanted to be," Abdul murmured into her hair. "Never leave Me, Nica," he said in a soft rasp. "Please...come back to Me."

Her mouth sought his, their lips clashing with the passion that had always existed between them. Abdul lowered her to the ground as they kissed, their tongues hungrily touching as he laid her beneath him.

He ran his callused hands all over her breasts, breaking the kiss and staring down into her beautiful face while he gently but firmly kneaded them in the way he knew she liked. She gasped when his fingers ran over her distended pink nipples, moaning when he lowered his face and took a plump one into his mouth.

"Abdul," Nicoletta said thickly, her eyes closing and her back arching. She pressed his face in closer to her chest, sucking in her breath as his tongue flicked her nipple back and forth.

"Spread your legs," he commanded from around her nipple in his sexy Arabic accent. He released her nipple with a popping sound and gazed down into her face. "I want to feel My pussy," he murmured, his eyes heavy-lidded as he settled himself between her thighs. "My pussy," he said thickly, possessively, poising his hard cock at her entrance.

Nicoletta shivered, knowing as she did how territorially Abdul had always guarded her. The fact he was the only man who'd ever been inside her had always made his territorialism all the more acute.

He sank into her cunt on a groan, his eyes tightly closing and his teeth gritting. *"Mine,"* he ground out. *"All Mine."*

Nicoletta moaned as he began making love to her, her stiff nipples growing impossibly more aroused as they brushed against his chest with each thrust. He picked up the pace of their mating, sinking in and out of her sticky pussy with a hunger that bordered on maniacal.

"Abdul," she gasped, throwing her hips back at him to meet each possessive stroke. *"Harder."*

His nostrils flaring, he threw one of her legs over his shoulder without missing a beat. He gave her what she craved, riding her body hard, pumping in and out of her as she moaned. His jaw hotly clenched as he pounded her mercilessly, fucking her faster. Perspiration soaked skin slapped against perspiration soaked skin, her tits jiggling beneath him as she begged and screamed for more.

"My pussy," he growled. *"Mine."*

Nicoletta cried out her orgasm as Abdul rode her, sinking into her tight flesh over and over, again and again. He fucked her harder and faster and deeper and —

His teeth gritted as he tried with all that he had in him to keep from coming. He wanted the moment to go on and on, to keep sinking in and out of her forever. He fucked her harder, animalistically, moans echoing throughout the jungle cavern that were as tortured as they were filled with pleasure.

Always there had been this between them. Always.

"I'm coming," he rasped, unable to hold himself back another second. His nostrils flared and his muscles tensed as he repeatedly slammed into her pussy. *"Nica."*

He came on a territorial roar, his body convulsing, his cock jerking and spurting inside her. Nicoletta threw her hips at him, frenziedly milking him of seed, while he groaned and came.

It was a long while before they moved, a long while before their breathing became normal. They clung to each other the entire time, two haunted souls whose ghosts could only be put to rest by the other.

"I love you, Nicoletta Isabella Carlotta Kan," Abdul murmured. His gaze found hers and held it. "I will always love you."

CHAPTER 7

He had known almost from the beginning that he was changing, knew too that Sinead was as well. He had no notion how Malifé's hired thugs had gotten to his first wife, yet clearly they had. He could see the changes within her happening as surely as he could see them within himself. Thankfully, Nica had been spared. So too had his daughter, Nellie, and his son, Asad, whom Nica had bore him.

When Abdul had first realized what was happening to him and Sinead, he had hired the best scientists he could muster within the Hierarchy to find a cure. Day and night they toiled in their labs, a ten million yen reward the prize they raced to claim. The scientists thought they had found a cure...

They had been wrong.

Sinead grew worse, her bouts with madness nearly overwhelming her on several occasions. Abdul himself had injected her with what he'd prayed to Cyrus was the cure, only to find that the alleged remedy made her grow worse. And Nellie...

There was something in the way she would look at him, a haunted expression in his daughter's young eyes as she stared at him. It was as if she knew her mother was sick and she blamed him for it. The fear he saw in her innocent gaze when she beheld him was enough to break his heart.

Abdul wondered, not for the first time, if his daughter's memories had been tampered with. He realized his own memories *had been erased, for try as he might, he could not recall what had led to his and Sinead's infections. And so if his memory had been altered, perhaps Nellie's had been too…*

And Sinead's as well.

Sinead, Abdul thought, sighing as he raised a chalice of spirits to his lips and sipped from it. Poor Sinead. She had never wanted to become his wife as she had always preferred the company of women to the company of men. She loved Abdul – as a friend – but she could never be in love with him.

And yet, in a world where women could make no rules, Sinead knew she would never be free to love another female. Creagh O'Malley had wanted his sister to be owned by a Master who would respect her, respect also the limits of her love.

And so Abdul had married her. Sinead had given him his Nellie and been a good mother, so he'd never regretted the union. And then Sinead had found Nicoletta for him.

Ah, Nica, as long as I have breath to breathe, there will never be another love for me but you…

* * * * *

Two days later

"I know You are nervous to see Nellie again," Nicoletta announced as they left the cave hand-in-hand. She frowned at the scratchy makeshift clothing they'd fashioned for him out of animal skin, brushing a patch of dirt off the tunic sleeve. "Yet rest assured she will be happy to see You." Her smile was warm, gentle, just as it had been in the old days when she'd given her love to him freely.

It was time to begin the journey through the jungle and into the heart of the rebel Underground catacombs.

Within days Abdul would be reunited with his firstborn child and her husband. A new destiny was unfolding for all of them, a future he could not control or foretell. It was at once exciting and frightening. But whatever was to come, his beloved wife would be at his side. For that, Abdul would be forever grateful.

Things between Nellie and himself wouldn't be so easy as Nicoletta imagined and Abdul knew it, though he conceded now was not the time to upset his wife with what was to come. But, no, it would not be so easy...

Nicoletta had not been the only one he'd turned away from in an effort to keep the madness from claiming him. He had hurt Nellie too. She had wanted his love despite it all, despite what he deeply suspected were faulty beliefs that he had a hand in her birth mother Sinead's infection and eventual death.

While different, the wounds inflicted on Nellie were cut just as deep as the wounds that he had inflicted on Nicoletta. Back then, when infection had been a new disease and nobody had any guesses as to how it might be cured, Abdul had done the only thing he could think to do to keep from succumbing to it.

He had refused to feel. He had refused to show love or accept it.

In his heart, he still knew it had been the only way. He had told himself over and over again that one day — someway, somehow — he would find that cure and all would be as it should again.

But then one year turned into two, two into a decade, and a decade into twenty-five years...

No. Nellie's forgiveness would not come easily or quickly. But he was determined to earn it. He wanted his life back, a life that had been on hold in lieu of a quarter century long nightmare.

A nightmare that was still not over. Until he was cured and his family again stood as one, it would never be over.

"Cease Your worrying, Abdul," Nicoletta chided him. "I can read You true, You realize." She smiled. "Nellie still loves You."

Abdul raised Nicoletta's hand to his lips and kissed it. His cherished Nica was more beautiful than even he had remembered. Naked, clad only in her matrimonial nipple rings and chain, his brand on her right buttock for the world to see, everything — at least between the two of them — was once again as it should be.

"I hope you are correct," he murmured.

She inclined her head. "I am. I know You doubt me, but I am. And what's more, I think she might be able to cure You. I distinctly recall her stating that the serum the Underground scientists had obtained worked on those who have not yet fully turned." Her eyes were filled with excitement, with hope. "You have not yet fully turned," she breathed out.

Abdul nodded. Had he fully turned there would be no man to speak of left within him. "No. I have not." He sighed, admitting, "The only good thing to have come of the past twenty-five years."

She returned his sigh, knowing nothing could be said to that for it was the truth. They walked in silence for a while, clutching the other's hand as they made their way deeper into the jungle — and soon into the catacombs that would reunite him with his eldest child.

"I have much to explain to you," Abdul said, squeezing her hand.

Nicoletta shook her head. "No, You are wrong." She came to a halt and swung around to face him. "You've told me plenty and the rest I have figured out for myself."

His gaze searched hers. "Do you forgive Me?" he murmured.

"I do," she whispered, her heart in her eyes.

They had a long road to haul but they would travel it together. She stilled, a thought occurring to her. Her gaze narrowed on a frown.

"I have but one question to put to You and by Cyrus I swear You had best have the right answer."

His forehead wrinkled. "You have successfully gained My attention," he slowly drawled. "Go on."

She grunted. "Dumb, Dumber, Dumbest, and Hopelessly Moronic," Nicoletta hissed, making him grin at the names she used to refer to his other wives. "Will You keep them?"

He scratched his chin, pretending to give the matter some thought. He chuckled when she swung around and began stomping off, his arm snaking around her and drawing her back into his side.

"No," he said simply.

Nicoletta's chin notched up, her expression smug. "Good," she sniffed.

Before Abdul knew what came over him, he was laughing, the first laugh he'd entertained in more years than he cared to remember. Throwing his yelping wife over his shoulder, he made his way through the jungle, both excited and tense over the prospect of being reunited with his daughter.

Abdul Kan was a man with many regrets. Confiding his secret in his wife that they might battle it together would never be one of them. Giving his other wives their freedom so that the only woman his heart had ever cherished could know happiness was no sacrifice at all.

Always there was Nicoletta.

There could never be another.

EPILOGUE

Later that night

"What does *ana wahib* mean?" Nicoletta whispered, her head on Abdul's chest.

She couldn't get the question out of her mind for he'd called her and only her by that name for as long as they'd been married. Her face came up. "What does it mean?"

His smile was gentle, his eyes filled with tenderness. "It means my one," Abdul murmured. He lowered his face and softly kissed her lips. "My only one."

She searched his gaze. "As You are mine."

Abdul made love to Nicoletta in the cave they took shelter in that eve. He was the same husband she'd cherished with her whole being in the early days, the same husband she had always prayed would one day return to her. She was not afraid of the beast that dwelled within him, nor would she leave him to wage the battle against it alone.

As Abdul sank into her, possessively impaling her flesh again and again as he moaned and made love to her, she vowed to herself that come what may, she would be with him always.

She had left Abdul that she might find her destiny. Ironically—joyously—it was in Abdul that she had found it.

There was nothing quite like the love between a man and a woman. Love for all others can be fierce, even border on the maniacal, but the love between a man and a woman carries a hunger, a longing — an intensity — unlike any other.

"I love You," Nicoletta whispered again and again as her husband made love to her. Twenty-five years, good memories and horrid ones. Children and soon a grandchild. There was more between them than mere words could say.

And yet she tried. She smiled, cried, and told him over and over again just what was in her heart. "Oh how I love You…"

About the author

Critically acclaimed and highly prolific, Jaid Black is the best-selling author of numerous erotic romance tales. Her first title, The Empress' New Clothes, was recognized as a readers' favorite in women's erotica by Romantic Times magazine. A full-time writer, Jaid lives in a cozy little village in the northeastern United States with her two children. In her spare time, she enjoys traveling, horseback riding, and furthering her collection of African and Egyptian art.

Jaid Black welcomes mail from readers. You can write to them c/o Ellora's Cave Publishing at P.O. Box 787, Hudson, Ohio 44236-0787.

Also by Jaid Black:

- Death Row (serial)
  - The Fugitive
  - The Hunter
  - The Avenger
- God Of Fire
- Politically Incorrect
  - Stalked
- Sins Of The Father
- The Obsession
- The Possession
- Trek Mi Q'an series
  - The Empress' New Clothes
  - Seized
  - No Mercy
  - Enslaved
  - No Escape
  - No Fear
  - Dementia
  - Guidebook
- Tremors
- Vanished
- Warlord

- Anthologies
  - Taken
  - Things That Go Bump In The Night
  - Warrior

Why an electronic book?

We live in the Information Age — an exciting time in the history of human civilization in which technology rules supreme and continues to progress in leaps and bounds every minute of every hour of every day. For a multitude of reasons, more and more avid literary fans are opting to purchase e-books instead of paperbacks. The question to those not yet initiated to the world of electronic reading is simply: why?

1. *Price.* An electronic title at Ellora's Cave Publishing runs anywhere from 40-75% less than the cover price of the <u>exact same title</u> in paperback format. Why? Cold mathematics. It is less expensive to publish an e-book than it is to publish a paperback, so the savings are passed along to the consumer.

2. *Space.* Running out of room to house your paperback books? That is one worry you will never have with electronic novels. For a low one-time cost, you can purchase a handheld computer designed specifically for e-reading purposes. Many e-readers are larger than the average handheld, giving you plenty of screen room. Better yet, hundreds of titles can be stored within your new library — a single microchip. (Please note that EC does not endorse any specific brands. You can check our website for customer recommendations we make available to new consumers.)

3. *Mobility.* Because your new library now

consists of only a microchip, your entire cache of books can be taken with you wherever you go.

4. *Personal preferences are accounted for.* Are the words you are currently reading too small? Too large? Too...**ANNOYING**? Paperback books cannot be modified according to personal preferences, but e-books can.

5. *Innovation.* The way you read a book is not the only advancement the Information Age has gifted the literary community with. There is also the factor of what you can read. Ellora's Cave Publishing will be introducing a new line of interactive titles that are available in e-book format only.

6. *Instant gratification.* Is it the middle of the night and all the bookstores are closed? Are you tired of waiting days — sometimes weeks — for online and offline bookstores to ship the novels you bought? Ellora's Cave Publishing sells instantaneous downloads 24 hours a day, 7 days a week, 365 days a year. Our e-book delivery system is 100% automated, meaning your order is filled as soon as you pay for it.

Those are a few of the top reasons why electronic novels are displacing paperbacks for many an avid reader. Welcome to the Information Age!

As always, Ellora's Cave Publishing welcomes your questions and comments. We invite you to email us at service@ellorascave.com or write to us directly at: P.O. Box 787, Hudson, Ohio 44236-0787.

Printed in the United States
1543600001B/136-147